OF LAND

THE FOUR REALMS

THE GUARDIAN MOUNTAINS
Realm of Sky

Muninns Home

Taiga Province

Desert Province

Ki...
Re...
Realm...
In-Be...

The Mound

Whispering Woods

Eldenroot Grove

'Esis'

VERDANTVALE
Realm of Land

Deep Jungle

Hills of Yo...

MARSH
LANDS

SACRED
FOREST

SEABORNE
Realm of Sea

CONTENTS

Dedication	VII
Copyrights	X
Prologue	XIII
1. Awakening	1
2. The Lonely Forest	14
3. All the Colors of the Sun	27
4. A Fateful Encounter	46
5. The First King	56
6. Spirit of the Fox	70
7. Harvest Festival	83
8. The Berserker & The Flame	98
9. An Oath to Keep	114

10.	Tree of the Valley	132
11.	The Powerless	152
12.	Whispers of the Forest	166
13.	A Loss in the Jungle	182
14.	Twin City Atlon	198
15.	A Tint of Orange	220
16.	The Start of a Journey	238
17.	Hills of Yoid	258
18.	Night of the Wolf	278
19.	The Stranger in a Strange World	298
20.	Where the Water Meets the Land	311
Index		335
Acknowledgements		337
Chapter		339
Also by		340

To those who wonder
To those who dream
To those who see the sunlight through the leaves

"The whole earth is filled with awe at your wonders."
Psalms 65:8

Four Realms Saga
of
The In-Between Chronicles

OF LAND

S.J. GRAGG

Copyright © 2024 by Shelby J. Gragg

All rights reserved.

No part of this publication may be reproduced, distributed, or transmitted in any form or by any means, including photocopying, recording, or other electronic or mechanical methods, without the prior written permission of the publisher, except as permitted by U.S. copyright law. For permission requests, contact sjgbookcollections@gmail.com

The story, all names, characters, and incidents portrayed in this production are fictitious. No identification with actual persons (living or deceased), places, buildings, and products is intended or should be inferred.

Book Cover by Tiffany L. Gragg

1st edition 2024

*These are not stories of the past
but prophecies of the future.*

PROLOGUE

The large-horned creatures ambled around the grounds of the old forest, looking for plants, berries, or other tasty treats hidden beneath the undergrowth. They watched over the land and protected the balance of all those within their domain. While they searched for food, they listened to the trees and to the wind as it spoke to them in a language known only to those who knew how to listen for it. The forest whispered its secrets to the guardians as they continued through the lush green.

A small one who was new to the world lay protected in the grass and the tall weeds close to his mother. He was the first to be born in centuries, and with his birth, an era of change was among the land.

For when he was born, another quiet force, ancient and long forgotten, awoke from the depths.

I

AWAKENING

Ringing.

The kind of ringing that rattled her skull when she heard it. The kind of ringing that produced a headache almost immediately.

Constant. Agonizing ringing.

Where is it coming from?

She discovered the source of the sound when attempting to caress her head with her hand. The ringing became a sharp stabbing sensation that waved over the entirety of her skull. Her face scrunched through the pain. With her eyes still closed and her mind slowly waking, she began to move.

Reluctantly, she held her right temple and pinched the bridge of her nose with her other hand to see if the pressure would relieve some of the throbbing.

It didn't.

She steadily opened her eyes, hoping the pain would recede. It was hard to see. She blinked a couple of times in an attempt to clear her vision. Everything was blurry. All she could make out were the colors of light and the dark silhouettes of the surrounding objects.

The girl looked up to see a small bright light shining down on her, illuminating the inside of a strange glass dome. Underneath her, a soft, blue gel-like lining covered the surface, with a few thick wires extending outward from the pod.

The pod was a nearly perfect fit for her, except that it was built for someone slightly taller, extending a few inches beyond her feet. The girl tried to calm, tried to steady her breathing so that her eyesight could adjust and her mind could focus on getting her out of the small, enclosed tomb.

Once the pain had receded a bit, she pressed her palms on the cool smooth glass that laid above her. As she gently pushed on it, the glass popped open with a click of the latch and a hiss of stale air, as if it had been politely waiting to be opened the whole time.

Still confused, and with a spinning head and a nauseous stomach, she sat up in the darkness.

The light from her pod illuminated a small section, revealing scattered debris, shattered glass, metal trinkets, rocks, and concrete blocks with protruding metal at various angles.

Another pod, just like her own, was crumpled inward next to her, with no sign of the occupant.

I wonder if anyone I knew was in it.

The girl had felt familiarity in all the things she had seen, but whenever she thought deeper into why she was there or even the simple question of what had happened, her brain pulsed in tune with her heart. Even through the pain, she felt the aching of sadness and loneliness creep up on her.

She looked down at her clothes to see if what she was wearing would help jog her memory. She had on dark, tattered jeans with a brown belt to hold them up, a solid-colored tan t-shirt with black letters in the center of her chest, and black high top converse. The color had faded from them all, leaving them a shell of their once former vivid hues. Her fingers trailed across the characters printed on her loose tucked in shirt. *A.R.K.* marked her, but feeling them did not help discover their unknown meaning. Her memories and the meaning behind the letters were caught in a net like frenzied fish trying to escape their fate.

Attached to her arms were more smaller wires that seemed to push a transparent red liquid through them. She grabbed at the weakened tape stuck to her skin and cautiously pulled the thin needle out of her arm, putting it on the side of the squishy blue gel underneath her.

Her eyes had nearly adjusted completely now. Looking back down towards the small light to where she had been sleeping, she noticed the thicker wires trailing from the light. After passing through a luminous tablet, and descended through a fissure in a wall constructed of uneven and fractured concrete, which emitted a vibrant orange-red illumination.

The girl reasoned that the collapsed area was not the way out and she continued to look around, now noticing another light. However, it wasn't the glow of a machine, rather the glow of distant sunlight. Reluctantly, she made an attempt to place her legs over the side of the pod, but her weakened state caused her to move sluggishly. She noticed how emaciated her legs were, only to look at her arms and see they were just as skeletal. Feeling her bony face, she realized that, in the pod, her body had diminished greatly from the lack of use and nutrients. The girl put her hands on the blue substance and lifted herself out. When she put her full weight on her legs, she crumpled to the ground like a lifeless corpse.

She grunted as she hit the cold, hard stone.

For a moment, the girl laid there, sapped of energy. With great effort, she managed to stand up, her legs trembling unsteadily beneath her. Her legs wobbled as she braced herself on the side of the pod to make sure she wouldn't collapse again. After feeling more confident in her abilities, she took a step. She could feel the blood creeping down her legs, sending pins and needles to her feet.

Mindful of the glass and other sharp objects on the surrounding ground, the tired girl made her way toward the sunlight, using the nearest chunks of rock to help hold herself up.

She edged her way toward the destroyed pod next to her own, concluding that it was already empty when someone smashed it. Peering through the shattered glass roof, she found no trace of a presence. With a sigh of relief, she turned and went towards the small, orange light where the thick wires ran under the rocks. Kneeling down carefully, she looked in the small hole and saw a machine humming in a low tone. Believing it was wise to avoid the unknown, she rose with a slow pace. Her head was spinning, but with a deep breath she began towards the sunlight.

She made her own path through the catastrophe, working to get past the avalanche of rocks. She tried to make sense of her surroundings. Her dizziness made it hard to concentrate on anything. The girl stumbled, her hands catching her before she fell. She sucked in a rapid breath of the damp, moldy air. Looking at her now red and skinned palms, the girl got back up and wiped her hands on her jeans as she unsteadily climbed over the rocks and cement.

When she got around the largest part of the debris, there was a bare section to sit for a moment and gather strength from her rock-climbing endeavor. During her rest, the girl took in her surroundings. To her disappointment, there wasn't much. The things she saw were identical to what she had seen moments ago. The only noticeable difference, it seemed, was that someone had been here before her. Debris had been moved aside to make the path more accessible.

Someone was here? Are they still here?

Thoughts raced through her mind, leaving her feeling both anxious and eager.

After a quick pause, she decided to keep moving forward, and eventually got to the entrance where rays of sun glittered across the ground, beckoning for her to join it. The way out wasn't difficult, but upon seeing it, she didn't believe it to be the actual exit of the building. The entire side of the building had been demolished, leaving a large gaping hole littered with rocks, cement, and green leafy overgrowth.

Lucky me. The girl thought as she worked her way over to it.

The easiest way to get out was a giant tree, blended seamlessly into the side of the building, its roots twisted and broken into the rock.

She saw her hope for escape and kept going.

At first, she believed her imagination or lightheadedness caused her to hear rustling, which could have been tricks of the mind, especially considering the state she was in. However, in her peripherals, she felt as though she could see something moving into the darkness as she passed.

The best course of action, she thought, was to ignore it and to leave as fast as possible. If she could reach the entrance, she would be okay. Reassuring herself, she sought the natural light, tinted with a green glow that beckoned her towards its haven.

As she hiked over, and around the debris, she could feel eyes on her. The feeling of being watched was undeniable, leaving her to wonder who or what was lurking in the shadows.

Her anxiety swelled. She sped up her pace but fumbled, awkwardly losing her balance. As her heartbeat rose, her head spun and her stomach twisted until she could hardly walk without the world softly swaying. In the building's yawning mouth, the tree made its home along the crumbling edges of the entrance, its roots flowing down into the cave like a waterfall.

The girl grabbed the bottom roots of the magnificent evergreen to steady herself just as her vision doubled. She noticed that the roots were damp from the morning dew.

The need to escape the dark cave grew more intense with every step she took closer to the light.

She had climbed only a little way when a low guttural groan crawled up from behind her. Her hands slipped down the wet roots of the tree bark, and for a moment, there was only air and the space between her and the wild pounding of her heart against her ribcage.

Her breath was knocked from her lungs as her back smacked against the rocky cave floor. Rolling over on her side, the girl stifled her small cry of pain. Warm blood flowed from a thin gash on her arm and dripped off the palm of her hand as she clasped it to her chest. She folded over, her knees to her stomach, and focused on the beat of her heart and the burn in her fingers.

And finally, the girl snapped.

Holding herself in a tight ball, she cried quietly to herself. Stifled by the terror of the dark, she struggled to release the pent-up emotion in her chest.

Crying for as long as she did, the tears wash the dirt away from her face in small streaks. Her throat tightened and ached from her fear.

The pain receded from her head as she thought about the people she did not remember and about all the things that eluded her.

Is this really happening? Am I dreaming?

So many other questions raced through her mind, hopping from reason to reason.

Her eyes closed, heavy from releasing all of her emotions simultaneously. She had given up. She laid on the ground, her body trembling uncontrollably.

The girl did not know how long she had been laying there, but after a while, she opened her eyes and sat up. Using her shirt to wipe off the excess amount of smeared blood that covered the fresh cut, which had turned into a dull pain.

The girl heard the groaning again, then looked for the origin. Looking back, the way she came, nothing stood out to her, but turning to the left was another section that she had not come from. Reluctantly, the girl got up to see if this was where the sounds were coming from. She glanced past the corner into the darkness and heard more than one source of the strange noises.

She squinted her eyes and saw something terrible.

A section of the fallen building jailed them.

Some were dead, others deformed and darkened like shadows of what they once were.

Humans.

Some of their heads had morphed and intertwined with various plants or fungi. Others were as dark as the walls of the cave they were trapped by, and she could only see their bodiless shadows. The rest were a confounding mass of deformed fangs, horns, bumps and thorns, the stench of death and mold, gagging her.

The girl covered her mouth and nose with her hands.

She looked down at her feet and could see the crushed bones of the dead underneath her. She stifled a terrified cry once more.

As she frantically backed away from the corner, her heart raced with fear.

They had not seen her yet.

The frantic girl shuffled backward, her feet brushing past small rocks and pieces of metal and glass. Her body flushed with heat and sweat beaded on her forehead in the intensity of the moment. Her eyes stayed pinned to the corner, unblinking as her mind begged her to not look away from the sleeping peril that had laid before her.

Once the girl felt the thick tree roots press up against her back, she grabbed at them, her fingers trembling. Intertwining her fingers into the roots, she stared into the darkness for a moment longer before facing the sunlight above her. Tears brimmed her eyes and her back ached with terror as her body screamed at her for facing away from the existing danger.

The girl started back up the roots of the ancient tree.

This time she was more careful with her footing, digging the tip of her shoe in between the steady roots and the rocky wall. However, adrenaline quickened her pace as her body leaned naturally towards the beckoning light. She reached the top. Gripping onto the last bit of the edge, her fingers dug past rocks and dirt filled her fingernails when she pulled herself up out of the basement of the devastated building.

With little strength remaining, she clumsily flopped up and rolled away from the entrance. Keeping the mouth of the cave in her line of sight, the girl escaped. She lay on the plush pillow of grass, her eyes closed with the sunlight warming her eyelids and her clothes damp from the dew. She imagined herself emerging from the cave like an evil that seeped out of the shadows. Her decrepit and now bloodied body resembling the monsters below, making her wonder if there was any difference between herself and them.

The girl looked around the area. She was in a small field of tall swaying weeds, with chunks of rocks jutting out that she thought might have been a part of the building once, overgrown with trees and flowers further out. She looked back towards where she had emerged and she saw the spread out, gnarled roots of the tree slicing an opening at the rock. The letters 'ESIS' broken apart and scattered among the rocks and tall grass.

Her head throbbed once more as memories swam just past her grasp, trying desperately to fill the gaps in her mind. She looked away from the old crumbling building, now just a prison for those poor creatures.

Around her were temperate trees of all varieties and sizes with lush greens, a crisp, clear sky and wildflowers sprouting everywhere. The sun shone through the leaves, and the wind blew morning shadows gently through the dancing trees.

She went over to the rocks protruding from the ground and touched the soft and plush moss that covered them. The girl sat down against it to rest, breathing in the forest's life. Smelling the grass, the fresh air, and even the dirt, she took another deep breath while soaking in the sun's rays against the warm rock. As the girl took in her surroundings, she basked in the sun's natural light and realized she could not hear any animals. There were no birds chirping or the chittering of other small creatures. It was as if the forest was holding its breath.

Loneliness crept over her as she tried to remember anybody that she might have known before. Hopefully, she could find clues as she kept going.

The girl noticed a small path was across the field that led into the forest instead. This was the only clear path besides the one that would take her back into the building. She grimaced at the thought of returning to where she just had escaped.

The girl put her hand on the rock and hoisted herself up from the ground. Her leg had fallen asleep, and it took a couple awkward limps towards the trail until it felt awake again.

As she got closer to the little trail with the line of trees looming over her, the dense leaves of a large bush rustled near the edge of the forest. The girl stopped and hunched over in the shin high grass. She heard the rustling again, turning towards the bush. Her eyes narrowed as she waited for whatever it was to make the first move.

The rustling stopped as she took a step towards it. Suddenly, came the fearful screams of children.

Taken aback, she saw three figures rush out of the bushes and move toward the opening of the trail.

Are those... children?

Her mouth gaped for a moment.

She took a step and immediately became lightheaded again. She held out her hands for balance.

This can't be right? They looked... weird.

The children were dressed in ragged solid-colored clothing, but most importantly, she noticed, one had small horns while another had a face like a dog with whiskers and a snout. She stood there, hesitant. One resembled a girl. She looked back, their eyes met.

"Wait!" She cried out when they took off.

But the small creature had fear plastered on her face as she ran faster to catch up with her group.

The little girl had fox ears, a fox tail with burning hazel eyes, and at the end of her dull-colored dress, she saw fox legs. As they vanished into the forest, the lonely girl laid back down and faced the scattered clouds and treetops with a tired huff.

2

THE LONELY FOREST

The sun reached its peak in the azure sky, and the heat was nice at first until it beat down harder on her, creating beads of sweat on the small of her back and under her matted hairline. She fidgeted uncomfortably as she wiped her forehead with the back of her hand. After a long rest by the mossy rock, she reached the tree line and spotted an entrance to the mysterious woods. The opening was decorated with two mangled oak trees guarding the entryway.

Behind the oak on the left, she peeked into the forest, letting her eyes adjust to the dim light under the shaded foliage. She could see the sunlight breaking through on the covered path, coaxing her in, making stepping stones of light on the ground. Ever so slowly, she made her way past nature's gate and on her way.

Her stomach let out a disgruntled rumbling as it echoed its emptiness. As she thought about eating, her stomach responded with another louder gurgling. To draw herself away from her hunger, she looked around the forest trail, wondering if anyone was in earshot.

Maybe I can find some berries or mushrooms to eat.

"Pfft," she laughed out loud and rolled her eyes. It was comical how little she knew about finding food in the wild. Just to be safe, she decided to steer clear of anything that might look suspicious.

In spite of her hunger, the girl continued to walk down the shaded path and deeper into the forest, where quiet life brimmed all around her. She could hear the birds from above and the chittering of other animals. Even though they weren't in sight within the dense wood, she could still hear them communicating and buzzing with the news of the mysterious creature that walked about.

As she looked up, she could discern the different species of trees. Beautiful maple trees, towering pines, and sturdy oaks dotted her view. Farther off where the trees met the land, she could see deep purple wildflower patches scattered throughout. Around her walking trail, ferns and bushes mixed with tall colorful weeds.

The sweet aroma of pine, wildflower, and fresh forest air was a relaxing presence. She breathed deeply and noticed the crunching leaves under her feet. Her thoughts trailed back to the ruined building and those disturbing creatures shuffling in the dark. The girl overcame her fear after the terrifying events of her mysterious past. She turned her mind to more hopeful thoughts.

Like finding help.

The girl came to a fork in the trail. The left path jutted at a sharp angle, and the right path turned slightly the other way. For a moment, she stood there and looked towards the left.

This path doesn't look too out of the ordinary.

Then looked straight forward to the right trail.

And this one looks no different either.

She shrugged and continued straight on the path to the right. As she picked up her foot to continue walking on, out of nowhere, a black snake with opalescent, shimmering green scales slithered its way out of the ferns and down the path.

Without hesitation, the girl instinctively twisted towards the left path instead.

I thought the left path was more appealing anyway.

It had been a while since she began her trek through the woods when she noticed a clearing ahead of her. As she walked closer, she heard a loud, crisp snap. Surprised, she looked down to discover the crumbled bones of skeletons. She picked up her foot and dread seized her stomach as she realized she stepped on a forearm.

She gasped, backing up frantically. Her eyes widened and her heart raced as the realization flooded in. Bones littered the glade she had stumbled upon.

The skeletons had all become part of the forest, buried beneath the grass. The path was dotted with so many of them, making them impossible to count. Some skeletons were entangled in the roots of trees, but the majority of the remaining skeletons were scattered throughout the clearing.

It must have been some sort of battlefield.

She thought when she saw the shattered old bones with rusted weapons stuck in the ribs and skulls.

The girl spotted swords, axes, a couple of daggers scattered around, and some other unique weapons that she had never seen before.

As she walked into the clearing, observing her surroundings, she noticed something that spiked her curiosity. The girl saw a massive heap on the far end of the meadow.

It's some type of mound?

There were abnormal chunks of stone emerging out of the ground, forming spikes. Baffled, she narrowed her eyes and began walking towards the bones, weapons, and tall, wild grass. The closer she got, the more she could comprehend what she was seeing. It was the bones of a human, stabbed in the back by spikes. Its arms sagged as its head looked longingly up toward the sky. Nature had overgrown the almost pristine skeleton. Strange vines kept its bones together like sinewy green muscle running over it. Shin high grass and wildflowers grew all around it, as a tribute to the lost soul. The closer she approached, the more desolate she felt.

She stopped in her tracks to observe further. Velvety purple mushrooms, with white stems and white spots that resembled stars in the night sky, poured out of the eyes and mouth of the skull.

Stabbed into the ground as praise, or maybe an offering to the fallen warrior, was a staff made up of a strong and hearty looking metal and decorated with a calligraphy of leaves and vines that twisted around itself. It also stood a little taller than her, with symbols down the middle that she did not recognize.

The longer that she stared at the staff, the more it called to her. It felt wrong to disrespect the person's grave, but also it felt as though all of existence itself was calling out to her and telling her to pick it up. Her body moved on its own as her hand drifted toward it and she was pulled closer by an unexplainable force.

Warily, she reached her hand out and grazed her fingers over the staff, touching the strange symbols. The metal was warm from the sun and instinctively she wrapped her hands around the center. With as much strength as she could muster, she pulled it out of the rocks and vines. The stone crumpled, toppling onto itself, as she worked to rip the vines from its home. Once she succeeded, she rested it back on the ground.

It's much heavier than I thought.

She ran her fingers along the twisting metal, wondering how much work it took to make it look so sinister yet so beautiful.

Adjusting to the extra weight, the girl picked up the staff again, this time inspecting the engravings that lined the middle of it. They were unlike anything she recognized and seemed to make up a sort of foreign language.

As she gazed at the staff, a horrified scream of a child echoed in the distance.

The girl snapped out of her trance and took off towards the call for help, completely forgetting what she had taken from the grave. Adrenaline pushed her weakened body forward as she made her way through the grim battlefield. Dashing around the skeletons and rocks, she made her way toward the scream she had heard. Once she got to the edge of the meadow, she heard another cry further into the forest.

The girl came across a decent sized running creek. She made a mental note of the fresh source of water as she trekked through its coolness and to the other side.

The crying had grown louder. She scanned her surroundings, hoping to see where it came from. She continued to walk, her head swiveled anxiously for the cry or the danger that had caused it. The crying stopped, and she stopped as well to listen. She could hear sniffling as she rounded a massive oak tree, but there was still no sign of anyone. The girl turned and looked down to see that the tree had a rotten hole at the base of the trunk and in the hole, a pair of hazel eyes reflected back at her.

"Where are you!?" Cedar ran, stumbling over the nearly invisible roots and rocks that blocked her path.

"Hello?!" She jolted to a stop, and her eyes overflowed with tears. She continued looking for anything similar or a hint to where she needed to go. All the children she was supposed to watch had vanished.

Cedar forcefully stomped her foot, feeling the urge to express her frustration, yet her mind was consumed with terror and longed to release a loud cry for someone to notice. Her thoughts turned to the defiled monster they had seen in the forbidden meadow. She picked up her pace to a jog. It had crawled out of the gnarled roots of the guardian tree. The tree that warned all of those who saw it, not to enter.

She'd heard stories of the shadows and of the monsters that dwelled there, but thought they were stories to warn children off from falling into the cave.

She passed a babbling stream and realized she was closer to the village than she had thought she was. Slowing down, she hiked through the pine scented forest, jumping over roots that swam out from the ground and dove back into it like a tentacled creature of the sea. Her attention was drawn to a rather large tree that was hollowed out at the bottom by rot. She rounded the old oak and looked inside the small wooded home.

"Are you in there?" She asked.

As she peered in. A loud, angry snort echoed through the forest behind her. She turned in alarm and let out a shrill screech that rang through the forest, followed by a deafening silence.

It ran at her, charging with speed and precision. The small girl, not thinking, backed into the hole to evade the beast. Pushing herself as far back against the tree's trunk as she could, she watched, mortified, as it collided with the old tree. Its stout ivory tusks jammed into either side of the narrow entrance. The boar barely missed her. Agitated, it swung its stuck head violently side to side, throwing loosened bark every which way and releasing its tusks from their trap. It squealed in outrage and circled back, trotting the other way and out of sight.

As it disappeared, she heard the crunching of leaves coming from the other direction. It sounded as if someone ran towards her.

The sound stopped, and the forest hushed once more.

She held her breath, waiting.

The lanky shadow that had crawled out of the forbidden cave earlier cautiously walked in front of the tree. It held the golden staff now, and the girl shrunk even further down into her hiding spot. As she watched it, she noticed it had strange blue clothing on and was covered in blood and grime.

As the pale monster turned, her heart stopped. It kneeled down, grabbing the rim of the entrance to her hideaway, and set the shimmering staff on the soft fallen leaves. It peered into the darkness with curious grey eyes.

The human stood, frozen in terror, not knowing if this was the source of the cry for help or the danger. Time slowed down as she crouched there. Her eyes adjusting to the darkness. The sight of a child's face gradually became clearer, and with it came a sense of unease that settled in her stomach. As she took in the sight before her, she could feel her mouth gap in astonishment at the what she saw. The child's appearance was a blend of human and fox-like qualities that showed in her long red ears that protruded from her wavy red hair.

It's the little girl from earlier.

A sigh of relief left her chest as she recognized her. When she went to take another crouched step forward, the little girl in the tree started crying again.

It's me, she's scared of me?...

"Hey, hey, hey, it's ok," the girl said as she put down the staff and crouched down onto the ground to meet the child at eyesight. She moved in at a slow pace with her hands out. She was trying to show the little girl that she meant no harm. The child was teary-eyed but seemed to understand, staying on the cautious side, she stayed in the tree.

The child began speaking at a hurried rate, and in a language she could not understand. Even though the words were jumbled nonsense, she understood the pointing and yelling that came next. They heard the crunching of leaves and branches snapping on the forest floor.

The girl whipped around now facing the green woods with her back to the tree, and she saw what the child had been trying to warn her about.

Her blood ran cold, and she swallowed.

A couple of trees past, was a boar. It stood knee high and was embellished with husky muscle and large white tusks. The creature's stomach sported a deep brown fur, while its back was a mosaic of light and dark colors of green. Its surface covered in a lush growth of shrubbery that included a colorful assortment of dandelions, flowers, and mushrooms sprouting from its body. However, she couldn't dwell on its appearance because the boar's frustrated squeals filled the air.

She looked down at the staff slowly and grimaced when she realized it was just out of reach. Keeping her back to the tree, she moved deliberately, glancing back and forth between the screeching boar and the staff. The girl could feel the metal on her fingertips as it let out an unholy squeal and charged forward.

The girl was frozen in fear. Her brain screaming at her to move but her body felt heavy. She heard the small girl crying behind her. The human girl turned to look, and they locked eyes. The fear in the child's eyes helped her understand what needed to happen. She was the only one who could act in this situation. She needed to be strong now.

The girl snapped back around to face the wild boar as it raced towards them. The girl grabbed her staff and stood. Unsure of what to do, she braced for impact.

The boar closed in on them. The girl bent over from the weight of the metal staff and held it out equal to the boar's body. As it got to them, her loud cry of fear matched the boar's angry screech, shocking the woods with their battle. She thrust her staff forward, hoping for it to find its mark. They clashed.

The girl was thrown backward into the tree trunk, her breath taken from her. Her staff raked upwards, ripping the bark off of the tree and halting her movements. The collision skewered the boar with the staff, its golden tip emerged from in between its ribs, dripping with blood and matted with a few flowers that once lived on its back.

One of the boar's tusks pierced the flat of her thigh and she screamed out in pain, struggling frantically while trying to push it off her. As she pulled the tusk out of her thigh, blood oozed out.

She grabbed at her fresh wound. The soft touch of her hands in the opening sent agony like lightning down her leg. Blood gushing out of it in thick spurts. She looked back into the hollowed tree to see if the child was safe. She was still in there, unharmed but with a wide-eyed, shocked expression across her face.

The girl fell to the ground, holding her new wound. She scrunched her face in pain and tried to hold back tears. The child crawled out of the tree and tried to speak to her while pointing and prodding at the wound.

Through a pain-stricken grimace, she looked at the child and said, "I.. DO NOT....... UNDERSTAND YOU." She struggled to respond through the pain and her staggering breaths.

The small girl stopped talking and looked at her, concerned. *Maybe she's trying to help.*

The child grabbed her bloody hand and pulled, helping her up. The wounded girl tried to get up and walk, but when she put pressure on her left leg, she crumpled back down to the damp forest floor.

She grunted in pain again when the child helped her back up. Then the little girl used herself as a crutch to help her walk. They hobbled silently away from the dead boar and the tree, back towards the creek she had passed. Once they got there, the child let her sit down at the water and they began washing the injury. The girl winced while watching her blood billow like heavy clouds in the cold water's current.

The water washed away the blood, revealing a golf ball sized chunk missing from her thigh. She looked at it, disgusted and unsure of what to do. Immediately after her thigh was cleaned, blood dribbled back down toward her knee. She looked at the child who had taken charge.

The red-haired child, however, did not blink. She pulled something out of the pocket of the satchel that was wrapped around her side and began chewing it. She added more of the plant into her mouth, smacking her lips together in the struggle to turn the plant into a paste. The child must have thought it was an adequate amount because she spat it back out into her hands. The wounded girl watched in shock as the child smacked the mysterious glob straight into the wound.

"UGH!" The injured girl made a disgusted noise.

She quickly went to remove it from her leg, but the little fox girl smacked her hand and furrowed her brow disapprovingly. Upset, she sat back once again with her legs laying out in the cool water, allowing her new young medic friend to finish her work.

3

All the Colors of the Sun

The small child noticed the cut on her arm and proceeded to put the goopy healing paste on it, as well. While she did that, the human girl decided to clean off as much of the blood and grime as she could. She dunked her hand upstream, cupping the water in her weak hands and gulping down handfuls. An awareness came upon her, she felt the crisp water coarse through her body as she washed the dirt off of her face and arms,

Afterwards, she dipped her feet back in again to enjoy the refreshing water running through her toes. They rested by the stream for a bit, and the little girl rummaged through her satchel for a moment, pulling out a strange fruit that seemed to look like an apple. Motioning it towards her, she took it and smelled it.

It smells fresh.

Giving it one last look over, she took a cautious bite.

"Huh, that's so weird..." the girl laughed and looked at it again. It tasted sweet and grainy like a pear.

Hunger hit her almost as hard as the boar had after her first bite. She then finished it quickly in a few more bites. The juice from the sweet unknown fruit dripped down her chin and dotted her shirt as she finished the delectable treat and she used the water from the stream again to wash off the stickiness.

The two tried to communicate with each other on and off again during their time at the stream, but to no avail. The little girl's words were incomprehensible. Just like the fruit she ate, the boar, and the monsters, she wondered if she would ever truly understand the new world that she awoke in.

The girl looked at the child, examining her ears and tail in confusion. The child saw her and said something in her native tongue. She scooted closer to the injured girl, putting her shoeless foxlike feet into the water too. Smiling, the older girl put her hand out with her palm up in a gesture, asking for the child's hand in return. The red-haired child stared for a moment at her smooth pale palm, then put her hand out on top of hers. She had claws, not fingertips, and realized the child's arms and legs were a fox's as well and not human. The only feature that was human about her was her face and body.

"Cedar, ccc-eeeddd-aaaa-rrrr," the fox child spoke again, gesturing to herself.

The girl snapped her eyes up to meet the child's, no longer looking at her clawed hand. She furrowed her brow into an understanding look, and they exchanged a knowing thought.

"Cedar," repeated the injured girl as she nodded once. The girl smiled and laughed heartedly at finally being able to communicate through the veil.

The child prompted toward her. She wanted to know the girl's name now. She opened her mouth to tell her but came up short.

My name? What's my name?

Perplexed, the girl made the ugly realization that she did not know her own name.

She looked back up at the child with a pained smile and gave her a confused shrug.

Cedar gave a sad expression and stood up, looking at the sun. It was the time to travel again.

The child held out her hand to help her up, and she added pressure to her leg. Cedar cautiously let go and, after the success of standing by herself, she tested her ability to walk independently.

The pain in her leg pulsed, but the newly placed wrap kept itself in place.

At least I am alive, and there's now a place for me to go instead of just wandering in a giant forest, she thought to herself, sighing. At that, a new thought came to her mind.

"My Staff!!" She exclaimed while looking desperately around for it, but it was nowhere in sight.

Alarmed, Cedar jumped and looked at the girl, worried. Then the injured girl, wobbling on her leg, trying to stand by herself, made a whooshing noise along with a swish of her arm to indicate the staff. The red-headed girl, saying a few unknown words, pointed back towards the boar where they left it.

She bit her lip in concern. The staff was special to her now and she would not disrespect it by leaving it in the bloodied, decomposing corpse of a wild boar.

They looked at each other and she tilted her head back the way they came. Cedar nodded, and they began their slow march back toward the incident. When they made it back, the injured girl tried pulling the staff out of the boar unsuccessfully. It had lodged itself deep into the body of the now dead animal. Grunting, she grounded herself with her good leg and hoisted her wounded leg onto the boar. She pulled with all the strength she could muster. Cedar stood behind her and wrapped her hands around the staff as well.

With their combined strength, they pulled. She could feel her heart beating in her thigh, the pain growing along with it, and her face contorted in the struggle to rescue the staff.

Nothing happened at first, but leaning further back, she felt the slightest movement. Then, with a wet sickening sound, the staff came out of the boar's body, bringing along more blood and tufts of fur with it. The girl grunted as she fell to the ground from the momentum, falling on Cedar as the staff landed in her lap.

Ugh.

She looked down at herself, holding her arms out in disgust.

The sight of her, covered in both her own blood and the boar's blood, was enough to make anyone mistake her for a real monster.

The girl laughed, shaking her head ironically as she got up using the staff to steady herself.

There's no point in caring anymore.

She watched Cedar pick an interesting spruce stem off the boar's back. The girl looked at her, confused. Cedar shrugged, putting the plant in one of the many pouches of her useful satchel and patted it snuggly. Then Cedar pointed in a direction the girl had not gone yet and started walking, beckoning for her to follow. She used the staff as a sturdy walking stick as they started their way to Cedars' home.

There was no trail this time. They walked straight through the forest, following what was hopefully a young child's decent tracking skills. The girl gradually followed behind, trying to conserve the little energy she had left. Along the way, Cedar would see plants she liked and stuff them into her satchel. Sometimes, she would point at a fruit or plant higher than her reach, and the girl would use her staff to knock them loose from the branches above.

Dusk settled, and the sun was setting in the forest, turning everything a beautiful deep orange-red. Cedar picked up her pace, making the girl think that they were close.

The girl smelled the village first, beginning to salivate she breathed the scent in deeply. She could smell meat being cooked on a fire. The smell of cooking herbs, spices and meats was overwhelming to her senses.

They came out of the forest and into a clearing, where they saw a small village at the bottom of the hill.

Mud, clay, stone, and wood beautifully crafted the houses into one and two-story homes. Everything that was made of wood or clay had designs etched into it, and each structure had ribbons in the colors of red, blue, and yellow. The whole town was a painted masterpiece. Colorful banners shaped as animals flying everywhere, connecting rooftops and buildings together. She could see the knee high wooden planked fence surrounding the town that ran the entire border of the village and around fields. They came out of the forest on the other side of the farmland. She noticed that the town was on the opposite side of the opening and that the forest surrounded them on all sides.

The girl hobbled out of the security of the trees and into the field of golden wheat, where she could see farm animals that were grazing and lazily sitting in the dusk sun. A shepherd, who was a half sheep, half man satyr, saw the two girls in the distance. He dropped his shepherd's nook and took off towards the village.

Yelling and waving her arms, Cedar tried to get his attention, but his face showed only worry at the human girl as he continued to run away. Cedar grabbed her hand, glancing at her solemnly as they quickened their pace.

The injured girl's mind turned back and forth with the thoughts of how this town would react to the sight of her, fret filling her stomach with uneasiness.

From Cedar's reaction earlier, what would these people think of me?

They made it to the main road that leads into the village and could see people gathering to watch the spectacle. They were all wearing dull-colored garb like Cedar, some however had shining jewelry around their heads or neck, or swords strapped to their waist.

She held tighter onto her staff when a couple of men came running up the hill, shouting. Cedar ran towards them, yelling as well, but once they met, the warriors pushed past Cedar, drawing their circular blades and continued to run at the girl.

This is it. This is where I die. She thought, holding her staff up and slapping a determined expression on her face. She slashed her staff out as a warning when they got within a close distance.

They stopped, encircling the bloodied girl, grabbing her staff from her faster than she could react.

"HEY!" She yelled, snapping at them, but the warrior's weapon went to her neck.

They pushed her forward into the town. People of all species and sizes looked at her, terrified. She didn't understand how she could stand out so much in a crowd of people who look nothing alike. As she overlooked the crowd of fearful bystanders, a thought came to her.

There are no humans...

Cedar spoke sharply towards the warriors, trying to push herself in the circle to get to the girl. But just as easily, they pushed her away. Cedar and the girl's eyes met. The guards pushed her forward harshly, causing her head to whip back at the sudden movement. Cedar gave her an exasperated look and sprang off like lightning towards the other direction further into the village.

The girl, defeated and alone again, looked down to the cobblestone road as they walked. She thought she had finally made a friend, but just as quickly, she was gone.

As they trudged along toward what seemed to be the center of the bustling village, she stared at the ground. Trying to ignore the whispering and shock of the onlookers.

I guess I really am a monster to them.

They made it to the center of the town, where there was a fountain with a majestic deer and a tall pine tree that decorated the middle of it. Behind it was a quant building that looked like a place of worship because of the bell at the top and mosaic windows dressing alongside the walls.

A short, chubby goat satyr with olive-colored skin and two thick twirling horns stood on the stairs of the fountain. His arms were crossed and looked at them with a stern expression. The warriors opened up the circle as they tied the girl's wrists together.

The chubby satyr came up to them, his cloven feet clopping on the cobblestone, and looked at the girl with a curious disgust.

"I don't look that bad..." she mumbled, looking down, examining herself.

Everyone around her gasped or awed at her words. At that, the man barked at her in his language.

The girl returned his look of disgust and retorted in a sarcastic, annoyed tone. "I... do not... understand... you..." they glared at each other for a moment in silence.

He motioned to the warrior next to her. The guard grabbed her shoulder forcefully and pushed her knee in, causing her to kneel. She snapped a look at the man holding her down. He was a mix of dog or some other type of canine. He raised his circular weapon above his head. Time slowed as she began to understanding what was happening, she looked around desperately as struggled weakly to escape.

Where was Cedar? Did she really abandon me?

"Cedar," she whimpered.

"Cedar help me!" She cried out as tears streamed down her cheeks.

All she saw were looks of horror and others avoiding her gaze. Empty, she closed her eyes in defeat and continued crying as she slumped to the ground.

When the warrior had raised his hands, ready to slice down, a shout came from the crowd. She looked around to see where the voice of hope came from. Cedar ran up, pushing through the villagers. Panting and waving her hands wildly, she put herself in between the guard and the injured girl, glaring venom at him.

A woman followed through the crowd. She had warm brown eyes that matched her long brown hair, and she looked a little older than the human girl. She also wore a type of red garb that stood out from everyone else's. The girl observed that while the woman appeared mostly human, she had fox-like characteristics, resembling Cedars, but with a brown color.

Cedar stood next to the girl, showing off the spruce plant to everyone and speaking fiercely. The brown-haired woman in her deep red dress came up to the girl, cut the rope from her wrists, and helped her stand. Cedar and the goat satyr began arguing with each other while he jabbed his finger at the girl.

How many times have I almost died today? She thought, drained as she watched the interaction.

A deep bellow rang throughout the valley of the forest. She covered her ears in shock. The call shook the entire village along with the nearby trees. It stopped and for the first time since she had arrived in the village, it was dead silent, no one was looking at her. They stared past the temple and into the forest.

Wide-eyed, she stared in disbelief. First she saw the horns, the gigantic horns of a moose, the two of them spread out like massive velvet shovels with many pointed ends on both. Next, the long snout of the biggest animal she had ever seen emerged from the woods behind the temple and towered over the townspeople, calmly making its way towards the commotion.

Her mouth gaped open at the enormity of the moose, fearfully she backed up, ready to escape from the massive creature. The brown-haired woman gripped her arm tighter, and the girl looked at her with wild eyes. She simply shook her head and looked back at the commotion.

At its huge hooves, another woman walked along beside it. She graced a long flowing dress that trailed on the ground behind her and the sleeves hid her hands. The exquisite garb was fashioned in all the colors of the sun, from the sunrise to its setting. Adorned on her midriff were three jewels of fire, two of equal size and one much bigger sitting neatly in the middle. Her oddly pitch black hair flowed downward past her waist. She had a small V shaped band on her forehead that disappeared in her hair, with a white fire opal marking the center.

All the townspeople kneeled once they arrived, except for the girl. She stared up at the giant creature, with her face plastered in fear and astonishment. She couldn't tear her eyes away from the two who had made their dramatic entrance.

Her mind raced, and her breathing picked up. Her chest ached, and she clutched her heart, bending over as she tried to breathe. The woman holding her noticed and set her back down. Cedar, the two women, and the moose were now watching her. Then the moose looked at the adorned woman and back at the girl.

"*Quiet now, little one,*" a soft, soothing voice came to her.

Where did that come from?

The girl looked around for the speaker.

"*Girl, look at me,*" it said sternly.

She glanced at the moose, but continued her search for the speaker.

There's no way.

She doubled back to the moose and could see its eyes on her.

Did... did the moose just speak to me? She thought, blinking in disbelief.

"*Yes,*" the moose began to lie down, "*the moose did just speak to you.*"

She looked around for confirmation, but everyone was still kneeling.

I don't understand what's happening? She covered her face, the panic setting in, she began to hyperventilate.

"*I am speaking to you directly. This is how I communicate to all.*"

"How!? How is that *possible*!?" She exclaimed out loud to the moose.

"*I don't know. I am just an old moose... I was alive during your era and have been alive for thousands of years. This is something that began a long time ago. Breathe child, calm down,*" he chuckled and continued to look at the girl.

My era? You know what I am?

Surprise captured her attention from her surrounding predicament.

What is going on? Where are the humans then?

"Let's get you settled first, and then we can talk more. This is not the time nor the place to discuss such tragedies."

The girl could hear the old moose's bones creak as he rose.

The adorned woman waved her hands in the air, and everyone took one last look at the mysterious blood-covered girl and dispersed. She then went and spoke to the warriors. The one who took her staff handed it over to Cedar and they took their leave as well. The olive-skinned satyr looked displeased but did not argue as he left with his men.

Cedar took the girl's hand and led her behind the moose with the other two women through the rest of the village. A forest home hid right behind the temple, on a small growing hill. The ground had turned into a soft moss layer with different clover and grass scattered throughout the area. A pond with a small trickling waterfall decorated the front of the curious cottage. They sat down in what seemed to be an outside cooking area. The girl saw a rounded clay-covered oven, a garden of herbs and other plants near a freshwater well.

The adorned woman spoke hurriedly and quietly to Cedar as she glanced between the two of them. Afterwards, the others stayed in the cooking area while Cedar led her to a bathing room inside with a large bamboo tub. She left the girl there to look around the room and came back moments later with a pair of tan colored clothes. Cedar let the water trickle into the smooth tub. When it was full and steaming, she motioned to the bath for her to get in and gave her a kind smile as she shut the curtain.

Once she had left, the girl hesitantly climbed into the hot bath and felt her muscles melt into the hot water. She grew tired and let out a sigh of relief. She doubted how long she had been in there, but when the water grew cold and dirty with mud and blood, she decided it was time to face the odd new world. Begrudgingly, she stood, dried off with the fluffy towel that sat waiting for her, and grabbed the fresh clothes that Cedar put out.

The girl thought back to the pod she emerged from earlier that day and let out a small sad whimper at seeing her shriveled and damaged body in the mirror on the wall. She touched her ribs and arms, feeling only bone. She closed her eyes, turning away from the pain of what she had become.

When she slipped the soft clothes over herself, she examined them. They had leafy green vines sewn into the bottom of the sleeves and pant legs. The texture between her fingers felt coarse, but the material itself was soft and comfortable. She put the pieces on and the outfit turned out to be a top that was a closed neck with loose arm sleeves, and loose pants that went to her ankles. She tied the pants with a couple of extra loops of string to keep them from sliding off. The colors were a mix of brown and tan, with a dusty green for the leaves. Looking down at the loose clothing, she wondered whose they were.

Maybe these are the brown-haired ladies' clothes. She thought to herself.

Satisfied with the outfit and ready to rejoin the curious people she found, she walked the way she came, using the wall and furniture for help and guidance. The hot bath lessened the intense pain, leaving a dull ache in its place as she made her way through the home.

I guess it's not miracle water.

They all watched her when she came into view. She sat next to Cedar at the stone and wood table. Cedar gave her back the freshly cleaned staff.

"How are you feeling, little one?" The moose gazed down at her.

Speaking plainly and out loud, she responded with a tired shrug.

"I'm here," she said as she crossed her arms over the table.

"Can you just tell me what is going on, please? It has been a very long day," she shook her head and meet the moose in his old, dark eyes.

"First, tell me your story, where you came from, and what has happened to you since. We are all very eager to hear," he responded.

"Wait... they can't understand me though, so how will they hear my story?"

"I am translating what you say back to them telepathically. As I am speaking to you in the old earthen tongue, I speak to them

in their native language. You are not the first to come here with a different dialect."

The girl sighed, "At this point, I should've expected that."

Her universe has twisted and turned into something entirely different. If she could recall her past, it's highly unlikely that any of this would be part of her memories.

She stretched her arms forward and drummed a small beat on the table with her fingers, then she rubbed her face, trying to recall the beginning of her curious tale.

As the sun finished setting, the girl told everyone what had happened so far. At some point, the brown-haired woman got up and began prepping for dinner, Cedar was still sitting, and the adorned woman was nowhere to be seen.

After she had finished talking, they all sat in silence contemplating, and wondering what it could mean. Then the girl asked a simple, yet extraordinarily complex question.

"What happened to my people?" She asked. "I... I need to know."

He starred at her for a moment, thinking of the safest response.

"It is a tremendously sad story to speak of, but these are your people, or rather, your descendants, in a manner of speaking."

With his head, he motioned towards the fox women around her.

"Those monsters in the building," he hesitated, *"...are also your people."*

She sat patiently, trying to take it all in as he continued with his story.

"Almost two thousand years ago, I was of normal size, at least what you perceived as normal during your time," he paused to think again.

In his old, weary voice, he began, *"I am not a human like you, and I did not understand your world. But my story begins when I was grazing a forest meadow. There was an immense flash of heat and light. The next thing that came was a smell different from anything that ever was. Your people... the humans... died. Or mutated. That is what the surviving animals like me noticed. It was not just you humans, though. All around us, the world began to change. Some things were sudden like the monsters, but other things were slowed, like me and this new civilization you see around you. It was not until many years later... I am uncertain how long, though, that I developed a way to communicate with others. When all this first started, it was chaos. So much fighting, so much pain and sorrow, we call it the Thousand-Year War or the Great Despair. Then the first king came. He defeated the shadows and united his people. That was when I was appointed as Chief of the 7th Province for my help in the war, and it has been peaceful since."* He looked down at her with knowing sorrow in his eyes.

He ended his story with two stomach-wrenching sentences.

"Your kind has not been seen since the victory against the mutants and the shadows. As far as I know, you are the only pure human I have seen since the time of Great Despair."

Silence filled the air. She stared at the patterns on the table, not wanting to see pity in their eyes because it was just as palpable in the air. For a while, it was silent, no one wanting to be the first to speak.

"How am I supposed to respond to something like this?!"

He stayed silent. The girl wiped away the tears from her face.

"How long have you been chief of this village?" She thought to him.

He looked at her with no expression.

"How *long* HAVE YOU BEEN CHIEF?" She yelled and slammed one hand down on the table. Cedar jumped, and the brown-haired lady stopped cooking, turning around to watch.

"549 years." He responded with no emotion in his voice.

The girl covered her eyes and laughed, shaking her head.

I was asleep for almost two thousand years.

She caressed her hands in her lap and laid her forehead on the sun-warmed stone table.

"Why?" Her voice cracked.

It was the only thing she could think to say. It had felt as though her body had given up on her and her mind was following behind. She closed her eyes and cried, letting her tears drip onto her hands. Her throat and eyes stung.

The delicately clad lady gracefully glided out of the cottage with something in her hands. Once she got to where they all were sitting, she set down a lovely teapot and a porcelain cup to match in front of the crying girl.

Everyone sat and watched as she poured a dark and steamy liquid into the small smooth cup. She put it in front of the girl, and to the girl's surprise, she gently stroked her hair and pushed the tea closer.

Their eyes met and even though they had interacted little since they had met, she could see kindness and understanding coming from them.

"Drink. This will calm you," the moose said.

She took the warm cup into her hands. Bringing it to her lips, she sipped the tartness of green tea, instantly feeling the soothing warmth travel through her body.

"And sleep well," he finished.

Panic set in when she realized she was the only one drinking the tea. She looked around through the blurriness to see all of them watching her. Hastily she stood wobbly. Cedar went to catch her, but the girl pushed her away.

Is this a trap?

She should have known.

She only made it two steps before she fell onto the soft ground. She felt the moss on her fingertips, and the last thing she saw was all the colors of the sun.

4

A FATEFUL ENCOUNTER

a couple months later

"SAMMII, Samihanee!" A voice boomed down the hall.

She woke gradually, opening her eyes and rolling over to face the windowsill, and looked up to the open room ceiling with the morning sun dripping in. It had been a chilly night, with beads of precipitation glistening the wood paneling. As the sun came up, it became a fresh summer morning.

Sam thought back to the first week that she met Cedar and her family. After the first couple of days, they created a name for her.

Samihanee.

A FATEFUL ENCOUNTER

Since she did not remember her actual name and instead of calling her 'girl', they gave her that one. She was unsure how she felt about it though. The family explained to her it meant 'the lonely forest' and after a while, they had shortened it to 'Sam' or 'Sami'.

"Sammmmmiiii! Breakfast is ready!" Atlas hollered.

A little boy with hair as pitch black as his mothers, squealed and popped his head in from the arched curtain entryway. He ran up to the bed and crouched into a pouncing position. Instantly, Sam rolled the other way to dodge the tiny boy's pointed feet which dug into the spot where she was lying only moments ago.

"Atlas... you are getting too big to jump on people." Fern, the brown-haired sister, groaned as she walked in after him.

"And *you're* too old to have any fun!" Atlas retorted, sticking his tongue out.

"Oh, ya! Well, I'm not!!" Sam flung the cover around Atlas, making him into a small teddy bear burrito. She tickled him as he struggled to get free, and Fern covered her mouth, giggling.

Atlas and Amos, their father, were not there the first day she had met Cedar, Fern, or their mother Lin. She met Atlas and Amos a week after they had come back from their hunting and fishing trip in the wild. Sam had noticed Atlas took after his father, who took on the form of a grizzly bear man. With a stocky build and thick brown fur coming from his arms, legs, and back. Both have small bear tails, and, for the most part, looked identical.

Atlas was the definition of the cute teddy bear, but Sam could tell he was much smarter than he let on. However, he seemed to enjoy playing the part others wanted to see. Amos, on the other hand, is sturdy and stubborn, but something inside him melted when he interacted with Lin or his children.

"Alright, alright, mom told us to come wake you, breakfast is ready!" He said in between gasping breaths.

"Hmmm, you got off lucky this time but next time you won't!" She released the boy from his blanket prison. He jumped out and ran down the hallway to the kitchen with loud, thunderous footsteps.

Fern looked at Sam as she got up from bed and fixed the big feathered comforter the way she always did when she woke up.

Fern sighed.

"The bigger he gets, the harder it is to handle his excitement."

"He definitely has grown a lot since I first met him." Sam said, smiling as she put her hair up into a ponytail. Fern nodded in agreement and they walked to the kitchen together.

The first few weeks were a hard change for her. Sam didn't leave the cottage or the yard surrounding it. Despite her slow recovery, she would go outside to the patches of deep green clover in the sun, spotting the dancing flowers and grass. Looking around, she sat and watched the village life go by from the forested hill they lived on. As she would sit and watch, all the emotions that grabbed at her for attention came closer in the silence. Sadness did not let her look up towards the sky that beckoned for her happiness, and dread brought moments of breathlessness throughout the months. During these fits, she ended up spending most of her time in the room that was given to her or in the comfort of others. Cedar's family helped lessen the overwhelming anxiousness she felt when she entered her own thoughts. They had been so welcoming and understanding, but interacting with the rest of the village was much different.

They explained that when she had first come to the town, the villagers were terrified and thought she was something they called a 'Shadow'. Shadows and Mutants were the monsters that she had seen in the cave the day she woke. These were creatures of the past that were left behind to roam mindlessly. The villagers feared them along with the dark cave and did not wish to upset the peace. That is why it remained forbidden to that day.

After a while, she got used to the difference. It became easier for her to take in her surroundings and the feelings that dwelled inside of her diminished, waiting to re-emerge. The Chief decided it would be best for her to be put in a class to learn the language and to hopefully make friends with the village. Unfortunately, Sam found that learning the language was much easier than making friends out of her wary neighbors.

"Sam, good morning." Lin chimed in as they walked into the kitchen. The wooden cooking utensil in her hand scrapping across the pan while Cedar and Atlas were at the table, already eating. The rich and salty smell of peppers, onions, eggs, and potatoes lingered in the air.

The forest is calm this morning.

Sam enjoyed going on walks in nature and silently investigating the strange new things she found around her. Peace came as she watched the trees sway in the breeze of the morning.

A lot of the plants looked the same from what I can remember, but some are new and unlike anything I had ever seen.

She thought curiously as she spotted a clump of deep salmon petals that formed the shape of petite bells. She smiled to herself as she continued on her small, creek-guided adventure.

She stepped onto a fern-covered boulder and looked out into the clearing, where she always went to sit and think. She knew this was her spot because she would always follow the creek from the cottage to the clearing that it ran through with a clean sight of the open sky.

Listening to the water sing its never ending song, she sat cross-legged in the clover and moss next to the bank and watched it glisten over the tiny rocks and brown sand that called the bottom of the creek home. This was where she came to get away, clear her thoughts and process everything she has been through and seen.

Loneliness seeped closer to her as her mind trailed in a straight line from thought to thought, leading back to what it had always led back to. She sighed and laid on the cushion of grass, looking up at the cloud-dotted summer sky.

How can I miss something that I don't even remember?

Only Cedar, her family, and the Chief were kind to her, whereas the others in town treated her as a monster or fully shunned her presence.

I wish there was something I could do to get these villagers to see I'm not as horrible as they think I am... or nothing's going to change.

She picked at the innocent grass in frustration as she lay there chewing on her bottom lip in concern.

Her mind led her back to the first time she found the spot by accident, and she laughed to herself. It had been springtime, and the flowers were in full bloom. That was the beckoning call for Sam to leave her nest of safety and travel into the unknown. She walked through the forest that whispered to her from behind the cottage one evening. Following the colorful wildflowers and the newly vibrant trees, she began searching for something. Unsure what it was, she continued through the woods. Taking off her shoes, she walked into the water of the creek that led her further away from the new world and into a more ancient one.

As she stopped to look around at the dense greenery and the water, a mother bird chirped sharply at Sam. She looked around for the bird and found in the tree that sat next to the creek laid a twig nest with light purple eggs resting in it. Sam admired the oddity she had discovered, not noticing the chirping that grew louder and more agitated with her movements towards the nest.

All at once, a bright shimmering purple bird flapped its small wings in her face, startling her and causing her to trip and fall into the water. Surprised by the unanticipated reaction of the bird, she looked up in shock as another less glamorous bird joined in the fight. The two flapped their wings madly and chirped sharply at her as they guarded their nest. Chuckling in embarrassment and feeling her face flush with heat, she got up. But as she did, the two continued to fly at her. Ducking and covering her head, she ran barefoot splashing through the water, away from the two protective parents.

Once she found that she was finally clear and now drenched, she saw a clearing that the creek ran through, where she could sit and bask in the sun to dry.

As she continued to torment the clover, grass, and weeds in deep thought, a rustling came from bushes on the other side of the small creek. Interested in the commotion, Sam propped herself up onto her elbows and calmly waited.

A curious creature came up to the water and started drinking. Sam tilted her head to the side, intrigued. The little creature had no fear of her. Its slender body resembled a deer, but it had a long, skinny tail with a tuft of brown fur at the end, like a lion's tail. It also had a small set of almost invisible horns. The predominant color of the creature was a muted shade of green, with patches of brown and black interspersed, and sporadic white spots dotted across its back.

Sam stared at it for a while in bewilderment. It didn't seem to notice her until she tried to get up. Swiftly, the beautiful creature pranced back into the ferns and out of sight, letting out a bleat of alarm.

"Oh no, I'm sorry. I didn't mean to scare you," Sam said in a gentle voice to it.

She crouched down while making soft clicking noises with her tongue, trying to coax it back out from the safety of the bushes.

It popped its head out and looked at her with the same curious look that Sam had given it. She picked some berries from the bush closest to her, in hopes that it would like them, and called out to it again. The creature cautiously crept up to her. They met at the water's edge. She tossed the berries close to it and waited. Gently, he started nibbling on the berries as she sat watching the interesting creature's movements.

"Now, what in the world are you? I think you remind me of a deer, but there is something else that I don't recognize." She said, inspecting it more, noticing odd pearly scales hidden in the short, patches of fur.

After it grew comfortable with her, the creature ate from her hand. Its tongue was rough like sandpaper and tinted purple. As it finished eating, it crossed the water and laid down next to her. Surprised, she reluctantly moved to pet it.

"Wow." She breathed.

"You're so soft!" She chuckled as she tried to maintain her eager excitement. It responded with a tiny bleat, looking at her. Sam saw that its eyes had no whites but were a deep brown with green and tiny speckled dots near where its pupils were. She sucked in a breath.

She could see the mass of the universe in the tiny creature's eyes.

Then a thought came to her.

Ajax. *His name is Ajax.*

She said the name out loud, "Ajax."

The creature stared back as she said his name. He put his head on her leg as she continued to pet him until he dozed off to sleep.

Thoughts of heading back to the cottage tugged at her mind, but Sam hesitated as she glanced at Ajax, who had been peacefully sleeping for a while.

Poor little guy. I don't want to wake him, but we can't stay here forever.

She moved around enough to stir him from his slumber. He bleated sleepily at her and his tired eyes blinked a couple of times.

"Bye, little Ajax, thank you for spending time with me today." She stood and waved to him as she began her journey back. However, it did not take long for her to notice that Ajax was trailing close behind her.

"You have to go back to your parents." Sam said, shooing him away. She kept walking on, but he was insistent on joining her.

I don't know if this is a good idea..

She thought for a moment, wondering what to do. Then, decided that it would be best to see what Lin and the Chief had to say.

"Alright then, if you're gonna come with me, you gotta keep up." Sam patted her leg. He trotted happily up to her and stayed close to her the rest of the way back.

5

THE FIRST KING

Samihanee reached the hearth with good timing as the Chief and Lin were sitting for tea with the family. As she approached with her new companion, there was a wave of expressions from astonished to confused that passed through the group. Not knowing if this was a good sign or bad, she stopped in her tracks and quickly, before they could react negatively, she blurted out.

"He just found me, and I might have fed him... and he won't stop following me. He doesn't seem dangerous," she paused for a breath while she fidgeted with her fingers, then continued, "so I thought it would be fine-" looking around at their faces, then looking to the ground she said. "and I didn't know what to do... so... here we are-" She fumbled through her words, flustered.

She felt anxious about their reaction but optimistic that they would be kind enough to accommodate not just one additional life, but now two.

Sam gave him a reassuring pat on the head, which in turn reassured herself as well and he bleated back at her. The Chief chuckled. Lin stood and made her way over, and the rest of the family followed, crowding around to get a look.

"Sam, do you know what this animal is?" Lin kneeled down in her blue garb.

"No. He looks like a deer mixed with some other animals, but I've never seen anything like him before. I tried to shoo him away, but he won't leave, as you can see." She added with a light chuckle.

"Sammi, he's a Qilin. They are known as the guardians or protectors of the forest. These are creatures of *legend*. It's said that the forest sends them to people it believes are worthy. To see one is rare, but to have one come to you is something else entirely. In all the stories, the guardians and the people, they come to end up doing great things." Fern said as she beamed at Ajax.

Cedar and Atlas played with him, laughing as they ran chasing each other.

"I think his name is Ajax," she said.

"When I saw him for the first time, the name came to me."

Sam looked at Lin and Amos, who were standing there now, admiring the strange being.

"Do- Do you think he can stay? With me, I mean..." She stammered hopefully. "I'll take care of him and you won't have to worry about anything. I just need to learn what he eats and how to care for a.." She stopped and deliberately tried to pronounce Qilin. Giving up, she continued her speech of persuasion, "for him in general. I don't want to burden you with this and I know I'm technically a *guest*, but he came to me and I think he is meant to stay with me." She looked at them pleading.

Amos came up next to Lin and looked at her. "The Qilin are beautiful and rare creatures, they themselves aren't dangerous... but faunanoid will hunt them for their pelts, scales, and horns. They have many mystical properties. The Qilin can protect themselves, but a baby like this can be picked up. He should be safe in the village and in the forest under our care, but anywhere else..." He didn't finish his sentence as he looked at her doubtfully.

Lin continued where her husband left off, "He seems to have chosen you though, and as long as you can understand the weight of the responsibility of taking care of a baby Qilin and protecting him, he will be loyal to you more than any other creature or person in this world."

The Chief walked over to Ajax. When he leaned down, Sam could hear the creaking and moaning in his old bones as he touched noses with Ajax. The little Qilin seemed to liked him. He trotted around the large moose and laid down next to his hooves. Cedar and Atlas, glued to his side, sat down and continued to brush their hands across his pelt as they cooed at him.

Chief looked over at Sam. *"He is very excited to have finally met you."*

"You can talk to him?" Sam asked, astonished, and looked up at the giant moose in disbelief.

"Unfortunately, no, but I can understand him in a sort of way as I can with most animals."

Sam shook her head in disbelief as she sat down and poured herself a cup of tea. As the tea steeped, turning into a warm honey hue, she sunk into her thoughts and processed where the day took her. The sun had reached the hottest part of the day, but with it getting close to winter, the temperate air enveloped the grounds subtly. Fern, Amos, and Lin came and sat down next to her at the table. They all watched the little creature play and trot around like he had always been a part of the family.

After a while, Lin collected Fern and Cedar to go practice their dance ritual for the upcoming Harvest Festival. Cedar explained it was a celebration of the past year's harvest and asking for good yields for the next year. Sam decided to join them to watch the practice while learning more about its festivities.

As Sam had thought, it was a changing of seasons celebration with their ritual dance as the main event. There were good luck customs to uphold, plentiful harvest tokens to make, along with food, drinks and games to celebrate.

It seems like it was going to be a really fun festival!

Sam twirled her hair as she walked behind Cedar, listening to their conversation.

Maybe I could finally meet some new people too.

She bit her lip, trying to stop the tears that brimmed her eyes from escaping. After a couple of deep breaths, she managed to conceal her loneliness behind the smile that she had been practicing for almost a year.

They talked on the way to the giant gazebo where they would dance on the stage in front of the village and its inhabitants. On the walk, Sam noticed the village buzzing in excitement about the coming festival as the days passed by.

There was also talk of a celebration happening in the King's Realm, but that was going to be marking the end of summer, signifying the celebration of life.

Cedar explained it as a type of race where you have the three species of faunanoid on one team. The land fauna will race on foot up treacherous terrain. The sea fauna will race in the water into a labyrinth in the depths. Lastly, the air fauna will race in the sky with floating obstacles in a competition of grace and speed.

"But this time is different!" Cedar said, bursting with excitement, her hands waving to match her energy.

"The princess has come of age! So after the race is won, the King will choose which nation the princess's husband will come from! It has been a tradition passed on since the beginning of their reign!"

Cedar slumped down, "I wanna be a priiiiinceeeesss!" She whined.

Sam chuckled.

"You're more important than a princess," Fern scoffed, motioning the thought away as she walked up next to them. "*You're* an Elemental apprentice priestess, even I am just a *regular* apprentice priestess," she said sadly. "Be a little proud of your heritage, please."

Cedar rolled her eyes at Fern. "Sorry..."

"Elemental?" Sam looked at Lin curiously.

"Yes, a long time ago when Elementals still mingled with faunanoid, some had children together. And sometimes those children and now the generations after have the powers of the Elementals. I am a descendant of a fire Elemental. Cedar received the gift, but unfortunately, Fern did not. Sometimes, it skips generations or is random," Lin explained, glancing at Fern sadly.

"Fire Elemental? What does that mean? Like you are the symbol of fire?" Sam was still confused.

"No, we control fire." Lin stopped. They had reached the wood and stone gazebo. Lin put her hands together in front of her chest and concentrated. Without warning, her hands separated, and a spark of flames ignited eloquently on both palms. Sam stepped back in alarm when she felt the warmth of the flames kiss her face.

"Umm-" She watched dumbfounded, staring at the flames trickling upwards toward the sky. Her mind jumbled as she searched for her next words.

"That's.... not something normal humans have or could *ever* do-" Sam fumbled with her words, still mesmerized.

"This is a relatively rare occurrence in our world too, but it has been around since the beginning of the Elementals." Lin put her hands together and smothering the innocent flames.

"The Elementals fought in the Thousand-Year War. They helped us rise and protected us when we needed it the most. After the war finally ended, they went into recluse, and they have been gone ever since. The only sign of their existence now is us, their descendants, and the one Fire Elemental who stands guard at the Tree of Knowledge." Fern added.

So there are Elementals now? Thoughts raced through Sam's mind. She pinched her nose as a headache began to form.

"We will talk about this no more for now. Let's focus on the dance." Lin looked at Sam, worried, but twisted her attention back toward the reason they were there.

Cedar and Fern climbed onto the stage, Sam sat on a stone bench with Ajax, and Lin stood in front to instruct.

"Alright, you may begin." Lin waved her hands for them to start, her dress sleeves reacting dramatically to the movement.

The girls began by slowly dipping into a plie as their hands went close to the floor. They graced the stage as ballerinas. But Sam could see Cedar had trouble with balancing and moving in sync with Fern. It was clear Cedar needed to practice more before the festival. She was supposed to use her flames in the dance as well, but was still far from doing anything her mother had shown her. She only produced tiny sparks of evidence of being a Fire Elemental.

The dance was mesmerizing when performed perfectly. It gathered the attention of bystanders. The faunanoids would stop and watch the peaceful dance, but once they saw Sam, they flashed her a look of distaste or fear and scurried back to completing their daily chores or tasks.

Sam sighed. Rejection seeped back in. She wished there was a way for them to understand her. Sam looked down at Ajax, who was content just being near her as he slept underneath her legs, then back up at the people who had taken her in. She came to the thought that she didn't need the acceptance of the others, especially the ones that looked at her with the prenotion of her character, even though they knew nothing about her.

The two dancers continued for the rest of the afternoon, only stopping now and then to rehydrate and talk about how to fix mistakes in the routine. Once the sun began to dip lower in the sky, they walked back home and stopped through the small market square to buy some food for dinner.

The square was cobbled, with a quaint fountain in the middle where children ran around, tagging each other. The village well was off to the left side, and a small inn sat at the end of the market. Most of the faunanoids homes were scattered throughout the fields. However, there were some in the small village as well. She could see the temple's spire with the bell placed in its center behind the marketplace and the road that led back to their cottage. As she looked over the village, a feeling of annoyance washed over her. A familiar short satyr graced her eyesight and was making his way over to them with the look of unyielding perseverance.

It's like he can sense my presence.

She made a frustrated sigh and side-eyed Cedar. Cedar looked back and saw him marching up towards them and groaned in response. Lin and Fern continued chatting with the merchant, unresponsive to the situation.

"Mom, we've got company," she said through a face of regret.

Just as she finished speaking, he joined them at the fruit stall.

"Good afternoon, Captain Ryner." Lin and the stall merchant said in unison. Lin gave a small head bow as she spoke.

"Afternoon Priestess," he said with a curt nod, "and Vice, your fruit looks fresh as always. I just came over to check on things, and make sure everything was alright here." He perused the fruit.

"How's the monster girl? She looks like she is getting used to the village now." He sneered, laughing at his own joke as he stared at Sam and adjusted his belt that Sam could see was struggling to stay on.

Everyone looked uncomfortable and unsure how to respond. Sam pursed her lips and furrowed her brows.

"You know I can understand you, right?" She retorted back.

"That's why I said it, stranger, just making sure you understand your place in this. You're not a part of this village and the only reason you are still here is because the Chief and the Priestess vouch for you." He smirked, adjusting his sword in its leather holster.

Sam replied, this time in English, crossing her arms. "Well, you're a greasy looking mole rat with goat legs." She raised her eyebrow with a stern face, not backing down from his gaze.

He stepped closer, his cheeks blazing red against the cool tone of his skin.

"That's enough! Both of you." Lin held up her hands, ending the dispute. "Ryner, please be kinder to our guest. The disrespect is unwarranted, especially after everything she has been through."

He was silent for a moment, obviously unhappy.

"For you, Priestess." He grunted.

After that, he stiffly bowed while eyeing Sam, then turned and made his way back the way he came.

Sam rolled her eyes. "What a rude, short man."

"He isn't usually like this," Fern responded. "You did arrive to us in a very intense way. He just wants to protect this village, even if he is incredibly rude."

"Yea... yea, I *know*- I just wish your people understood that I'm not some scary monster. Everyone is still so distant from me." Sam looked at the ground. She didn't want them to see the tears forming in her eyes.

Cedar hugged her sympathetically, while Fern gave her a look of pity.

"Give them time. These are good but *cautious* people. It is how they have survived for so long," Lin said, resting her hand on Sam's shoulder.

"Maybe at the festival, you can meet more people and make some friends," Cedar added hopefully.

Sam looked up. "You're right, thanks." She wiped the tears away, and they began their way back home with dinner.

When they returned, they prepared the food outside at the table while the oven heated. The others sat as Sam convinced Fern to let her help cook.

After all, I can't depend on this family forever.

Amos had gotten back in time for dinner, along with Atlas, from collecting wood and working on some other minor projects around the village.

"So, can someone explain this Thousand-Year War to me, please? I am still confused," she said as she crunched down on a carrot.

"And how can a war last that long? And we still need to discuss this Elemental thing too," Sam said sarcastically, pointing the cooking utensil at them.

"It might be too much to take in right now... why don't we start with the Elementals and worry about the rest at a later time?" Lin stood up and walked into the house, not giving much choice to the matter. Sam sighed in defeat as Lin came back out with a tea set. She began her story as she poured tea for the table.

"The Elementals are as old as the story of the dragons. None truly know where they came from or began. They were always just there. When our world was new and the faunanoid still roamed feral, they were plagued with the shadows of the old world and horrible monsters that slaughtered for no reason." She stopped, sipping her steaming tea.

"It was a time of death and sadness. Our ancestors could barely survive. One day that changed, though. The Elementals appeared, and like a beacon of hope, the faunanoid rallied with them to rid the world of the chaos. There are many types of Elementals. You have seen fire, of course, but there is also water, air, earth, and much more. It is hard to name them all, and a lot of them have not been seen since the Time of Great Despair." She looked at Sam.

"There is even a legend about an Elemental who can control nature and an elemental who sees the unseen," Lin said in an eerie, dark voice.

Sam took in a sharp breath. A chill went down her spine and excited bumps raised along her arms. It was almost too much for her to believe.

How did they exist at this time, but not in mine?

Lin continued, "The Time of Great Despair came to an end when a group of Elementals found the heroic King Arthur. He and this army battled together and brought an end to the last Shadow. After the war was over, the Elementals crowned him as the King to unite *all* faunanoid across the Realms, and we have been at peace under their rule since." Lin ended her story with another satisfied sip of her tea.

"Why did they choose him to be the uniter of all the Realms?" Sam asked.

"Well, that is because he was the first and only faunanoid found to be of all the Realms. He was of sky, land and sea." Lin said.

In unison with what she said, she touched her forehead, put her hand on her heart and pulled her hand away like she was grabbing a string from her chest.

Sam looked at her questioningly.

Fern, understanding her confusion, responded, "Each motion represents one of the Realms. The touch to the forehead means the mind of the sky, the hand over the heart means the body of the land and the pulling away from the heart represents the soul of the sea."

"Wait, so he was the only one to *ever* be from all three Realms?"

"It has been attempted but with no success, the ancestors of King Author are the only ones to have these traits." Amos replied.

Sam put her hand on her temple pressure point.

"You were right, Priestess Lin. I don't think I can take in anymore information. My head is hurting," she chuckled.

Everyone laughed. "You don't have to be so formal, Sammi. You are a part of our family now. I think that it is appropriate to say," Lin added with a warm smile.

Sam nodded, smiling at everyone in turn. She turned back to the food she was preparing with the feeling of happiness filling her body. Fern leaned in and affectionately nudged her with her shoulder.

"Alright, I think we are done with dinner. What do you think, Sammi?" Fern wiped her hands off on a rag and put them on her waist, looking admiringly at the food.

"Yes, I think so too!" Sam said as she started putting the dirty cooking utensils in the sink, and Amos gathered the plates.

6

SPIRIT OF THE FOX

SAM STARTED HER CLASSES while trying to find a place where she belonged in the new world. She kept her staff cleaned and would find herself staring at it as she dozed off, wondering, speculating about its past. In hopes that it might magically give her an answer for her many questions.

Ajax was an immense comfort and became inseparable from her when she was in the cottage or when they went on their many explorations. She felt their bond and understanding of each other grow every day with their time together. Sam observed that there was a mutual understanding between them, as if they could both sense each other's thoughts and emotions.

Ajax had a lingering loneliness about him, that Sam was all too familiar with. She wondered about his own family and where he came from.

She thought of what her parents might have looked like, trying to remember anything. She squeezed her eyes shut tighter, as if that would help her more in remembering the lost ones.

Nothing.

There was nothing to grab onto. She could feel it right past her grasp, with an impenetrable wall of fog guarding what she was looking for.

She breathed deep, drawing attention back to her surroundings. Ajax was napping next to her, his stomach rising and falling in a slow, comforting motion.

The farmers' field was golden and beautiful in the afternoon. A gold glow hovered above it from the fall sun's warm light. Now that it was not as hot, it was more enjoyable to sit on the hill outside of town and watch the farmers and people move throughout their lives. Just past the town on the other side, she could barely see her home, the little cottage hidden in the forest's shade. The town's folk were eagerly setting up the festival that would be for the next three days. They would hold a celebration of the last year's luck and plentiful harvest for the first two days with games and food. Then, on the last day, there would be ceremonies for luck and good harvests for the following year.

"Heeeyyyyyy!" Cedar yelled, waving wildly.

Fern and Cedar trekked up the hill. Ajax woke from the commotion and bleated at the welcome disturbance.

"Took you long enough to wake up,"

Sam chuckled and rustled his head; her fingers lingered on where she could feel his horns growing in.

She looked at them both, smiling.

"Hiyya."

"We were going to the forest to pick some herbs and mushrooms for the festival. Want to come with us?" Fern asked.

"Sounds like fun. This would be a good time to learn what is *edible* in the forest and what's *not*." Sam snorted a laugh as she stood and dusted off the bits of grass and wispy seeds that had stuck to her pants. Ajax shook himself too, as if copying her movements. And they all started for the forest.

"Are you excited about the festival?" Cedar asked as they were rummaged the forest floor. "We can't wait for you to see the actual ceremony." She looked up from poking through leaves and smiled at Sam.

Sam picked up a light brown mushroom and handed it to Fern. "Of course I am. You guys have been working a lot this past month," Sam said with a light chuckle. "Some harder than others, though." She glanced at Fern jokingly and laughed.

"I am working just as hard as Fern!" She frowned, crossing her arms and looking at the two of them with a stern face. Fern smiled, laughing along with Sam.

She was excited. Saying it out loud helped her feel more sure of that. But she felt the nervousness on the edge of her thoughts as she wondered what was going to happen or if she would accomplish her goal of making more friends. With a smile on her face, she reassured herself that everything would be alright. Squatting down, she brushed away a pile of leaves to resume her search.

They had gathered a good deal of mushrooms and interesting-looking herbs when Sam finally looked up and took in her surroundings. She stretched her arms and looked at the sky. The tree leaves were a burnt orange, which complimented their off white trunks that were slashed with thin slits of black. Something caught her eye. It was a clearing. She turned towards it for a better view.

A clearing with skeletons littering its meadow.

The mound.

The fossilized skeleton cried upwards towards the sky with so much sorrow.

"Sammi?" Fern whispered quietly beside her. She turned to her, meeting her warm brown eyes, and realized that she had unknowingly walked to the edge of the forest and stepped into the clearing.

"Yea?" Sam said with restrained tears in her eyes.

"Are you alright?" Fern whispered again, looking at the figure.

"It looks like they died a sad, painful death," she released the breath she didn't know she was holding.

"This is where I found my staff... where I met Cedar." Sam pointed in the other direction, her mind returning her to the memory of rescuing her from the boar.

"Yes, she told me. You were brave, especially for being so weak back then," Fern said as Cedar joined them. "You were very malnourished. I am surprised you made it out of the forbidden cave."

"You know, there is a story about this skeleton. It is said that their soul is trapped here, and that is why anyone that sees it is also filled with sadness. The warrior waits to be released from their suffering, but no one knows how to help them-" Cedar paused for a moment, the air became uncomfortable with grief.

"But they died a warrior's death. See the bones around their feet?" Cedar pointed. "Those used to be the mutated ones." She paused again before studying Sam.

"At least they died protecting what they believed in."

Fern leaned in, "It is called *The Statue of the Fallen One*, and it is also believed that this warrior fought with the first king, King Arthur."

A memory struck Sam. The image of a knight in shining armor holding the great sword Excalibur blazed in her mind.

"That's weird I just remembered, in my time, there was also a King Arthur. In the stories, he was supposed to be someone who fought for all that was fair and just. He was supposed to have been a good king." Sam said.

"Hmm, interesting. I wonder if there is any correlation," Cedar pondered.

Without thinking, Sam whispered so quietly that the others almost didn't catch it, "My mom used to tell me stories about him." She closed her eyes. A glimpse of curly brown hair brushing against the wind flashed before her. She heard a chuckle as soft and gentle as wind chimes.

Just as it appeared, it vanished.

Fern gasped. "What, Sammi? What did you say?" She gawked at her, wide-eyed.

Sam looked up at Fern. "What?"

"You just said that your mother would read you the stories about your King Arthur!" Cedar said excitedly and grabbed Sam's shoulders, shaking her. "Did you remember something?"

She looked at them, trying to recall her words. Her eyes grew wide with recognition.

"I did! I did! My mother read me old folktales and mythology from ancient times! We studied history together!!" Sam laughed and tightly hugged Cedar.

I remembered something! Finally, something to hold on to. She began to cry and laugh with joy.

"Sam, that's amazing!" Fern exclaimed, "But there was a word you said. I do not understand. Mythology- What is that?" she asked.

"It's the study of old religions from way before even my time, and stories about monsters and creatu-..." Sam trailed off, looking at Fern and Cedar's foxlike features.

"What?" They said in unison as they looked at her.

"Nothing." She laughed, scratching her head awkwardly. "I'll explain it to you later. Are we ready to head back? Did we get enough food for the festival?" Sam took a breath, feeling the weight fall off her chest. She thought back, recounting each minute detail of the small memory.

"Yes, it probably is a good time. We still have to make our family's dish for the celebration." Fern dug through her woven twine bag.

Sam took one last sorrowful look at the fallen one and began walking back to the town with the feeling of assurance. They made their way out of the autumn forest and down the steep hill towards home.

Little did they know, glowing green eyes watched their every move with patient anticipation.

Dusk drew near as the food was finished and the festivities began. Small children ran around the square in delight with kites pattering in the air close behind them while vendors sold their sweet or savory foods and festival goers enjoyed the activities.

The discomfort and weary expressions were clear on the few that shot Sam looks as they walked down the street. While a few remained skeptical of Samihanee, the majority of the faunanoid were gradually getting used to her presence.

Sam and her adopted family walked into the square. Cedar, Fern, and Lin dressed in their traditional garb and braided their hair into a ponytail that stuck out of a bun, which they adorned with beads and autumn colored bird feathers.

Lin wore a long, elegant dark red robe with a deep orange to yellow ombre ribbon tied around her waist, and her hands hidden under her long sleeves.

Cedar and Fern, on the other hand, wore robes that went only down to their knees. Colors of brown, tan and white covered the robes and took the attention of all. The ribbon tied around their waists was a black ombre and all three of them wore wooden sandals with leather straps.

Amos and Atlas came dressed in their fancy attire as well, which included a shirt tucked into some dark brown slacks. To match with the girls, they had small braids with beads and feathers in their short, dark brown hair.

Sam turned the bead in her own newly braided hair and thought back to earlier.

"No, I don't think it's a good idea," Sam said uncomfortably. "From what you said, the beads were meant to mean what province and family you're from and the feathers symbolized your ranking," she said, looking at Lin. "I have neither," Sam looked away, upsetting herself.

Lin tenderly touched Sam's chin and pushed her face up to meet her dark, keen eyes. "Whether you want it or not, you are a part of this family." She smiled at Sam and put the bead on the table with a soft metal clink. "It is here for you to decide. We will meet you outside when you're ready."

She hadn't realized how much she had grown with these people. They had been there for her for so long. Sam thought about her old life. The thirst for the knowledge of what was gone had grown daily, but she was becoming accustomed to her new life amongst these strange people.

Sam glanced at her own body. The weight she had lost during her time in the pod had been gained back. Eating well and taking care of herself had left her with a strong and lean physique. She no longer had to worry about resembling a skeleton from the forbidden cave, with her face now glowing with a healthy complexion.

Her clothes she arrived in were long gone. She now wore clothes fit for the fox and bear family. Similarly, she felt new from what she once was when she woke.

Still, her mindset and goals were the same.

A deep blue robe veiled her, with a black ombre ribbon around the waist, to match Fern and Cedar. She also wore the same uncomfortable sandals that they had to dance in. She looked down at the bead that confiscated her eyesight. It demanded to be worn, to be seen by the world, no matter the lack of feathers in her tightly braided hair.

Her fingers absentmindedly twisted the bead in her hair, but the smell of a cooking fire and the hum of the surrounding people abruptly awakened her senses.

Fern clicked her tongue to grab her attention.

"Hey," she whispered closely, "I know you're nervous, but stop twisting the bead in your hair. You're going to split your hair off." Fern gave her a hug. "This is supposed to be fun!" She said.

Cedar squealed, making Sam jolt, and ran up to her friends near a booth decorated with masks and what seemed to be fireworks.

Atlas ran off, and Fern, squeezing her hand, went with Lin and Amos to stroll the food vendors.

Too bad Ajax had to stay home.

Out of nervous habit, Sam seized at the bead and twisted it a couple times before catching herself and forcing her hand down to her side.

Cedar beckoned Sam to join her with her friends. Sam furrowed her brow and looked around for an escape, but once she realized she was socially obligated, she let out a sigh and headed over. Noticing that the group consisted mostly of teenagers and some children, Sam's eyes darted around the festival, searching for Fern. In the crown, she spotted her, now walking with her own friends.

A couple of the young faunanoid shuffled uncomfortably at her arrival, but two of them attempting to be nice, introduced themselves.

"I'm Jeremiah and this is Elaine." A bulky sheep satyr waved shyly and motioned to himself and the girl standing next to him. The small girl nodded politely, avoiding eye contact. As Sam greeted them, her eyes hesitated on Elaine. She was a goat satyr with light brown fur. The girl's face was familiar and reminded her of someone. As her eyes lingered, she felt unsettled as she noticed the uncanny resemblance between her olive-colored skin and brown eyes to those of someone else she knew.

"Wait.... are you related to Ryner?" She asked.

The girl blushed and let out a sudden sheep's bleat. Shuffling and looking down in embarrassment, "Yaaaaa, he's my dad, sorry 'bout him." Elaine grew redder. "He can be a lot. But he- he means well, he just worries too much." She stammered.

Sam snorted. "Is that what you call it?"

She tsked, regretting her harsh reaction to the timid girl and let out a sharp breath as she leveled her anger.

"It's fine." Sam smiled genuinely and shrugged. "I guess I would understand if a talking monster showed up out of nowhere like I did."

"To be fair, you were covered in mud and blood and walked like a skeleton." Cedar chimed in, imitating how she thought a skeleton would walk.

Everyone in the group awkwardly laughed. The difficult situation unfolded, her chest lightened. The infectious laugh spread through her and she felt like she hadn't truly enjoyed herself until then. The commotion subsided, and they resumed their shuffling side to side and hushed conversations.

Sam nervously bit her lip, feeling the smooth bead in her hair between her fingers, desperately searching for something else to say. As she pondered, she struggled to recall the feeling of being surrounded by a group of friends engaged in a captivating conversation.

At this rate, I'm going to tear my hair out like Fern had said.

At that moment, Jeremiah saw the bead in her fingers. "Oh wow! Priestess Lin gave you a bead? That's an official family crest!"

Cedar punched him in the shoulder playfully. "Of course she got a bead. Don't be rude. She has been with us long enough, and if she can handle Atlas's bickering, then she is a member of the fox and bear family!" She nodded proudly and folded her arms stubbornly. Sam laughed a little, not sure how to respond.

One of her satyr friends retorted. "Then I should get to wear one as well." Everyone laughed. Cedar blushed and laughed in a mocking tone.

"Are you going to buy something or not?" The vendor of the mask stall glared at them, annoyed. Most of the group disbanded, talking and laughing off into the crowd.

"O hey!" Cedar exclaimed. She touched Sam's arm for her attention.

"Hold on! I have an idea."

She rushed over to the masks and looked them over.

Sam joined her, looking at the exquisitely intricate masks that laid on the platform and hung from the stall. The masks were made either from clay, wood or porcelain and glossed with paint. A few had designs of swirls, leaves or flowers on them, but most of them were animals or monsters with tusks and fangs, painted to bring fear into those who saw them.

"Ah! Here we go!" Cedar declared triumphantly.

She picked up a mask, its light cobalt blue color shining with silvery white accents on the face, ears, and fur tufts.

It was a blue fox.

Sam's pulse jumped, but she stayed silent as Cedar continued her task.

She delicately put it on Sam's face. It only covered the top half of her face, leaving her mouth and chin out.

Sam touched the mask on her face and could feel the smoothness of the paint and the indentions of the carved designs. Behind the mask, she felt a sense of anonymity and freedom to conceal her true identity.

"There!" Cedar said, proud of her handy work.

"We might be red and brown foxes, but the blue fox represents the spirit. And I know on the inside-" She haltered as she fluffed out Sam's hair and untangled a thin stray piece.

"You are one of us."

7

HARVEST FESTIVAL

The next day, the festivities continued with crafts and wares to sell. The village was quaint, but still big enough for there to be a variety of weapons, clothing, jewels, and trinkets to be sold by traveling merchants. Many visitors came from neighboring provinces to enjoy in the multitude of festivities.

Lin had told Sam the previous night that with all the strangers in town, it would be best for her to wear the mask. She understood, of course, but there was a part of her that felt sadness tugging at her heart. She had to cover who she was because these new strangers would notice her.

This reminded her of the creatures back in the cave she came out of when she had woken up. Those creatures, the horrible mutated beings with no thoughts, only hunger. Those were monsters. Though, on some level, she felt the mask connected her with the people that took her in and had protected her.

With her hair adorned in the bead and braids, and her new mask set comfortably on her face, she eagerly looked forward to going out for the second day of the festival.

During the stifling afternoon, the festival was not as crowded, so Ajax joined the merry group. While Cedar, Lin, and Fern rehearsed for the upcoming ceremony, Amos, Sam, Ajax, and Atlas strolled through the square and vendor aisles in search of something entertaining.

"So- have you been enjoying your time during the festival?" Amos asked.

"Of course, it has been so surprising to see all of this. I don't think I have ever done anything like this before!" Sam replied.

Ajax and Atlas ran in circles, chasing each other on the cobblestone road.

"The ceremony sounds interesting. Has Cedar been able to use her fire before?" Sam turned and looked up at Amos through the holes of the fox mask.

Amos stifled a laugh. "No. She tries her hardest, but all she can achieve is a wee candle spurt." He picked up Atlas and held him to keep him from running into anyone.

As she looked at the two of them, she noticed that Atlas looked like a tiny version of Amos for sure. Amos was tall, no doubt, but he was incredibly bulky.

He definitely also resembles a bear.

"Lin has mastered the way of the flame, but she also has had many a year to practice." He continued as they browsed through a stall with some very peculiar armor.

"How long have you and Lin known each other?" Sam asked, picking up a piece of armor with a cloth hood and examining it.

"Ooooooooo, since we were small, about Atlas's age, we grew up here in this village. She went away, though, for training in her art, and I stayed here farming the land and travelled a little. Nothin' special really," Amos said in his burly accent.

"We used to fight all the time before she left," he chuckled. "But when she came back to take over as Priestess, I couldn't seem to find my words."

Sam smiled. "That's really sweet. I am happy it worked out for you two, then."

Amos gave her a distant smile as he added.

"Also, I never really thanked you properly for watching over Cedar that day when the wild boar attacked. It must have been difficult. You seemed so defeated and tired when she brought you to the village." Amos stopped walking and put his hand on her shoulder. "My family means the world to me, and if anything happened to any of you, I don't know what I would do with myself." Amos and Atlas reached down and hugged Sam.

She choked back her words, "Any of... us?" A small stream of tears hid behind her mask.

"Samihanee, I know you have your own family to find answers for, but you are a part of our family now. So, yes... any of you." They released her. Atlas playfully patted her head, and she looked down at the road.

She cleared her throat as she struggled to calm the sea of emotions inside her. As she did, she became heavily aware of the surrounding people. Her cheeks bloomed in embarrassment at the thought and weight of the stares.

Amos and Atlas chuckled together and continued walking past the shops while Sam composed herself. She took a deep breath. There were still so many things she needed to know about her past. As she looked up at the two of them walking away, she felt something in her heart that made her feel calm.

The night had grown near, and dusk was blanketing the horizon. The people left their chores and daily routines to enjoy the cool night of fireworks, food, and games.

"SAAAAM, HEEEEY!" Cedar screamed from across the crowd, intriguing everyone to turn to get a peek, which made Sam blush. Cedar ran up as Fern and Lin followed. "We thought it would be nice to have some dinner before the festival picked up and the crowd got worse. They did well with their training today." Lin relayed with a basket of delightful, fresh smelling food on her arm. Sam's stomach growled and explained to her it had been a while since she had eaten.

"YES! I'm SOOOOO hungrryyyy!" Atlas rushed over to his mother, snatching at the basket.

She pulled it in the air just in time.

"No," she said sternly, "Where are your manners, Atlas? Let's go find a spot to eat, then we can enjoy this meal."

"Hmph!" He crossed his arms, displeased, but promptly started looking for a place for everyone to eat.

The family soon found a quiet place to rest. They began eating, and the fireworks started soon after. Atlas ooed and awed in between giant mouthfuls of bread and cheese, but inhaled the food down rapidly to play with his friends in the festival's games. Sam watched him run off excitedly with a group of his friends.

Sam fed Ajax some of her food, laughing every time he would bleat expectantly for more of the delicious fruit. They sat, watching as the fireworks popped in the distant sky in its many bright colors while they enjoyed each other's company and prepared for the next day, the ceremony.

After some time, Cedar became antsy to walk around and enjoy the games and shop. So they strolled about looking at all the things that the girls hadn't seen during their practice. Cedar bounced through the road passionately when she spotted the new clothing that was being sold that day by a vendor from the desert province. Lin had wandered away, looking at some old relics that had to do with the Elementals, and Fern had gathered near the spices to browse for anything unusual.

Sam was happy to tag along with the girls. She glanced around momentarily and noticed that Amos had disappeared.

Probably looking for the weapons stall.

She rolled her eyes to herself and thought about how they had all been so predictable in their interests.

I wonder if there is anything here I would have liked before I lost my memory.

Her eyes danced over the unique items to be bought and the different hobbies being pursued in the stalls as she waited for something to catch her eye.

Sam put her hand on her staff and felt the engravings that ran down it. Thinking back to Amos, she wondered if she would ever get to train properly and learn to use it.

Maybe Amos could train me. Does he know how to use this type of weapon?

The sneering face of Ryner flashed in her mind, making a face she snorted to herself.

He would never train me.

She sighed.

I guess I can ask Amos after the festival is over.

"Sam, let's keep going this way," Cedar said. She held a bundle of new colorful clothes in her arms and a mischievous, burning look in her eyes. Sam laughed to herself as she followed the child with the shopping problem.

As they continued exploring, Sam saw more stalls with various items to sell, exotic plants, beautiful mosaic lamps, and soft linens. While on the other side, she spotted blacksmithing, pastries or wonders that Sam had never seen before.

The night had fallen, so the sky was lit up with scattered fireworks and lanterns glowing on the street. The cobblestoned road was beautiful, with the lantern light dancing on it and the occasional color splashed by the firework. She looked all around her, full of people talking, laughing, and admiring the beautiful art that had come from all over. Sam was stunned by the beauty that lingered around her.

She didn't realize that a stench had crept up behind her.

A voiced cleared their throat.

"Oh, sorry, I wasn't payii..n..g," She moved to get out of the way but trailed off as she realized who it was.

Ugh.

She rolled her eyes in annoyance.

"What?" She retorted back.

"Where's your leash, monster?" The gruff goat man retorted back.

She glared at him, not breaking eye contact while also noticing that he was right. No one else was with her.

Where is everyone?

No one was nearby to help. This was her battle to fight.

She looked away, ignoring him.

"You know, you're not really a part of the fox. They are just being generous. Once you are gone and out of this village, everyone will forget about you. You don't deserve that bead." He spat and pointed harshly at the bead that rested delicately in her braided hair.

Fury lit inside of her, her chest erupting in anger. He knew that she was no threat. That there was no danger in Sam. And yet he still went out of his way to make unnecessary comments and linger on the lies of what he believed about her.

"Don't point your smelly fingers at me, goat man!" Sam growled through her teeth, backhanding his hand away from her and getting close enough to him that she could see the fear creep into his eyes and smell the stale sweat on his body.

"What's your deal? Why do you have to treat me like this? Is this fun for you?" She snapped. Sam's finger poking into his chest like a metal prodder with each question. She could feel her blood boiling and her face burning. He backed away, stumbling for words, but regrouped quick.

"How dare you touch me!" He roared. He came in close again and in a stern voice. "You are a danger to this village! You came from the shadows, and this will not end well for anybody that you surround yourself with. If you really cared for them, then you would leave!" He pointed to the forest. Before she could respond, he breathed out heavily, turned around and stomped away, disappearing into the crowd before she could counter.

Sam couldn't think. The world spun around her, voices merging and lights blurring. She ran behind the stalls, behind the people, behind the houses, trying to find a place that wasn't a crowded jumble of eyes and sounds.

She slid down against a moss-covered stone wall. She took the mask off and looked at it, her breathing rigid and irregular.

No matter how hard I try... I can never be one of them.

The mask fell from her hand, clinking against the small gravel, and she covered her face and cried.

She had lost that battle.

Sam cried to herself, afraid of the world to notice her as her tears were drowned out by the laughter of the festival.

She cried until she couldn't, holding her arms for comfort. The mysterious forest darkened by the night, being the only witness to her vulnerability.

He is right.

She gazed up at the stars. They shone so brightly, seeming different from before. Hazily remembering that before the pod, during her old life, the stars seemed so sad and dim. Now, they danced in the night sky, celebrating along with the festival.

She sat there for a time, her eyes wandering the forest and the stars, watching for anything to tell her what to do, listening for guidance, or for something to give answers.

The guidance didn't appear.

There was a scuttling in the fallen leaves.

Instantly, Sam threw her mask back on, snapped her head in the direction of the noise, and she made herself a shadow against the wall. Blending in with her surroundings, she watched as a drunk couple walked past her. A cat faunanoid and sheep satyr giggled and laughed with each other as they steadied themselves and headed to their home for the night.

Now with her eyes heavy and swollen, she picked herself up and started towards the cottage.

I have moped long enough.

Content in her sadness. She walked the long way, avoiding the festival and the people, mainly to not run into Cedar, Lin, or Fern. She wouldn't know how to explain what had happened and why she had utterly failed to defend herself.

She made it to her room, took the mask off, placed her staff back, and slumped into bed. She stared out the windows at the town and fell asleep to the dim light, the fireworks and silhouettes of the village.

Come morning, Sam walked into the main room, groggy from crying. Lin, Cedar, and Fern were madly running around, getting ready for the Ceremonial dance that was that evening. Their hair was re-braided and graced with feathers and beads in it just like before, but their wardrobe was different. This time, their gowns were similar but more formal, decorated with fall colors and more feathers. They were chatting earnestly about the big day they had practiced so long for. Fern turned to look at Sam as she walked into the room.

"Good afternoon! Sam, where did you go last night? We missed you! I found some wonderful herbs for cooking and healing that I wanted to show you." Fern jumped to her feet and ran into the kitchen.

"I had a crazy, weird headache, so I turned in early." Sam said dismissively and yawned, hoping they wouldn't catch her lie. There was no reason they needed to know about what happened.

Lin turned to her while fluffing a bow on her robe. "Oh, I'm sorry. Did you want any tea to help calm the pain?" She asked tenderly.

"No, no, I am all good now," Sam replied, smiling. Lin looked at her a moment longer, in quiet caution, and then turned back to her gown fluffing.

"Okay, dear, just let me know then."

Fern returned with the herbs and explained to Sam their names and their uses while they all finished getting ready. She took this as an opportunity to distract herself from the event of last night.

Cedar squealed in excitement when her makeup was finished.

"This year is going to be different. I can feel it! Sam is here, and I have been working so hard on my fire summoning! I might be able to make a spark during the ceremony!" Cedar squeezed Sam.

"Hey, hey, hey! Chill out, Cedar, you're going to ruin your-well, you're *everything* if you go around acting like that." Fern shot her a look while she put the herbs away. Cedar rolled her eyes but stopped and fixed her mushed attire back to its previous glory.

After they were dressed and ready for the ceremony, Lin fixed Sam's hair and the three of them left for the platform to help set up for the night. Sam said she would join them to help once she finished eating a very late breakfast.

She sat at the wooden table inside, in her hands a bowl of broth with vegetables and chicken. She grabbed some bread and cheese to go with it, thinking back to the night before as she ate.

She scorned Captain Ryner for the rift he had created in her between her and the people she grew to care about.

She shook her head.

No, this is just him trying to get inside my thoughts and make me leave, and I am doing what he wants.

The soup and bread received the blunt end of her thoughts as she ripped into her brunch.

I can't let him win. He is just a nasty old man with problems.

She stood fast in frustration, wiped her hands on her cotton pants and put her dishes away before heading into the village. Ajax bleated tiredly as he trotted out of her room to join her on the journey. Sam chuckled in response to his obliviousness.

"How 'bout you stay here today, mmkay? You look tired, and there isn't much you can do down at the ceremony. So get some rest and we will see you tonight." She patted his head and then headed out the door. Ajax laid his head on his legs like a dog and watched her leave out the door without taking him, her staff, or her mask.

She jogged down the small, grassy hillside toward the village. Getting closer, she could hear the excitement humming. She passed the stoned mosaic square and rounded the corner to see the gazebo being cleaned and decorated by Amos, Atlas, and a couple of others. The girls made it before her and ended up doing some minor jobs to help. Sam arrived to Amos lifting a beautiful backdrop and hanging round lanterns. The others were setting up big drums and interesting-looking stringed instruments to each side of the platform.

Sam helped wherever she could, hanging up lanterns and finishing the floral decorations for the background. A couple of hours later, with time to spare, the set was complete and the stage ready. Sam could tell the ceremony was about to begin as the crowd trickled in and the three dancers disappeared.

Sam scanned the crowd for them. She wanted to wish them luck before the dance started. Amos caught her eye and pointed behind the stage. Waving thanks, she rounded the corner and was caught by surprise by Cedar crying in her mother's arms.

"What's wrong?" Sam came up to Lin, concerned.

"I'm never going to call the fire, Sam." Cedar looked up, tears streamed down her face, smearing her fragile makeup.

"This year won't be different. I will never be good enough to call the flame." She covered her face back up. Lin patted her head, running her fingers through the unbraided parts of her hair, and Fern frowned, not knowing what to say.

Sam sighed and embraced Cedar.

"Listen, the fact that you *might* be able to control fire is something that is ridiculous and amazing in itself. I'm sorry that you're having trouble with it," Sam leaned in, "but what's going to happen if you can't do it during this ceremony? You will just have to keep practicing and get stronger until you do. Right?" Lin and Fern agreed with her and Cedar took a deep breath in.

"I guess if you cannot summon the flame, I will have to *disown* you as a daughter," Lin chimed in sarcastically.

Cedar softly chuckled and looked up through her hands, her face full of pleading sadness.

"You've waited this long. What's one more day?" Fern said, rubbing her back reassuringly.

Sam looked at Fern, recalling their conversation about her not having the ability to control the flame.

I wonder how she feels about this.

"Thanks guys, I'm just so nervous. I wanted to do well this year because you're here." Cedar said, wiping her tears away.

"Don't worry about me. You all have been practicing so much for this dance. That alone is going to make it amazing." Sam said.

Cedar nodded, smiling a little. "I am going to do my best for you."

"Now then, we got that settled. Sam, if you don't mind, we are going to get her fixed up and begin the ceremony. We are already running behind." Lin looked up at the sun's setting position.

"Of course, I'll be sitting with Amos and Atlas. Good luck guys!" Sam set off for her seat, eager to see what the ceremony would hold.

8

THE BERSERKER & THE FLAME

BOOOOOMMMM..

Silence took the crowd. Three drummers on one side of the stage, three on the other, began reverberating their drum sticks on the sides of the noble drums. They pause, letting the echo pass the through faunanoid and through the village.

BOOOOOMMMM...

The first drummer held his sticks high in the air, pausing again for effect. Then slammed them back down on their target. All the other drummers joined in rhythm.

BOOOMMM... BOOOMMM... BAA...BOOMMM BOOMMM..

The thundering drums shook the village. In perfect harmony, the two in the middle on both sides were delivering powerful blows to the center leather, creating a deep, resounding impact. Then the pairs on the outside of the middle drummers hit the wooden sides of the drums, creating the crackling sound of thunder. Goosebumps ran up Sam's arms and down her legs from the immersive music that the drummers took part in. Her chest beat in tune with the vibrations of the drums.

As they played their introduction, Lin came out from the left side, her head and eyes down, strolling to center stage gracefully to the beat of the large drums.

Her elegance captivated the crowd. Fern followed behind. Cedar came out from the right side, creating a triangle on stage.

The drummers stopped. The last beat echoing in everyone's heart.

Silence.

Then below the stage in front, the people with the stringed instruments Sam saw earlier, played. Soon after a gentle flute, joined in the cloud of harmony that took the audience.

Lin moved first, then Fern and Cedar together. Raising and lowering their arms in time with the music as they moved in circles.

They lowered themselves to the ground and picked themselves up again, facing the sky.

The three of them danced in rhythmic motion for a minute more.

Amos looked over to see Sam's awed expression and nudged her. "This is a representation of them asking for a plentiful harvest next year, the part after will be them giving thanks and celebrating the past year." Sam nodded in silence, not taking her eyes off of them for a moment.

They returned to their original spots, took off their colorful shawls and let them flutter to the ground. The flute and harp played, as one drummer came and took the pieces of clothing off stage before the next act of the dance began.

The drums created a soft beat that continued until it grew as loud as before. The girls looked down, holding their hands in front of them. Once the drums got as loud as they could be, Fern and Cedar both stomped their left foot in time with the beat, their arms now out, balancing them as they moved harshly.

Lin twirled. As she got faster, her dress opened up to reveal colors in the trim that even Sam hadn't know about. Her twirling created patterns, and she danced around the stage elegantly in a flash of colors.

Cedar and Fern in time joined her, they danced in synch throughout the stage stomping, jumping, and twirling an abundance of rainbow and feathers, the crowds body echoed in beat. Sam had seen nothing as fierce and fragile as their performance.

As the beat grew, so did the excitement of the crowd. She could feel the others around her holding themselves from movement.

Cedar and Fern backed up and began stomping with the drums again.

The crowd grew restless and eager. Sam looked at Lin peacefully standing in the center, then she looked at Amos, her eyes asking if the dance had ended.

Amos glanced at Sam, giving her a wink, he turned his attention back to his wife.

This is it! The part everyone was waiting for, the fire summoning!

Sam watched, holding her breath in anticipation. Her hands fidgeting in her lap.

Lin's head was down. She looked left and stretched out her left hand. Swiveling her head to the right, she reached out her right hand. Then, the Priestess brought her hands back together, enclosed.

Suddenly, she separated her hands with the beat of the drums and when she did, flame erupted from her palms.

The crowd took a breath in, a sporadic few clapping or whistling at the sight. The drummers slowed down, the flute and the stringed instruments picked up into an entrancing tune.

Lin made a half circle with her hand and the flame followed, sitting in her palm, dancing in the day's dusk. She twirled in a circle, and it grew bigger, creating a circle of flame around her. Then she produced another flame on the right hand and created another ring of fire around her.

The crowd cheered and stomped to the beat of the drums as well. Lin twirled faster, creating a swirl of fire all around her. The dress giving off all of its colors and the color of the flame blending completely as if they were their own symphony of majesty.

A trance enveloped everyone. The music hit its pinnacle and then stopped abruptly. Lin fell to her knees and extinguished the spiral ring of flames as the last of the drum beats echoed through the village square. At that point, Fern and Cedar got on one knee as well.

Come on Cedar, you can do it.

Sam, Amos, and Atlas leaned in. This was her time to shine.

As they got down on one knee, Fern raised her right hand and Cedar raised her left hand.

The crowd waited for a moment with deep expectation. Waiting to see the remarkable Priestess child create a spectacle as well.

Nothing happened.

The air filled with silence. She could see the hidden glint of dread in Cedar's eyes. Sam's stomach turned as she forced a smile. Their eyes met.

Cedar turned her face towards the floor beneath her.

Whooping and whistling brought Sam out of the sadness as she clapped along with the crowd of faunanoid.

Cedar, gathering strength, stood and in unison with her mother and sister. Exiting the stage the way they came.

The cheering died down.

As it did, Sam and the crowd of onlookers heard an unusual noise.

Crying?

Everyone looked around. Cedar, Lin, and Fern came around the stage, confused and searching for the source as well.

It sounds like someone is screaming-

Sam's face went pale.

It was bleating. The bleating of a baby Qilin.

Sam met Cedar's eyes. Her heartbeat quickened. She stood. The look of recognition struck their faces as they understood what the cry was.

"AJAX!" Sam shouted and pushed through the crowd. She stopped short. His fear-driven cries grew louder. Then she saw him bounding down the hill. His cry splitting the stunned air.

There, standing outside their home, hunting Ajax, was a massive timber wolf, and its calculating eyes flashed a luminescent, brilliant green.

The massive wolf had the pattern of black, gray, and brown. His large, bared fangs dripped with saliva and hunger. He let out a powerful howl, throwing his head back to make sure all knew his presence.

Terror and dread ate at Sam's heart, her eyes glued to the wolf and its movements. The beast leapt down the hill and over the wooden fence in one solid jump. Its legs, neck and back were strong and rippled with muscles under the short fur, and his large curved black claws looked as though they could cut through what they wanted with little effort. He prowled through the village square menacingly, eyeing the frozen travelers and people of the village.

A scream pierced the air, bringing all the tranced onlookers back to reality.

"HUUUUNTEEEERRRR."

The frightened crowd scattered, creating a panic and running in all directions, pushing, shoving, and trampling anything that was in the way.

Ajax ran to Sam, cowering behind her legs. He bleated at her in fear.

"Ajax! Are you hurt?" Sam got on her knees and skimmed her hands over his trembling pelt and face. She let out a sigh of relief.

He's shaken, but ok.

A horn blew from close by. It was the Captain. He bellowed for reinforcements. They gathered together and guarded the tunneled road that led to the gazebo, waiting for the massive beast to make his first move.

The cunning enraged eyes tracked any movement, as if he was looking for something specific and paying little attention to the nonsense around him.

"What is that thing?" Sam asked Amos. He had just finished instructing the others to seek shelter in the stores and houses. At this point, only Lin, Sam, and Ajax remained with him.

"He is the Hunter. He kills people and animals for sport." Lin grimaced, igniting her hand in flames. The three of them shot a look at Ajax.

"He must have smelled him in the forest and tracked him here." Amos continued.

"You must go. Keep him safe," Amos growled. He bent over, disgruntled and in pain.

Amos looked back at Sam. His face... changing.

Are his teeth bigger?

"Leave," he repeated himself in a deep, low growl. He turned back and started prowling towards the wolf.

What's happening?

She watched, blinking with her mouth gaped open. Her mind trying to make sense of the confusion before her.

Amos grew bigger and hairier as he walked toward the fight. In disbelief, Sam looked at Lin.

"Now is not the time Sam, we will explain later." Lin said as she also began towards the intruder, with flames now engulfing her arms.

"Stay back and stay safe. Hopefully, the Chief will be here soon." The flaming Priestess glanced at her once more before turning and setting her eyes on the battle.

Sam got inside the closest house and watched from the window as the battle unfolded.

The Captain and his men created a barrier of spears so that the wolf could not enter the rest of the town from the village square.

Amos, now as big as the wolf and on all fours, had shifted into a bear with spiked horns emerging from his head, neck, and upper back. Sam shook her head in disbelief, unable to tear her eyes from the strange situation. Her mind was uncertain, but her stomach twisted in horror as they paced around one another. Malice lurching off the wolf's body.

The predators circled each other. The Hunter stopped. He lowered himself and bared his fangs, spitting and growling fiercely. Amos stomped his feet territorially, cementing his place, and bellowed a deep and powerful roar.

Without warning, the wolf lunged himself at Amos's throat. His charge missed slightly.

Amos moved more to the side and used the opening to bite down hard on the wolf's rib cage, locking onto him as he flew past. With his weight as a counterbalance, Amos fell back and flung the Hunter. The wolf flew through the air, writhing his body to land on his feet. And dug his hooked claws into the ground, stopping his backward momentum, unfazed.

Ajax raced through the house in fear, pushing furniture, and knocking over belongings. A clay flower vase tipped off the table and before Sam could grasp it, it fell, shattering into many tiny pieces, drenching the carpet in water and wildflowers.

Sam froze. Looking back to the battle from behind the opened window, she could see the Hunter staring past Amos now.

He made eye contact with Sam and looked at Ajax, his pupils turned into dark slits. The Hunter had found its prey.

With one cautious side look and a quick leap past Amos swiping out his enormous paw, the wolf bounded toward the house.

Sam knew what his goal was, and it wasn't fighting Amos. Lin shot off a streak of fire, but not fast enough. It singed his fur, just barely missing him.

Panic bolted through Sam and sunk into her stomach, weighing her down.

I can't fight or run fast enough.

She closed her eyes.

Opening them again, she shouted. "Ajax, RUN!"

She pointed out of the house.

He bleated and began running, but when he saw that Sam wasn't following, he stopped.

"No- NO! GOOOO! I can't run as fast as you!" She pushed him a little, but it was too late.

CRASH.

The wolf's head came through the window, glass spraying everywhere. Gnashing fangs, flying in a frenzy. Sam moved away, wide-eyed, as she watched, her legs weak and her body frozen.

His front legs didn't make it in, he was too big. Sam and Ajax pushed against the wall in immobilizing fear.

The Hunter slowed his pushing against the frame of the house once he realized it was useless. Glaring at the two just beyond his reach, he snarled and tried to pull his head out. Savagely, he whipped his head and neck in all directions, trying to free himself, but it no avail.

Sam eyed the door and pushed Ajax in that direction. They ran out of the house. Looking back, she could see Amos bounding towards them as almost a full bear now. There was barely any human left in him as anger oozed from his expression.

They started down the main road, running past the fountain. The wolf crashed through the house, freeing himself of his temporary prison while sending chunks of wall and roof shooting across the village.

He closed in on them. Easily creating distance between himself and Amos.

Too fast, he's too fast.

Sam's breathing was sporadic, adrenaline coursing through her tiring body. Ajax kept pace just a few steps ahead, his cloven hooves beating against the stone. She could hear the Hunters breathing now. He was close. She dared not to look back. As she pushed herself to run faster, she could hear jumbled yelling from Cedar and Fern.

At the bottom of her eyesight, she glimpsed something gleaming in the sunlight. Pitch black claws scraped across her right upper arm, causing pain to shriek through her body. She lost her balance. Tripping and tumbling over the stone paved road.

Everything went in slow motion.

Sam rolled to a stop. Dirtied and bloody, she cried out in pain, grabbing her arm. As she grabbed at the wound in agony, the wolf effortlessly jumped over her, continuing the chase.

She couldn't think. She watched, frenzied, as the wolf chased Ajax further down the street past the fountain.

"AAAAJJJAAAAAAAAAAXXXXXXXX!"

Sam screamed louder and louder, expelling her frustrated helplessness through the rest of her energy. She yelled through her chest, she yelled through her raw anger, and she yelled through her uselessness.

She watched with horror, tears streaking down her face and across her vision as Ajax turned the corner and vanished behind a row of houses. The wolf followed, closing in on the small terrified creature, then he disappeared from sight as well.

She screamed again, loud, and full of exasperation and fear. She stumbled to get up, but Amos hurdled past her, disappearing around the corner as well, and Lin rushed to her side, quieting the girl's pain and working to stop the bleeding.

The ground shook, Lin and Sam looked up, alert.

The ground shook again.

Then came a loud bellowing sound that rang through the village. Sam covered one ear with her good arm and squinted, trying to see where the call came from.

She watched as the large horns and head of the Chief appeared over the roofs of the homes and shops where Ajax and the Hunter had vanished down. In his oval spiked horns lay the wolf, bloodied and bruised. He yelped as the Chief threw him as far as he could back into the forest. They watched as he hit a tree with the center of his back and fell to the ground, limp. With another loud and long bellow from the Chief, the wolf vanished, limping into the forest, blood trailing its footsteps.

"Where is he?" Sam struggled to get up but cried out in pain.

"Stay down. Let me at least stop the bleeding." Lin mumbled, returning her attention back to the swollen, bloodied arm. She put her hands on the claw marks and applied heat to it. Sam cried out at the immense pain, clutching Lin's arms to pull her off, but in seconds Fern had her other arm pinned down. The heat was searing. Sam flayed under them, trying to escape the heat and the pain. It pierced her flesh, as she cried out again in incredible pain. Cedar stroked her hair, she whispered soothing words to her as she tried to calm Sam. After what felt like an eternity, Lin finished cauterizing the wound, the blood dried and it scabbing on her skin.

Lin helped her sit up, lifting her from the stones and wrapped her arms around her, squeezing tightly. Sam looked around dazed, her body tired and her energy gone.

"I'm so sorry Sam. I had to stop the bleeding." Lin caressed her head and held her cheeks in her palms. Sam saw that there was blood staining Lin, Fern, and Cedars' dresses. She saw blood smeared on the ground and trailing through the cracks in the stones. Her blood.

"Do not move around a lot. That is not a permanent fix. I am NOT a healer. It needs to be cleaned before it can heal." Lin said sternly and helped Sam stand up. Pushing through the agony, steam rose from her arm and it pulsed as she took a step forward.

I need to find Ajax.

"Ajax." She croaked.

They led Sam to the end of the road as people had begun to leave the safety of their homes to observe the aftermath of the battle. Turning the corner, they saw the Chief and Ajax resting next to a pile of fur and blood that lay on the ground.

"Amos!"

"Dad!"

They rushed over to him to see what they could do to help. Ajax excitedly leaped up to Sam, restless to see her. They collided, she collapsed on him in relief as she wrapped him in her arms.

The town healers came over and started helping Sam with her wounds and helping Amos. After the situation was assessed, they informed them that he was ok except from exhaustion and a couple of deeper wounds.

Captain Ryner and his guards ran up. When he glanced at Amos, he saw him being attended to, his body covered in bandages, and slowly getting back on his feet.

He turned his displeasure towards Sam and Ajax.

Before Sam could think, and before he could blame her for the incident, she blurted out.

"Teach me to fight."

Everyone stopped and looked at the two.

He looked taken aback and hesitated to respond.

"*You*? Teach *you* to fight?!" He started. "This is *your* fault, to begin with. You should be exiled because of this, not taught to *fight*." He shouted, waving his arms around belligerently.

"She led the Hunter here. She is the real danger!" Captain Ryner continued, pointing at her, and looking around to gather the agreements of the villagers.

Sam held her arm and grunted in pain as she tried to move.

"Teach me to protect them." She said again, more determined.

He laughed exasperatedly. Looking around for anyone to say anything. Everyone remained silent and stared at the ground, avoiding the argument.

In the silence, a low growl emerged from Amos.

"You will teach her to wield her staff..." He grunted, trying to move to look at him, "or I will take your neck within my teeth and squeeeeezzzzeee." Amos said through a fanged and bloodied mouth.

Sam side eyed Amos uncomfortably. The air now felt palpable with the fury that seeped from him.

"I... am.... tired of the way you *think* you can speak to my family in such UTTER DISREGARD." He grew louder. "She is of bear and fox and how you speak to her is how you speak to ME." He shouted for all to hear. "You will not treat her like this anymore or you will know the rage of a Berserker." He collapsed back down into exhaustion.

The Captain's face went white in trepidation.

"You will do no such thing. Thank you, Amos, but it is time for you to get some rest." The Chief deliberately nodded to the healers and Lin to take him away.

He stared a moment longer at the small Captain with rage filled eyes, then he nodded and went with them, limping along the way.

"It is time for her to learn to fight, and to- 'protect' as she said. You will do what Amos says as soon as she is healed and well enough to fight." The Chief said to him. He got up and stared at Sam for a moment longer before leaving.

The Captain looked at her with bile and turned to walk away, knowing he had no choice in the matter.

Once he was gone, Sam collapsed. Cedar and Fern took her to their house to treat her wound and rest.

The festival was over.

The air was silent. No forest creatures sang their songs that night. All were still, all were hiding from the night of the wolf.

While a few thought of the uncertain days to come.

9

AN OATH TO KEEP

The days flew past as Sam waited to start her training. Amos, still injured, returned home after a week, for bed rest.

During their resting and healing time, Sam learned what it meant to be a Berserker. Some people in the new world, not all, had the ability to become more animal and less human. That was how Amos became almost entirely a bear. It also explained why he became so aggressive. Lin had revealed that it was a side effect of becoming a Berserker. The more animal he turned, the less of a person he became. Also, she said that if they go too far into their Berserker forms, then they cannot return to normal. The faunanoids will become the animals that they shifted into.

Sam would find solace in sitting and observing the gentle sway of trees and the tranquil flow of water in the forest streams. Her mind filled with contemplation about the intriguing complexities of the new world.

Sam thought back to the nights they spent sharing stories of the unfortunate people who transformed for too long or went too far into their animal side and could never return. The stories that made the biggest impression on Sam were those of the eagle that flew too high and the koimaid that sacrificed herself for her family.

In difficult moments, she held onto the faint memory of her mother. The helpful distraction was more than needed, and it was something to keep her from thinking about the overwhelming evidence of her vulnerability.

One morning Sam woke trying to resist the urge to itch her tight wound that was finally scabbing over. Antsy, she got out of bed.

She found Fern in the kitchen, humming as she mixed herbs together to make tinctures and concoctions of her own accord. Sam sat down at the wooden table and watched her as she used a short, smooth stone to crush dried plants into a matching stone bowl.

"What are you doing?" Sam asked, bored. Her fingers hovered over her scabs, resisting the urge to pick at them.

Fern looked over at her, smiling. "I didn't hear you come in. I am just making some spices that we were low on for cooking," she said. Grabbing some dried stems, she threw them into the bowl, "I'm crushing them into a fine powder and then I will mix some of this together with it," she pointed to an already crushed bowl of spices, "after that I will put them in one of those glass containers for storage." She used the stone to point at the glass jars on the top shelves while working.

"Hmmmm... can I try?" Sam asked, looking at her hopefully.

Uncertainty showed on Ferns face.

"Pleeeeeaaaassse, I'm so BORED." Sam dramatically threw her head down onto the table for effect.

She turned her head to see if her dramatic show worked. Fern raised her eyebrows and then rolled her eyes.

"Fine." Fern gave in. Sam jumped up with excitement.

"You can mix the herbs together that I crushed. Mix these two bowls but do not mix this in- it will ruin it." Fern pointed to the small bowls that sat on the table.

They worked for a while in silence, focusing on the task before them. Once Sam had mixed all the spices, Fern explained what to do next. Then she poured them into the jars and put a cloth over the top to store them.

"Would you like to come with me to the garden to water and pick some herbs? That probably isn't too strenuous, right?" Fern asked.

"Why not?" Sam shrugged casually, eager to get out of the house.

Outside, around the house, the sun hit the grass and helped keep it lush and soft to walk on with their bare feet. They had an entire garden full of fruits, vegetables, and herbs. Sam walked past it looking at all the alluring colors and shapes, some she recognized, a few she didn't.

They reached the river stone well, Fern picked up a clay pot that sat beside it and filled it with water from the pool. Then they walked back to the small spot where the herbs were planted. The layout of the herbs looked different from the fruits and vegetables that were planted in rows. Instead they were planted in a rising circular shape with small round stones supporting the elevated ground. The dirt hill came up to about mid-thigh height.

"Why is this different from the fruits and vegetables?" Sam asked.

"It helps with the growth of the plants, the small pond at the base give water to the herbs that need more, the ones that need less water, we planted at the top and I water them less."

Sam nodded as she tried to follow along.

While she was watering, Fern explained that each herb had its own benefits. Among the plants, some were suitable for consumption. While others possessed healing qualities, that can be used for a variety of purposes, such as soothing rashes, reducing inflammation, and acting as a disinfectant. Others can add a pleasant taste to certain foods and teas.

Fern pointed to one that was yellow greenish and had small pronged leaves on it. "This is the one that knocked you out when we first met you." She chuckled. "It's a calming herb, and you were just so exhausted that you just... fell asleep right there," Fern laughed.

A look of awe crossed Sam's face as she observed the multitude of intricate, small plants, amazed by their remarkable abilities.

I need to learn more about them and what else they could do.

She glanced mischievously over to her gardening companion.

"Fern... I know we said we would wait until I'm healed completely," she paused briefly before continuing, "but I'm ready and I want to learn about how to use these plants to help me," Sam earnestly eyed Fern as they cut and picked the small colorful plants that stuck out of the ground in plenty.

"Well... you have been doing good today, and your scarring hasn't reopened, so maybe we can start with the small stuff and work from there. I don't want you to overdo anything." She said as she wiped the beaded sweat from her forehead.

"Yes! I will keep an eye on it," Sam continued hurriedly in building excitement, "but I'm ready to get out of the house and do something!" She responded, her eyes gleaming with hope.

"Ok ok, we will start tomorrow." Fern smiled at Sam's childlike happiness. "It will just be me describing the benefits and uses for the plants around us. That's it, nothing crazy. After this, go and find some writing utensils and paper. I'll try to find some gardening equipment to work with once you're feeling better." Fern said as she continued to pluck and pull at the helpless greenery.

"It's about to be the cold season, so we are going to have to prepare the plants to make sure they survive the harsher weather." She nodded to herself thoughtfully.

Sam beamed with the new happy distraction as they continued to work in the small garden through the warm afternoon.

After a while, Cedar found them and joined in with finishing up the work. While sitting outside, they savored the tea that Fern had prepared, utilizing the herbs, fruits, and flowers they had gathered. Once Cedar heard that Fern was going to be teaching Sam, she begged to join the class as well.

Fern finished her tea and stood up. "Alright, it's settled then. Classes start tomorrow. Make sure to find the stuff I told you to get. I have to finish gardening and get some other things done." She gathered her delicate clay cup with the bowls of herbs they added to their tea, and then headed inside to clean up.

"We better go find those materials before *teacher* Fern gets upset," Cedar said sarcastically as she laughed.

Sam joined in as she got up. Finally, feeling better since the fight with the Hunter. During her time resting and letting her arm heal, she sulked in the stagnant water of her existence. Not moving forward or backwards, just floating, going nowhere. But this gives her a chance to do something, to be useful.

They took their cups inside, following Fern. Cedar grabbed the sack of coins she kept hidden away in her room, and they went into town looking for the collection supplies they needed.

Cedar could see the determination seeping out of Sam. She had never truly seen someone so ready to achieve a goal, big or small. She thought back to her own wants and was disappointed in herself.

Have I been trying hard enough to call the fire? Maybe if I tried harder like Sam-

Cedar was tired of being powerless. She wanted, no, *needed*, to become a wielder of fire. Sam was healing from her wounds, her mom was nursing her dad back to health, and Fern was keeping herself busy by taking care of the house. So, Cedar needed to find something to do as well.

The young flame apprentice found a quiet spot near the back of the house on the edge of the forest. She decided on a plush pillow of clover as she looked around for a nice soft spot to sit. She took a deep breath in, held it for a couple of strenuous seconds and then let it out slowly.

Just like mom showed me. And I have seen Sam do this many times before.

She closed her eyes, focused on her surroundings. The way the afternoon air smelled of moss and crisp autumn, the sounds of the birds, the wind whistling through the grass and the sounds of Fern chopping vegetables in the kitchen. She searched for it, that feeling that her mom described to her.

Calling out, asking for the spirit of fire to come to her. She felt for an answer, waiting for anything to happen. Moments passed, and she felt the same. She felt nothing but irritation grow inside of her. After a couple more unsuccessful minutes passed, she gave a huff and laid back, picking at the clovers that sprang out of the cracking dried dirt.

Why? Why me? Why can't I just DO IT?

She stood hastily, and in anger, kicked the dirt. Huffing and puffing, she dug out a small dent in the earth with her foot, letting her frustration out as a child would.

Someone chuckled behind her. Cedar briskly looked and blushed when she realized it was her mother. She rolled her eyes and crossed her arms in defense, then continued eyeing the spot she was destroying with the tip of her toes.

Great..

"Cedar," Lin started as she sat down on the ground next to where she stood. "Fire will not come to you if you ask it to. You need to be more demanding. Fire is life."

Her palm sparked a flame, and she let it dance as they talked.

"See how it moves and grows? It can destroy, of course," Cedar sat cross-legged, watching the flame grow, as her envy grew with it, "but it can also give way to new life. It is special this way. Some see it as a symbol of destruction, but I see it as rebirth. When I was chosen to become a wielder of the flame, I was told that the elements choose you, not the other way around. You need to show it you are ready, and strong enough to handle it, or it will burn you and everyone around you." Lin closed her palm, smothering the helpless, dancing flame.

Cedar covered her eyes with her hands. "I'm trying mom, I want this more than *anything*. I just don't understand what I am doing wrong."

Lin chuckled, "Then maybe don't try too hard. You might not be doing anything wrong, it just isn't your time." She stood up and put her hand lovingly on Cedar's head for a moment before heading back inside. She watched her go, leaving Cedar once again by herself and feeling more confused. Cedar looked up at the burning sun, feeling its heat lay on her and everything around her.

I have to be strong.

Resolve blossomed inside her.

If I have to be strong to be chosen, then I'll get stronger.

While Sam's wound had turned into a scar, the three girls entertained themselves with the impromptu herb and gardening class. After a couple more days, her bindings came off, and she was impatient to start her training.

After Lin gave her all clear, Sam was more ready than ever to get started and prove herself. The next day, when she woke up, she compulsively cleaned her staff and got into some clothes that she wouldn't mind getting dirty.

Her hair braided and out of the way, she joined the family in the kitchen and gulped down her breakfast while everyone watched nervously for the day to come.

"Maybe I should come with you to make sure it goes *ok*," Lin said reluctantly at the table.

"No no, I will be fine. Captain Ryner is going to have to get used to me eventually. Besides, I'm not scared of him." Sam snorted confidently as she finished her breakfast.

"Ok well- then just promise to keep an eye out for the Hunter or any-" she sucked her teeth thinking for the correct word, "rude neighbors." Cedar interjected. Her eyebrow raised as she tried to find the correct words to use.

"I will." Sam rolled her eyes and smiled. "Can Ajax stay with you? At least while I'm out." She got up.

"Yes, you know I love him, and Atlas will have someone to play with, too," Cedar said happily.

Sam nodded her head in thanks, waved goodbye and scurried out the door before any objections came her way. She was finally ready to start her training. Running her fingers over the small indentations of her fresh scar, she was reminded of her weakness. A spark of anger rose against herself. She gripped her staff and twisted it in her hand, feeling the ridges rake against her skin as she swiveled it in her hand. The sensation causing her mind to become alert.

Amos had told her she would train with both Captain Ryner and himself. The Captain would teach her the ways of the weapons and Amos would teach her how to fight and stay alive using the body. Amos was still healing, but in a week, they could get started.

Sam headed to the barren unused field outside of town where the guards trained and stopped at the top of the hill. She could see the Captain and his guard starting their morning routine. A twinge of nervous excitement went through her, landing in the pit of her stomach.

It is time for me to learn how to fight.

She took a deep breath and began down the nearly unseen trail. When she reached the group, they grew quiet and stood watching as she walked up to Captain Ryner. He had his arms crossed and already looked unhappy, with a scowl on his face.

"Hmph, you actually showed up. I didn't think you would." He started.

"Why wouldn't I?" Sam retorted quickly, leaning into her staff. She smiled smugly.

She felt ready for anything that he would throw at her.

He glared back at her. "Alright then, join in with them for our warm up and then we will get started with training," he said flatly.

Taking pride in her accomplishment, she joined the rest of the guard.

By the end of the warmup, she was hunched over, hands on knees, breathing hard, her lungs not capturing enough air. She could taste the blood in her mouth, and daggers stabbed her sides, while her legs stood on jelly.

She grunted as she slumped down on the hard, rocky dirt, staring at the sky.

"Was that too much for you, wee little monster?" Captain Ryner laughed.

A groan was her only response.

I don't have the energy for this.

"Well, we are just getting started. Today we are working on sword fighting, so grab a sword and get to fighting!" He barked at her. "You don't get the luxury of rest in a fight!"

Her arms were a brick wall, and her legs fought her the whole way, but she gradually got up and moved over to the weapons rack. Sam picked up a longsword dressed with a leather hilt, but as it gained its freedom of the weapons rack, its weight was too much and it yanked out of her hands, pulling her to the ground with it. The crowd laughed. Her face grew hot with embarrassment as she scrambled to stand.

She left the longsword where it fell and looked back for another smaller sword to grab instead.

"Since you have never fought with a weapon before, you can start with this," Captain Ryner laughed as he handed her a child's wooden play sword. Sam grimaced and scowled at him, but grabbed the sword and walked over to the closest person to her.

Her sparring partner was tall, and she looked to be a sort of shepherd dog. The guard had fluffy white ears that folded down and a tail that curved up to match. The thin, muscular woman looked down at Sam and smirked. Holding her sword, she motioned that she was ready to spar. Sam held up the wooden sword with frustrated energy. She locked eyes with her opponent.

I am tired of being treated like an outcast. If this is the only thing they see me as, so be it. I am going to go down fighting.

"Woof," Sam said flatly.

A look of rage sparked in her opponent's eyes. She struck hard and fast. Sam struggled to block, but her reactions were not to par. She was hit on the side of her ribs with the blunt side of the woman's weapon. It knocked the breath out of her and she fell to one knee, holding her side.

Desperation smacked her as hard as the weapon did. The idea of failing on day one wound around her heart, snaking circles in her mind.

She heard a snicker from her combatant. The sneer on her face gave Sam the energy to stand and face her once more. She held out her sword again, focusing.

"You should have stayed down, little monster." The guard growled and swung again.

Sam blocked the sideways swing, the wooden sword reverberating the echo of the clash. Gaining confidence in her microscopic ability, she stuck back, but the guard was again too fast. She dodged and hit Sam in the back of her head with the hilt of her sword. At that, Sam went down and stayed down.

She jolted awake, gasping for air, coughing through the ruffled dirt that puffed in clouds around her face.

"There she is. We thought Pele might've hit you too hard for a moment," Captain Ryner scoffed smugly.

Her head shrieked in pain. She sat up and stared past the crowd in defeat. With a wince, she reached back to touch her head and inspected her hand for any bleeding. Relief swept through her at the absence of crimson on her fingers

They aren't trying to train me, they're trying to break me.

She laid back down on the ground, her body outstretched, surrendering to defeat and shutting out the world around her. Closing her eyes on the cloudless morning, she thought of her next move.

The eyes of prejudice on her, she felt their gaze bearing into her skin, beaming through her as if they could see her innermost thoughts. Annoyed, the urge to be alone grew louder as each moment passed.

Her body heated, as her mind became obsessed with the thought of them staring. She grimaced with her eyes closed.

When it became unbearable and the exposure to the stares of the faunanoid was too much, she snapped her eyes open and shakily lifted herself using the wooden sword as a cane to get up. She met Captain Ryner's eyes as she stood.

"I'll see you tomorrow," she said.

And with that, she took her staff and the wooden sword with her.

"This is mine now. I'm taking this with me," she said defensively. And glared at each of them for any objections as she held it up.

"You can't leave, we only just started!" Captain Ryner yelled, throwing his hands into the air as she walked off.

Sam continued walking, not looking back or responding to his retorts. She couldn't let him see the tears that burned in her eyes.

Once she made it back to the house, Sam yelled in anger and threw the sword as hard as her body would let her into the woods. Letting her anger and revenge go with it. As she threw the sword, her shoulder stretched and popped awkwardly. Her frustration grew as she grabbed at the strained pain and stood there scowling at the woods where the sword had landed.

"Seems like you had a good first day," Someone spoke behind her.

She turned to see the Chief and Amos sitting cross-legged on the ground, talking to one another.

How did I miss him? He is like 18 feet tall...

She sighed, walking over to where they were and sat with them. She rubbed her greasy face with her hands and covered her eyes in exasperation. Her head still pulsing from the one-sided sparring lesson.

After a moment, she caught both of them up on what happened. Amos seemed upset, but the Chief chuckled. Hurt by his laugh, she crossed her arms and glared at the ground.

"I am sorry to laugh. He is acting in the way I assumed he would act because he is scared.." the Chief continued.

"He fears you and is stuck in his ways. I pity him more than I am angry with him, unfortunately. He acts like the small child

I remember him for. Do not hold it against him Sam, he has always been this way and he will stay in his ways for probably the rest of his life. His insecurities lead him," he stopped for a moment to look down at her, *"but the question is, will they lead you?"*

Sam looked at Amos, then back at the Chief. She vaguely understood what he meant but still wore the veil of anger towards Captain Ryner.

"Sam, I understand you are angry at him for the way he has treated you, but please understand that he is a child in his ways and will act as such. I am not giving him the excuse to do so, of course, but once you decide not to let children and their childish behaviors affect you so harshly, you will see how truly silly it is."

Sam sat, contemplating. She bit her lip as she forced herself to say what was bugging her.

"How can I let someone say and do all those rude and terrible things and not retaliate? I am going to stand up for myself!" She responded in defiance. Sam twisted her fist around the middle of her staff that was laying in her lap, digging her hand into the grooves.

The Chief chuckled softly again, no doubt seeing the confusion.

"One day you will understand, in the meantime..." The Chief looked toward the forest, where Sam threw the wooden sword, *"I would suggest practicing on your own terms as well. Wouldn't you agree, Amos?"*

After being quiet the whole time, Amos nodded in agreement.

"I will give you routines and exercises to start your own training, but first things first, that is not how you treat your weapons. Go get it and clean it." He added in a firm voice, pointing towards where it lay in the tall forest grass.

Displeased, Sam got up to get the sword and returned. As she cleaned it, Amos went over some day-to-day things that Sam could work on.

"Also…" Amos leaned back through an aching face and grabbed something that was behind him. "This is for you.. I saw you looking at it during the festival and wanted to give it to you at the right time. Since you're starting your training, this is something you will need to get used to," he pulled out a piece of cloth and metal. On further inspection, she noticed that it was the hooded chest piece she saw at the traveling armory during the first night of the festival.

The metal chest piece connected to a back metal piece by leather laced on the sides and a dark brown cotton cloth underneath it with the same-colored hood to complete the ensemble.

Sam marveled at the armor. Not having a tough hide of fur, claws, or sharp teeth, she was left almost defenseless. But this would be something that could help her defend herself in a tough spot.

"Wow, Amos, you got this for me? Thank you so much!" Sam said, admiringly stroking the welded floral design that traveled on the armpit and trim of the armor.

Amos nodded his head, happy that the gift was appreciated.

"Tomorrow, you start your own training, and then once I am healed enough, we can also begin your fighting practice. So, for today, why don't you get some rest?" Amos smiled.

Sam, feeling much better, agreed. Nodding goodbye to the Chief and Amos, she headed inside to show Cedar, Fern, and Lin her new gift.

10

TREE OF THE VALLEY

Snow fell softly through the weeks as winter arrived and the gardens and harvests of the fields died. This gave Cedar, Sam, and Fern more time to focus on their goals in mind. Sam focused on her weaponry and fighting skills, and in her downtime, she learned the art of botany and outdoor survival through Fern.

Cedar had time to practice calling the flame, with no luck she practiced mostly in frustration. Fern spent more and more of her time engaging in the priestess hood, just like her mother had done at that age. Ajax and Atlas grew bigger and stronger together during the cold season, both growing a thick coat of winter fur. While Lin and Amos carried on living as they had always done, upholding their lives and the lives of the villagers during the winter. The town was weary as they watched for any signs of the Hunter. Many believed him to be dead, but some felt that he watched from the shadows, waiting for the opportunity to strike again.

Therefore, the days of the cold were spent learning and growing. Sam had become proficient with the sword and bow during this time *'as a hunter should'*, Amos had informed her. She also spent this time getting to understand her staff and studying the fighting style that belonged to it. She knew she wasn't perfect or anywhere close to it, but that was not her goal. Her goal was to survive and protect those around her.

The snow fell dense but drifted gently to the ground one frosty morning as Sam had gotten up and dressed in thick furs to keep warm during her morning practice with Captain Ryner. She walked outside examining the white landscape, the trees carpeted with snow and the sun, a small thin dot, shining through the gray clouds, sending rays of light down on the village like rays of hope as the villagers begged for warmth.

Outside, she noticed they had a visitor. The Chief was lumbering his way up to their cottage, respectfully she waited for him. He arrived and laid down on the ground the way a horse or a cow would go to rest, to be somewhat the same height so that they could speak without strain.

"Morrow Samihanee, thank you for waiting. I wish to speak to you about something important. I have had a vision from the Seer, Muninn. She wishes that I bring you to her, so that she can speak with you on important matters," he said.

Cedar and Amos came out of the cottage together to see what the noise was. The Chief continued,

"Ahhh good morrow, you two, come along as well. We could use the company on this journey to the Seer."

"I believe that it is about a day's walk towards the Mountains?" Amos said thoughtfully. "It can be dangerous, so I guess I can tag along. Ajax should come with us, too. We don't want to leave the town unguarded with him in it. If the Hunter is still alive, then he would use this as an opportunity." When Amos finished speaking and went back inside to inform Lin of the newfound plans and to pack for the journey ahead.

"So be it," the Chief added, nodding.

"Maybe I can ask the Seer how to help me with calling the flame!" Cedar squealed excitedly.

"Cedar..." The Chief looked at her. *"You can ask her, but that does not mean you will get an answer, or even an answer you might want."*

Cedar sighed, "I know, but I have been working so hard, maybe she can help me with uncovering some secret to unlocking this power. I have to try." she said earnestly. The Chief nodded again and waited outside for them as they got ready.

Sam woke Ajax from his slumber by the fire. She went to her room and put on her hooded armor, covering it back up with a layer of furs.

If this is going to be dangerous like Amos said, then I am going to be prepared this time.

Accompanied by her staff, she also brought a small hunter's bow that Atlas had allowed her to use for training. Her gaze fell upon the fox mask, painted in shades of blue and white, resting on the stand beside her bed. With a pensive expression, she played with the bead in her hair. She made the decision not to bring it, reasoning that it would only be her and the ones closest to her. There was no need for her to hide. She grabbed a small bag of food and once everything was taken care of, they said goodbye to Lin, Fern, Atlas, and the small cottage on the hill as they set out for the Seer.

An hour had passed in the woods as they traveled in the high winter sun. The chilly winds seeped their way through the trees. They did not go the way of the mound or back to where Sam first emerged, but went a different route from the opposite side of the village. The trail was different. Most of the trees were tall and barren, a sparse few still had leaves and darkened the forest with a colder shade. The group marched lazily on a trail big enough for the Chief as they waded through the crunchy mid-shin snow.

Sometimes a cloud would part and sunlight would drift through, giving way for warmth that Sam basked in enthusiastically. She had noticed that the others did not get as cold as she did. Sam glanced at them thoughtfully, wondering if it might be because of the extra fur they had on their body.

Amos, being part bear, had scruffy fur on his neck, back and arms. Then Cedar, being part fox, had softer sleek fur around her fox like ears, feet and a tail. Sam, unfortunately, was the only one left with little protection against the weather. Realizing this, she twisted the coat around herself tighter.

Cedar interrupted the silence, "So the Seer lives near the mountain edge?"

Amos nodded. "Yes, we will be at the edge of our Realm and the Realm of the sky people. So we must be careful of any dangers from the beasts that lay between."

"Wait, Realms? Sky people? What does that mean?" Sam asked curiously.

"No one has told you about the different realms yet!? I thought you would have learned this already." Cedar said, mockingly.

"Well, we have talked about it, but I don't think I know everything." Sam rolled her eyes dramatically at her. Cedar laughed as she continued to explain.

"So, in our land there are four Realms." She put up four clawed fingers to represent the realms.

"We are in the Realm of Land, it is also called the Verdant Vale and we are the people of the land. There is the Realm of Sky, known as the Guardian Mountains, then the Realm of Sea, which is also called Seaborne, and last is the Kings Realm. Each Realm safeguards a different type of faunanoid, or people, and the King's Realm is where the High King lives. That Realm can accommodate all the different people of sky, land, and sea."

"Ok, so people of the Realm of Sea are like fish people? And people of the Realm of Sky are bird people, then this Realm is just animals that cannot fly or breathe underwater?" Sam responded.

"I guess to put it bluntly, yes, but the Realm of Land is heavily connected to nature and the land. The other Realms... not so much." She shrugged and ran her fingers through her hair in thought.

Sam nodded, thinking about the different Realms and what faunanoid or creatures they might hold. They continued to chat for a moment as Amos guided the pack through the woods. The Chief and Ajax took up the back, watching the forest whisper and talk about the newcomers in their wintery woods.

The only time they stopped was around mid-day when they ate. After that, they continued on until the forest lessened and could see the tips of the white-capped mountains even more clearly. The forest was thinning when they came upon a cliff with a small hut that fit snugly in one of the many deep crevices.

"We are here," the Chief said from behind the group.

Sam uneasily looked at the diminished dark hut against the rocky side of the cliff wall. A shiver ran up her spine. They approached it and saw smoke rising from a fire that sat in front of the home, cautiously they walked up and looked around for any sign of life.

"Seer Muninn!" The Chief called loud and clear.

"It is I, the Chief of the 7th Province, with Amos the Berserker, his daughter Cedar, the Flame Priestess apprentice, and Samihanee, the one you called for."

Ajax defensively bleated at the Chief.

"Of course, yes, I am sorry to forget. And Ajax the Qilin!" The Chief added, chuckling. Ajax looked proudly at Sam, who laughed under her breath.

Silence filled the air as they waited for a response. Nothing happened for an uncomfortable amount of time. The Chief settled next to the fire with Ajax. The rest went inside to see if she was there.

The small hut was a dark brown wood with grass and hay as the roof. Once they made it up the rickety stairs, Amos knocked three times. When there was no answer, he jiggled the handle, and they found that the door was unlocked. went inside calling for the home's resident. Reluctantly, Cedar and Sam glanced at each other and followed.

Decorated with drying plants and meats hanging from the ceiling in some select places, the small hut also had a plethora of books scattered everywhere. As soon as Sam laid eyes on the countless books, she realized that she had only seen a scarce few since she woke up.

This must be where they all ended up.

She snorted at her joke.

To see if she recognized any, she went over and looked at a stack of the tattered books that were almost as tall as her. She frowned as she flipped through a couple of them. They were in the new world's languages. With a gentle touch, she closed it, being mindful of the delicate old books, and carried on. The girls walked around. Cedar appeared disgusted by everything and reacted with audible expressions to the things she encountered or inadvertently came into contact with.

"Where's dad?" Cedar asked, grumbling.

Sam shrugged. "I think he disappeared when we came in here."

The hut was dimly lit, but the next room had a hearth that brightened the small dusty space. They found Amos investigating some oddly placed bookshelves touching the back wall. Cedar tapped Sam's shoulder and pointed to the floor. They saw scratches on the wooden planks where it looked like the bookshelves moved outward and opened. As Amos grabbed and pushed the bookshelves, Cedar and Sam looked at each other in regret. Fresh crisp air pushed through the crack, hissing past the three of them as the old bookshelves creaked open to reveal an entrance to a cave inside the cliff.

"Uuuhhhhmmmm no thanks. I'm going to be outside with the others." Cedar pointed backwards while she laughed uncomfortably and scurried out of the house with her arms close to her chest.

Amos and Sam made eye contact and Sam sighed, following him into the damp torch lit cave. Sam's heart pounded inside her chest as her mind raced through the many terrible theories of what could lie at the end of the secret tunnel.

She touched the walls of the cold cave and pulled her hand away quickly when she saw they dripped with condensation and algae. They followed the underpass for a bit, turning corners and walking carefully, prepared for anything that might jump out of the shadows or from the cracks in the darkness. By the second, Sam swelled with anxiety. Her eyes darted all around, trying not to miss a single movement, as she copied Cedar and wrapped her arms around herself for comfort.

They could see a light at the end of the tunnel, their anticipation grew. She could feel her heart pulling itself towards the light of reassurance, but she caught her pace and marched on with caution. Sam and Amos came out shielding their eyes, blinded by the brilliant noon sunlight, and when their eyesight adjusted, they saw a vast green meadow.

Sam gasped, holding her hand to her mouth. It was not what she had expected at all, and it was more beautiful than anything she had seen so far in the new world. She scanned her surroundings, taking in every inch of the beauty that beheld her.

There were flowers and plants of all colors that stood at least up to her thigh, a small brook twisted through the entirety of the lush valley that hid in the mountains, and at the very center was a gigantic dark oak tree with deep maroon leaves shimmering gold throughout the meadow. Its branches stretched far to the ends of the valley, brushing the rocky sides as it generously shaded the entire area.

Sam's mouth gaped open in speechless bewilderment. Dragonflies flew in a zig zagged pattern as they danced all around them, protecting their secret garden.

"I- isn't it... the middle of winter?!" She stammered.

"I bet Cedar is gonna be upset she missed this." Amos chimed in, chuckling in awe.

"O for sure." Sam breathed out her responce. As she said that, she spotted someone by the thick, above ground roots of the tree. The person seemed to not have noticed they arrived and was working hunched over by the roots that made a labyrinth of themselves in the tall grass.

"Hellooooo," Sam called out, waving to get their attention. The figure stopped and peered up. It had the face of a raven and a long black beak with glossy eyes that reflected the sun. It stood tall momentarily staring, Sam and Amos looked at each other again but now with a worried expression.

"Maybe I shouldn't have done that." Sam frowned.

Swift as the wind, the beaked faunanoid snapped a pair of giant, stark black raven wings open. With one strong motion, it pushed off into the high air and swooshed in between the branches of the giant tree, disappearing with a harsh rustle of the thick leaves.

Sam took a step back in shock. Amos, unmoved, took out a sword and prepared to fight. They looked up and through the spaces of the tree, and could see a shadow moving fast towards them. The faunanoid pierced the leaves, reentering the protection of the tree. When it was only moments from hitting the ground, it thrashed its wings in one large movement and caught itself, landing effortlessly only feet in front of the two perplexed onlookers.

Once the figure landed, Sam realized it was a rather skinny woman who stood straight and tall that looked to be in her 50s. The beak that she thought was her face was actually a type of mask like Sam's, animal like and hiding the lady's face.

She wore dark gray gardening gloves, a white tank top and dark brown breeches with a light purple half apron filled with plants, herbs, and roots of all sorts from the valley that flowed out of its small pockets. Her hair being dark brown, was streaked with the color of wisdom and braided into two long braids that flowed down to her apron.

"This is her." Amos leaned over and whispered as he sheathed his sword.

The Seer leaned forward, examining them up and down through her raven's plague mask.

"So, you're the human then, hmmm?" She finally spoke in a stern, rough voice. Sam winced. She got the feeling that Muninn might have been let down from what she saw.

Sam scoffed and looked at the ground, not knowing how to respond.

"Speak up, come on, we don't have all day to wait on you," the Seer said, putting her hand on her hips.

"Ye.. yes that's me.. I guess," Sam sputtered.

"Hmm," she said nodding, "well, I have seen many things but never one of *you* before. This is very interesting indeed."

She paused as she glanced at Amos, "When I had my vision of you, I truly thought I was going crazy, but when Chief told me it was true..." She pulled up her mask revealing a soft face with sharp bird-like features and eyes that were the color of electric blue.

Seeing the Seer's eyes surprised Sam, she was taken aback by the intensity of her stare. She stumbled for something else to say but fell short.

"Good morrow, Seer, the rest of our group is outside waiting for you," Amos interrupted the awkward staring contest as he gestured back towards the cave tunnel.

"Yes, I suppose we should go talk with them as well," the Seer responded, not taking her eyes off of Sam, like a predator who hunted its prey.

Amos turned sideways and gestured again for her to lead the way. Muninn the Seer walked forward and into the gloomy tunnel. They followed her back the way they came, through the darkness, then out into the hut, and finally back outside, where everyone else was waiting for them. The Chief bowed his head slightly to greet her respectfully. Cedar once again had a disturbed look on her face and seemed to ebb away from the Seer.

"Greetings. Thank you for coming so quickly. It was time for Samihanee to hear of the vision I had of her," Muninn said with a stretch and a ruffle of her massive wings.

Everyone waited in silence for her to begin. She cleared her throat.

"I saw you awake and emerge from the depths of your prison," she pointed at Sam.

"I see you fighting to find your place in a world that is no longer your home."

The wind blew softly, the Seer's sharp eyes glowed white.

"I foresee you being a force of greatness in this world."

She rose in the air as the wind blew harder. They all faced the gales of wind that began to blow. Amos sheltered Cedar, the Chief protected Ajax, Sam stood her ground.

"But Samihanee of the land. What I cannot see..." She opened her palm, and her braids and feathers flew violently around her as if they were alive and working to escape their captor. Muninn pointed at her again with the other hand, "Is if you-"

Sam grew tense.

"are a protector or a destroyer."

With her staff in front of her, she positioned herself against the wind. The others also began to understand the situation and moved in unison, trying to get closer to Sam, but the wind kept them from moving. Muninn raised her hand high in the air, ready to strike it down. The blowing wind found her palm to be the center of the storm. Ready for an attack, she defensively stood in place. She could hear Cedar trying to yell over the wind as Amos struggled to get close.

Out of nowhere, and as if the gusting wind was nothing but a summer's breeze, Ajax sprung out from underneath the Chief and leaped into action. He stood small before the

Wind Elemental Muninn. He made himself as big as possible, standing courageously between the two.

"Ajax MOVE." Sam bellowed, but the wind carried her voice away.

The Seer looked at him for a moment, floating in the air, and raised her eyebrow. The wind died down, her bright glowing eyes dimmed to their normal vividness, and she tenderly landed on the ground, as if to not want to disturb the grass around her.

"You take responsibility for this one and her actions?" Muninn questioned Ajax.

He bleated at her, challenging her.

"Very well, Qilin, if you say so," Muninn nodded in response to his bravery. "she is yours to be responsible for."

Sam's heart had jumped out of her chest, her legs weak. She used her staff for support as she regained her strength from the disaster that had almost occurred.

"Woah woah," Sam held her hands up. "What?"

"You were just about to-" She made a cutting motion near her throat coupled with the slicing noise. "Me!! And then you change your mind that fast!?"

Sam made a face and slapped her hands down onto her legs, bending over in shocked disbelief.

The Seer cracked a bemused smile, "In my many years of being here, I have learned to trust the Qilin, *whether* or not I agree with them." Her saddened eyes glossed over as a far-off memory showed behind them. The look just as quickly disappeared as she continued,

"So, I considered that I would decide here and now," she pointed to the ground. "whether that if you were good, I would help or if I thought you were a threat, I would...." She sarcastically copied what Sam had done only moments ago.

"Well, that's just great," Sam said joyfully sarcastic. "I am so glad you didn't off me in front of my friends!"

Sam looked around at everyone for conformation. Cedar's eyes bore into the ground avoiding contact, Amos sat down shifting uncomfortably, and the Chief sat, unphased by the interaction.

"I know you have had questions since you have awoken. Mainly you have wanted to get your memories back." Muninn said knowingly.

Sam's interest was sparked. She looked cautiously at the Seer. "Yeesss.."

"I am so the Seer of past, present, of thought, and prophecies.... from time to time," she weighed her hands, "because the will of people is neither here nor there, telling the future is as useful as preserving footprints in the ocean sand," she said, rolling her eyes.

"However, my visions of the past and present get hazy the further back they go or the more detailed I try to make them," Muninn continued on as she sat down on the nearest tree stump and trifled through with her plants. "Now, I have decided to help you, thanks to him," she nodded towards Ajax.

"But it would be best for you to *know* that I can only help you so much."

Sam let out a defeated sigh.

"Ok, at this point I'll take what I can get, I'm not picky and at least I'm not dead… so, I guess thank you- for that-" she said squatting on the ground and disturbing an unfortunate moss patch that grew there.

"You will not get what you want if you stay in the village," she added bluntly, "to get your memories and answers you seek, you must travel to the In-Between and speak with my brother Huginn," Muninn continued. "He is also a Wind Elemental raven, like me, but instead of thought and visions, he can see memories and he helps others with them." She finished talking and looked at Sam.

Sitting in silence, they had the answer to get what they wanted, but the solution was not a simple task.

Sam grew excited with awareness. "The In-Between, you mean the King's Realm, like the kingdom?" Sam asked. Muninn nodded.

"He lives near the castle, then?" Sam asked.

"This is unfortunately the hard part. No, he doesn't live near the castle, he lives *in* the castle. He works for the High King as his Seer and he works alongside the Fire Elemental that guards the Tree of Knowledge," Muninn said flatly as she trifled through her apron again.

Amos spoke up, "So, not only would Sam have to find her way through the Realms, but she would also have to find her way into the kingdom and into the castle to speak with your brother." Everyone seemed on edge with the daunting information that was laid in front of them. "Could he not just come here?" Amos asked.

"No, he cannot leave the Realm of the In-Between-"

Amos nodded, and Muninn continued.

"For his purpose with the King, but even if he could, he wouldn't- we are not on the *best* terms." Muninn threw some spices into the fire. With a puff of light brown smoke, the area gave off a calming cinnamon scent.

"The only way for me to get my answers is to do this. There is no other way?" Sam asked. Her heart thumped in her chest.

The Seer nodded. No words were needed to understand the task that now lay at Sam's feet.

"I guess I am going to meet the King then." Sam slapped her knee decisively and stood.

"If you plan on leaving the village... then the next spring thaw is the time to do it..." The Chief added. *"You will not survive the cold out there, and you cannot make it into the kingdom, let alone the castle, without a specific reason."*

Cedar gasped. Everyone turned to her in surprise. Sam had almost forgotten she was there. She had been quiet the whole time but now her eyes were bright with thought.

"The King's Journey!!" She snapped her fingers and looked at Sam excitedly. "That happens in the last time of the summer's warm season. If you leave by spring thaw, maybe there would be a way you could enter the Tournament of the

Kings Journey. The King grants a boon to those who win! You would just need to find one person of each Realm to compete in the Journey for you."

"I- don't know- that seems like a lot, just to get from point A to point B, I don't know this world well enough to convince someone to do that for me. It sounds risky," Sam responded, upset. She ran her fingers through the loose section of her braided hair and twisted the bead. "It's just too much," Sam frowned, looking at the ground, defeated she sat back down again.

"No!" Cedar said sternly, standing up suddenly. "I'll go with you. I know the way! We have gone to the Celebration of the First King before and we have traveled through towns and villages through the Realm of Land. We have made friends who can help us!" She desperately pleaded, trying to convince Sam.

"Cedar, you are too young to do this. You know how to survive, yes, but you do not know how to fight. I cannot leave the village alone at this time to protect you or Sam along this journey." Amos finally joined the conversation.

Cedar crossed her arms. "I can protect myself, I can do this, I can help Sam, I am not some helpless child anymore." She retorted disdainfully.

"I can continue to practice my fire calling until the time comes for us to leave, and maybe I can start weapon training or something. I can help with healing herbs and medicinal plants.

Sam will need that on the journey." Cedar turned to her father, continuing desperately.

"At this time, I do not give you my blessing for this journey. Sam may go. She has this task that she must do for herself, but you are not ready and that is FINAL." He stood, ending the conversation. Cedar's face flushed, and she furiously stared at the ground obeying her father's words.

The awkward silence filled the air as they said their goodbyes to Muninn and started their journey back to the village province. Muninn watched them leave, thinking about the dangers and the wonders that lay ahead in the two young girls' footsteps.

The group made it back to the village just as the sun set over the glistening white treetops. Over dinner, Amos regaled the rest of the family with what had happened that day. Lin agreed with Amos, which Sam could see did not help Cedar feel any less useless. She left dinner early and Sam soon followed, laying in bed trying to figure out a plan for the future and leveraging her options.

She could leave, go on a dangerous journey through the land's different Realms that she knows nothing about and hope she could get some of her memories back from before.

Or.

She could stay here and live a cozy life, maybe over time earning the trust of the people as she tried to find some type of happiness.

Peace or knowledge?

Sam sighed in frustration, unsure of what to do and realizing that overthinking would be unproductive. She turned over in her bed and pulled back the thick wool sheet that hung over her window and guarded the warmth in her room.

A breeze of cold air brushed in uninvited as she looked up to the stars, watching them shine in the winter sky, hoping that they would whisper the answer to her. Sam's eyes grew heavy with sleep and she fell into a slumber, watching the night sky twinkle as they spoke to her in their own language.

II

THE POWERLESS

"Let's go Samihanee!" A silhouette called to her, stretching out their hand. Sam tried to take it, but as she moved forward, the dark figure disappeared. Sam took a step and looked around, dazed.

"Hello?" She yelled, listening for a response. She kept going, searching all around her. A sense of disorientation took over her as she realized she had lost all sense of direction. Everything was black except a dull light ahead of her, leading her to where she needed to be.

Sam woke in a cold sweat, the chilly morning light peaked through the cracks of her covered window. Her eyelids dragged, and her tightly wound head punished her with grungy brain fog. Sitting up, she rubbed her face with her hands, wiping away the sleep. Adrenaline seeped through her, swiping at the fog and welcoming the sunlight. As she got up and walked down the hallway, Cedar angrily brushed past her and left the cottage, leaving the family staring in her wake.

"What's her deal?" Sam yawned and sat down at the table.

"She is still upset about our decision," Lin sighed.

"Cedar is too young to understand the dangers of travel. She will get over it," Amos replied sternly.

"Maybe you should talk to her Sam? She adores you," Lin looked at her earnestly.

Sam seemed a bit shocked. Cedar didn't seem to listen to anyone that much, and she also was adamant about going with Sam throughout the Realms.

"I mean, I can't *promise* anything. But I'll give it a shot."

"Thanks, that would mean a lot to us." Lin elbowed Amos, and he grunted a thanks. Sam could see that he was equally upset about the on and off arguments that were occurring between himself and his daughter.

After Sam had eaten, she got ready for her regular training day. Fern was out that day, so Sam had more time to practice with her weapons. She ran her hand up her scarred arm, feeling the toned muscle that now occupied her body, and thought back to when she had finally gained a healthy amount of weight. Her training with weapons had also seen improvements. Captain Ryner had been taking it easier on her as the time had gone on. He became more of a stern Captain towards Sam, rather than the disapproving fanatic, which she had taken as a victory.

Around noon, after she had finished her lunch, she noticed Cedar gazing into the forest, towards the edge of the trees.

"Whatcha doin?" Sam walked up, joining her. In order to prevent the staff tip from getting muddy on the damp ground, she placed it on her boot, then leaned on it.

Cedar looked at her through the side of her eye. "I'm thinking about things I can do to get my dad to let me go with you," she responded bluntly.

Sam laughed. "Cedar, your dad is as stubborn as you are. You really think he is going to let you go? It doesn't matter what you try to do. You could kill the Hunter and he would still find a reason for you to not leave!" Sam raised her arms out wide, exaggerating her point.

Cedar turned to her and raised her eyebrow. "Kill the Hunter?" She rested her chin on her knuckles in a quiet, thoughtful way.

"Nooooo, no, no. That's not what I said. Did you hear anything that came out of my mouth just now?" Sam said, baffled by the tunnel vision that she showed.

Cedar didn't respond. She stared into the woods. Her eyes revealed a plan being formed in the depths of her mind.

Sam sighed, turning to the woods as well, watching the calmness of the swaying, leafless trees. A minute went by in silence.

"Let's do it. Let's find and kill the Hunter, then we can finally show him I am ready to go." Cedar said. They locked eyes, and Sam could see ambition burning in them.

Sam raised her eyebrows and opened her mouth to say something, but no words formed. She latched the staff to her back and took Cedar by her shoulders so that they were facing each other, eye to eye.

"Cedar... Look at me..." She paused. "That is one of the dumbest, NO!" She put her finger up. "THE *dumbest* thing I have heard you say since I learned this language. We... in NO WAY... could ever *KILL* the Hunter." She made sure to emphasize the impossibility of Cedar's childlike mission.

Cedar pushed Sam's hands off and sucked her teeth. "We can- we have a month or two till winter's thaw, we can train, we can get stronger, then when it gets warm, we can track him down and bring back like a tooth or a fang. I bet he didn't even survive the fight from the festival, and we can just harvest that stuff from him and convince my dad we killed him."

Sam looked away. It wouldn't be a bad idea to get a fang or claw if he was dead, but that's a big chance to take. She couldn't say that to Cedar though. She was too stubborn and would take the idea and run rampant with it.

"Look, just don't do anything dumb. Let's wait until it starts to get warm and then make a decision. Maybe your dad will change his mind." Sam shrugged hopefully, trying to convince Cedar and the small part of herself that wanted to not go alone.

"Sam, I *want* to travel and see everything our Realms have to offer." Cedar said. "I know I can become strong. I just have to get past this wall that blocks me." She looked at her with pleading eyes. "And I want to be there for you. You're my friend- my sister." Cedar hugged Sam, soft tears trickling down her cheeks. "I cannot watch you leave, knowing that you would be like a child out there."

She didn't disagree with her. This world was new and dangerous. She didn't know what she would encounter. If she had to leave, though, it would be for a good enough reason, and figuring out her past could help her with her future. So, this opportunity that presented itself was going to have to be good enough for Sam. She would go, when the winter thawed, the snow melted, and the sun welcomed the plants and growth back, she would leave and journey to find herself and discover this new world.

But would I go alone?

Sam hugged Cedar back harder, scared of what was to come.

"Let's just- not worry about it for the time being. There is nothing we can do right now, so let it leave your mind and relax." Sam pulled away from the hug.

Cedar nodded as she wiped the tears from her eyes.

"I'm going to let you have some space to chill out, but let me know if you wanna talk about it more. Ok?" Sam said, unhooking her staff and holding it again, she ran her thumb over the grooves, calming herself.

Cedar nodded again, they gave each other a sad smile and Cedar headed towards the cottage while Sam walked the opposite way.

The rest of winter continued in silence on the subject, however Sam could feel it hanging in the air, like a heavy fog that clouded their minds.

Cedar started weapons training too and showed determination to find her strength. Lin and Amos believed that she had moved on, but Sam could see eagerness growing inside of her, week by week as the sun melted away the ice.

It was a temperate night. The full moon peeked through the scattered clouds. Sam lay in bed, sleepless. Her time was coming to decide what she wanted to do. She had spoken with Lin and Amos previously that week, about whether or not she had decided to go. When they asked her, she replied with uncertainty. Lin had urged her to make a decision within the next few days so they could start preparing her for the journey ahead.

As she lay, determining her fate, Ajax shuffled next to her and woke. He bleated and poked his head out of the curtained window.

"What is it?" she asked curiously, peeking her face out with him. As soon as she looked, she saw the white tip of a red fox's tail dip out of sight in the tree line.

Sam groaned in annoyance. "What could she *possibly* be doing right now?" She hissed to Ajax.

She threw off her covers, jumping out of bed and silently made her way out of the house after Cedar. She kept out of sight while tracking her, waiting to see what she was planning. Sam went deeper into the forest, guided by the light of the moon. Cedar only stopped when she got to the denser woods. She seemed to stare down at something. As she leaped down from the sturdy tree roots, Cedar effortlessly vanished from sight, melting into the shadows cast by a nearby tree. Sam came up crouching and peered behind the tree and to see her hunched over a giant dark mass.

Is that fur? It's kind of fluffy.

Sam squinted her eyes, trying to sharpen her focus on the situation unfolding before her.

Sam's mouth dropped open when the moonlight shone from behind a slow-moving cloud. Cedar was digging through the carcass of a large animal.

Internally screaming, she turned away, covering her mouth, gagging. Although her mind rejected the sight, she compelled herself to acknowledge its reality. She crept closer to Cedar to get a better view. The stench of death filled her nose and gave her confirmation that she needed.

"*Whhaaatttt'rree* you DOING????" Sam whisper yelled furiously while coming up behind Cedar.

Cedar yelped and jumped. With a knife grasped in her hand, she had blood on both hands from her mysterious and disgusting task. She looked at Sam, speechless and terrified, not knowing what to say. Sam stood up fully and repeated herself through the waving of her hands and disgusted grunts.

Cedar stammered, trying to push words out. Sam put her hands on hips as a disappointed mother would and waited for an explanation of the lunacy before her.

"It's- It's the Hunter." She pointed at the dead beast with her knife as tears started down her face. Sam looked at the lifeless creature uncomfortably as Cedar's plan put itself together in her head. "I asked around and some of my friends had said they spotted the Hunter dead, or at least what looked like the Hunter, so... I thought I would collect a trophy and pretend I killed him. Then my dad would let me go.." Cedar looked down, ashamed of her words.

"So, you were sawing off this dead animal's- very large claw..." she said in a shrill voice, "this is crazy." Sam fumed, tilting her head towards the animal. As she did so, she noticed darker wet patches on the animals' hide, covered by the night. She placed her palm on the animal. It was sticky and cold. She picked her hand up and looked at her palm, now red with blood.

"Were you cutting it up here?" Sam asked, growing on edge.

Cedar looked up and saw the blood on her hand. They made eye contact.

"No."

Cedar turned to the creature's hidden face. She pulled back its crumpled body and the mountains of fur. It was not the Hunter. It seemed to be a poor animal left for dead by its malicious predator.

They both took a sharp breath in and held it. Listening to the forest around them, they could now feel the danger in the air.

Sam whispered, "we need to get out of here."

Cedar shakingly got up and held her arms close to her chest, painting her forearms red. Sam looked at Cedar grabbing the clean part of her arm, then she froze. Terror filled her body. Her hair stood on end and the blood drained from her face.

"S..Sam?" Cedar whispered.

Behind Cedar, in the night's darkness, shone two bright green eyes.

Sam swallowed. The moonlight passed over the dense forest, gleaming down on the girls, the carcass of the animal, and then finally to the beast covered in the blood of his prey.

Cedar could see in her eyes that something was wrong. She turned swiftly. Instantly, the Hunter leaped forward. Covering the majority of the massive distance between them. Cedar fell to the ground, her legs giving up as she cried out in fear. Sam grabbed her and picked her up to run, but the beast was too fast. He towered above them, bearing his fangs. His fowl breath slapping their faces. Sam held her staff between them as their only form of protection.

"Sam..." Cedar whimpered weakly. Sam glanced at her, afraid to take her eyes off the wolf. Cedar's eyes glowed a hot white, and as she grew warm to the touch, Sam let go of her. Cedar looked at her hands, then down at her body, finally back at Sam.

"Sam, you need to get away from here." Cedar said firmly in a terror filled voice. Then turned towards the giant wolf, holding out her hands, blocking the path to Sam.

Afraid, Sam turned and ran. The heat in the air grew by the second. Her instinct screamed to get away. She dipped behind a tree and crouched down, protecting herself.

Cedar yelled, then she felt a massive heat wave pass by her and the thick tree she hid behind. There was a flash of light so bright that even with her eyes closed, it seemed as bright as a summer's day. Another stronger heat wave pushed her to the ground. The silence descended upon them a moment later, creating an eerie stillness in the air. The hush of the forest brought Sam out of her hiding spot. She caught a pillar of fire dim and disappear into the darkening sky. Cedar stood in the center of charred rings of burnt ground and destroyed forest. The whole area was singed by the signs of fire damage and the Hunter was nowhere to be seen.

A loud howl echoed through the forest, reaching the girls' ears, telling them that the battle was far from finished. Sam rushed her, Cedar's clothes were burnt and sparks were sizzling out on the edges of her sleeves. She felt warm still and looked weak, her eyes glazed and distant. Sam covered her in her overcoat and picked her up, carrying her back home.

As she stumbled over tree roots and rocks, Cedar mumbled nonsense. Sam glanced nervously between her and the path with each moment that passed. She quickened the pace as they escaped the dense part of the woods. The closer she got, the clearer she could see the family standing outside, their faces filled with a mix of shock and disbelief, as they stared at the aftermath of the flame pillar's destruction. Once they saw her, they ran to meet her. Amos took Cedar from Sam and looked at her in a father's worry.

"Quickly," Lin said, eagerly gesturing to the door. They placed her in bed and Lin examined her.

After a moment, Lin replied, "she will be ok, she just needs rest."

A sigh of relief passed through the group and Sam sat down, putting her head in her hands as she struggled to take in what happened.

"Why were you both out at night? What happened? What was that pillar of light?" Amos spat out questions frantically. Lin came over to attend to her injuries as well. Sam explained to them the story as Amos continued to eye Cedar in distress.

"It's because of me then." He responded half-heartedly.

"No, I tried talking her out of it. She is stubborn," Sam tried to reassure him.

"Hmm, just like someone else I know." Lin side eyed Amos.

Amos stood and rubbed the sweat from his forehead. "Go to bed Sam. We will deal with this when she wakes up."

She didn't argue. After all the excitement had passed, she felt hazy. She got up and sorely walked to the other room, collapsing on the bed.

About a week had passed since the incident. The entire village was buzzing with the news of Cedar being able to finally call the flame. In the life-or-death situation, she was able to summon it forth herself. She slept for a couple of days but had been practicing with Lin after she woke. Despite her now weak flame, Lin recalled vividly the intense presence of the flame that Cedar used that night.

Sam and Fern were engrossed in watching the practice, Amos and Atlas joined them after a while. In silence, they all savored the mesmerizing performance of light and heat. Eventually, Lin and Cedar called it a day and joined them, eager to rest.

"We should talk about Sam's journey," Amos said as they sat down.

When he mentioned it, Cedar's face went through a range of emotions. "Dad! I can call the flame now, and mom says I have a lot of potential, and I can use this to protect both of us. I scared away the Hunter, is that not proof enough?!" She said in proud haste, trying to get out the jumbled words fast enough to convince him.

He put a hand up for silence and once she stopped talking, she looked down at the table and scratched at the stone.

He sighed.

"You may go."

Sam smiled relieved, her mind reeled at the relief from the stress. Cedar snapped her head up from the table cheerfully beaming as she reached over the table to hug him.

He continued, "The Chief and I have sent letters to the different provinces, reefs, lakes, and cities that we have friends in. There are few in the different Realms, but a lot more here in the provinces, so they know to look out for you two and take you in if needed." He looked at both of them.

"We will be worried about you two, of course, but I think you have worked hard and showed dedication to achieve something you want."

Lin nodded in agreement, and added, "I also believe that this might help your powers grow stronger."

Atlas came over to hug them, digging his face into Sam's side, clearly upset that they would be leaving.

"So." Amos clapped his hands together. "Spring is here in two weeks, the fresh growth is upon us, you will leave then!"

Sam caught her breath.

Two weeks? Is that enough time?

Fern put a reassuring hand on her shoulder at her shocked expression. "You will be ready. You have grown so much and we will continue working until the day you leave." Sam nodded and softly smiled, trying to convince the others and secretly herself.

"We will escort you to the first city. We have been there before and know the path," Lin said. "A neighbor agreed to watch Atlas while we are gone, but Amos, Fern, and myself can escort you to the city. That will give us a chance to do some new year's trading as well."

Fern added in, "We also plan on taking Atlas to his first ever Tournament of the Kings Journey. So, we will see you at the King's City too!"

As Sam exhaled deeply, a wave of relief washed over her, easing her worries. At the very least, they would be with them when they left the village and supporting them however they could along the way.

Cedar and Sam thanked them.

Lin put her hand on top of Sam's gently. "You will get your memories back, Sam, I promise."

12

WHISPERS OF THE FOREST

THE WARMTH OF THE sun thawed the ice and snow that had blanketed the village for the last couple of months. Now spring had begun, sprouts of new budding grass grew and greened the fields. The farmers commenced their work plowing and seeding with their choice of vegetable or grain. The animals became more active, restless for the sun to awaken the life around them once more. Birds sang their songs, and the deer returned, migrating through, watching the villagers as they went on with their tasks. The forest grew back in its deep lushness and awoke again, whispering its secrets of life to those who listened.

With the arrival of fresh growth and change, it was time for Sam and Cedar to depart on their journey.

They woke up before the sun on their day of departure. Everyone packed the day before, only what was necessary for the trip. As they made their way through town, they bid farewell to a few group of faunanoid before leaving Atlas with his friends' family for the trip. Cedar ran to give her friends a hug, knowing she wouldn't see them for many weeks to come. Jeramiah and Elaine gave a soft smile and nod to Sam as they continued by.

At their destination, tears formed in Atlas's eyes as he ran to his mother, holding her, trying to persuade her not to leave. It took much convincing to calm him.

"We will see you again in no time, Atlas. And your mom and dad and Fern are coming back here in a couple of days. It'll be alright." Sam said, ruffling his coarse, dark brown hair. She picked him up and gave him a tight hug. Sniffling back a few tears, Sam placed him back on the ground and he watched sadly as they waved goodbye, not knowing when the next time they would truly see each other again.

They walked to the outskirts of town. No one spoke. They listened to their packs jangle and rustle with the morning birds. Sam noticed the Chief sitting at the edge of the forest line talking to someone. As they came closer, the figure came into view.

"O maaannn," Sam slumped over as she walked. "I was hoping I was done with this dummy."

It was evident that the Chief had heard her statement as he stood tall beside Captain Ryner, he responded with a light-hearted shake of his head.

"Good Morrow, my friends. Are you prepared for the journey to the City of Atlon? I have sent word of your arrival," he said.

"Yes, we have packed the necessities for the deep forest," Lin responded.

"This is a good opportunity to get some trading done for seeds, herbs, and maybe some... chickens." Fern gave a questionable eyebrow to her dad in hopes that he would agree. Instead, he gave a grimace of disapproval for more animals that would need to be taken care of. Fern shrugged it off with a smile. Sam caught the mischievous glint in Fern's eye. She knew that their conversation was far from over.

The Chief looked at Sam, bending his head and neck down to meet her at eye level. *"Are you ready to see what this new world has to offer Sam?"* His eyes sparkled with excitement at the wonders that awaited her.

Hesitantly, she replied, "As ready as I can be, Chief."

He nodded, understanding her answer to be genuine. Captain Ryner stood kicking the grass as the Chief spoke and after a moment he looked up.

"We will make sure to keep a weathered eye out for any dangers while you are away. I will also set out more guards at the forest's edge to watch for the Hunter." Captain Ryner said.

Amos gave him a curt nod in silent gratitude. Despite the lingering discomfort, everyone was gradually moving on from the unfortunate events at the harvest festival.

"Goodbye Chief. Thank you for everything. I am really going to miss you," Sam said faintly as she hugged him. She looked away saddened and waved to Captain Ryner.

"Thanks for the training."

She looked at him, and he stared at her for a moment. Then the corner of his mouth curled upwards into a smile. He bowed his head and mumbled under his breath.

"Stay safe, little monster."

With that, he swiveled and marched his way down the hill towards the village without a second glance goodbye to the travelers. A triumphant smile spread across her face. Sam took a deep breath, feeling revitalized. She looked at the little cottage hidden in the shadow of the tall swaying trees across the fields and looked at the village buzzing with its people. She felt a twinge of sorrow fill her heart as they walked away from the haven she had grown to love.

"Ugghhhh, my feet *hurt*," Cedar complained louder this time as she dragged herself on the trail through the forest. "How long until we get there!?" She continued dramatically.

"Well." Lin looked up at the sky, judging by the sun's position. "We have been walking for only about an hour, so I believe... two days." Lin looked back at Cedar. "We will get there tomorrow night *if* you can stop dragging your feet."

Cedar rolled her head back in annoyance but said nothing else. Sam interjected, trying to change the subject.

"He said we are going to the City of Atlon? What's it like?" She asked, kicking a rock down the trail.

Fern spoke up with excitement. "I love traveling to the twin city. It is so much bigger than our village and they have everything! We will reach the deep forest tonight, and then tomorrow night we will reach Atlon. The people live in earth homes and tree homes, not in cottages like we do."

Sam matched Fern's excitement as she imagined homes inside of the earth and treehouses in a jungle. Ajax interjected her thoughts by trotting around her as he tried to snap at a small flying bug.

"That sounds amazing. Will we get to see the insides of the homes?" Sam asked.

"Yes, we have sent a letter to the Chief. They will also help us with finding someone to journey with you to the King's Realm," Amos responded as he sharpened some small blades. "Hopefully, this new companion of yours will be formidable and able to protect themselves," he grunted.

"Speaking of formidable," Lin walked up to Cedar. "Why don't we practice your flame summoning as we walk?"

This seemed to cheer Cedar up. "Yes, please!!"

They practiced and sparks of heat warmed up Sam's side every so often as they continued on their way.

"How many provinces are there in the Realm of Land?" she asked curiously as she plucked a surprisingly tall blade of grass from the ground and slowly folded it as they walked.

"There are seven provinces, each with their own village, town, or city. Just like in the other Realms, except for the In-Between, the King's Realm is just the one kingdom and castle. The Realm of Sky has seven, so does the Realm of Sea. Each also has their own leaders to take care of that area." Fern responded.

"Some are safe, some are dangerous, especially right now. The Realms are on edge with each other, and the High King is having trouble maintaining the peace. That's another reason I am skeptical of you two being on your own," Amos said, looking at his blade. Sam watched as he nodded in contentment, put the small blade away, and then pulled out another one.

"I didn't know that. Hopefully, we can travel through unnoticed." Sam said, digging her fingernail into the leaf and feeling the stickiness of the juice on her finger.

Everyone nodded in agreement, but it still seemed to be a sore topic for Amos. Sam distracted herself by thinking about the different villages in the Realms and what they might look like. To change the subject back, she asked,

"What are the different provinces in the Land?"

A big flame passed over them, and they ducked in surprise. As it dissipated into smoke, they turned back. Cedar flashed an embarrassed smile and Lin frowned at her disapprovingly. Sam rolled her eyes and turned back around to continue their conversation.

"I have been to many of the provinces for trade or just travel in my youth. I traveled a lot before Lin and I were married." Amos looked up at the treetops thoughtfully, "There is a Desert Province that is harsh, near the mountain's edge. The Deep Jungle, where we are headed, then the Hills of Yoid. There is also the Sacred Forest of the guardians and spirits. The Queen of our Realm lives there, and no faunanoid is allowed to enter the sacred place. Then the last two provinces are the Taiga and the Marsh." He counted each one on his fingers.

"The Verdant Vale is a vast forest that takes up most of the Realm. Even I have not seen it all, nor do I want to. Some places are not meant to be seen and others are just too dangerous, like I said before."

Verdant Vale is the other name for the Realm of Land. Sam recalled the name from before.

After he finished speaking, they were quiet for a time. They listened to the birds call and the fire crackling behind them. Each of the travelers' heads was filled with different thoughts. Amos with worry for the young ones, Fern with excitement for the up-and-coming jungle province, and Sam with the wonders of the vast world around her.

As they continued walking, the woods grew lush and more dense. The sun shone sharply through the new leaves of the old forest. Sam noticed that some trees scattered through were taller and darker. They were great pines. There, laying at the base of the pines, were scattered pine cones from last season's drop. She walked off the path towards one that was particularly massive.

"What's wrong with this pinecone? Why is it enormous?" She yelled back to the group.

When she bent over to marvel at it, noting something odd. Not only was the pinecone massive, but lopsided as well, unproportioned to the others that sat around it. She cocked her head to one side curiously as she crouched down to pick it up to examine it closer.

Her hand felt the tip of the pinecones' sharp edges when, in a flash, the pinecone unfurled itself into a mass of face, beak and flapping wings.

QUACK, QUACK, QUACK.

The odd pinecone flapped its wings wickedly, scratching Sam's hand. Caught off guard she fell to the ground with an oomph.

"What the...." Sam scooted backwards as it spoofed itself up and hissed at her.

She could hear laughter in the background coming from the others. Fern walked over to help her up.

"Don't be silly, it's just a pineduck. They're like the chickens back home." Fern answered Sam's question. Then she ruffled through her pouch and threw some berries at the strange, aggressive creature. The pineduck cautiously sniffed and ate the berries, finally calming down. Fern went over and scratched its head underneath the sharp, pointed ends.

"I believe, by the loudness and sharpness of the quacks it made, that this is a female pineduck," Fern looked at Sam. "Males usually make a raspier and softer quack." She continued to pet it. The pineduck finished gobbling down the berries, mean-mugged Sam, and then turned her attention promptly back to Fern for affection.

Following the continuation of their journey, the little pokey bird trailed behind them, waddling closely but with enough distance to remain cautious. They paid her no mind, but attempted to shoo her away every so often.

After a while, defeated, they let her stay, and she was convinced to join the group as Fern continued to pluck little purple berries from nearby bushes and toss them to her.

Ajax curiously sniffed her occasionally but was given a hiss and a flap of the wings in response. This is how the rest of the afternoon was spent. Sam marveled from afar at the unusual prickled creature that seemed to have found Fern as a new companion.

They continued onward, the sun now dazzling, laying a brilliant orange and red on the rolling clouds in the sky, signifying nights approached.

"Does anyone hear that?" Cedar asked, stopping to listen. "It sounds like splashing and... laughter?" She looked in the direction she thought it came from. The group stopped and listened as well. Cedar was right. Left of the trail, they could hear laughter and splashing coming from a close stream. Lin shook the water canteen and looked at Amos.

"I guess this would be a good time to refill the water if there is a brook nearby," Lin suggested.

Amos agreed, and they headed off the trail towards the commotion. It was not far until they saw the trickling water gleaming in the dusk sunlight a few paces past the path. As they got closer, they could see a boy playing and hopping around in the water. He looked to be about Atlas's age, around ten. The little boy had bright yellow catlike eyes with dark skin and black fur covering most of his arms and legs, accompanied with him was a long ringed tail swishing back and forth vigorously as he enjoyed the water. He didn't notice them as he continued to jump from the shallow end of the small creek to the deeper end. He swam to the bottom and torpedoed himself upward through the water and into the air happily.

"Hello little one." Lin called to the boy as he crouched for another mighty leap into the cool evening water. With a startled jump, he spun around to confront the unknown individual who had spoken. Waist deep in the stream, fear paralyzed him, his eyes filled with uncertainty.

"It's ok dear, sorry to scare you, we are just here for some water," Lin said calmly. "What's your name?"

The scrawny boy didn't answer, but he took the opportunity to jump out of the water as quick as lightning, his sleek wet fur sticking to him. Then he pounced back towards the trail, not looking back. Sam cracked a smile and Lin gave a soft laugh.

"He reminds me of Atlas." She said, then she sighed, looking longingly to where the mysterious child ran away.

"It's okay Lin. We will be back to Atlas in no time. I'm sure he misses you very much, too," Amos said caringly, as he gave her a reassuring hug.

"Not to change the subject, but that was weird, right? Some random kid in the forest, no town or home in sight..." Sam pointed to the stream and then towards the way he left and looked around for confirmation. Cedar looked with concern at her father as well to see what he would say.

"No, there is an inn called the Stained Glass Tavern, a couple of miles down the road. It is the halfway point to the deep forest province. He and his family are probably staying there," Fern responded, putting down her new companion and watching her waddle to the water.

"Aye, he definitely looked like a forest creature with those sharp eyes. Those are the eyes of a hunter, for sure. I hope we didn't scare the poor lad too much." Amos said, scratching his beard and laughing.

Sam thought it was strange to see a cat-like creature enjoying the water so much, but she had seen weirder things that same day. She glanced at the pinecone duck wading into the cool stream, happily cleaning herself, and didn't think twice of the boy in the water.

They filled their canteens up with the clean water, and Sam splashed her face to refresh herself. Sending adrenaline rushing through her and making her more alert. She had gotten tired after the long day of trekking through the sun, hopefully this could take her the rest of the way to the tavern and then she could crawl into a bed for some much needed sleep.

After taking some time to rest and freshen up, they set off back to the trail, their energy renewed. The sun had set above the tree line and darkened the world around them as they saw the lantern light of a cozy three-story tavern come into view.

The tavern was nestled next to a hill in a small clearing of the forest, and was made from a combination of dark tree wood and smooth river stone. In addition, there was a wooden door that stood tall, was wide, and had a rounded shape to it. The windows that enveloped the oval door frame were stained glass windows with many intricate designs and colors on them. The designs were nature or of the different people of the land. She spotted centaurs, fawns, satyrs, unicorns, and other creatures dancing on the glass. On the right side of the tavern, away from the hill, there was a large, ornately designed bay window that offered a view of a charming small garden. The roof was shackled into a single point, and slightly jarred to the side above where the window was. A small tower hugged the hill that lay on the opposite side of the building.

Upon entering, they were greeted by a large seating area, scattered with tables and chairs, inviting them to relax and dine. To the right was a bar with drinks, and to the left were the stairs that lead upward to the rooms and to the tower.

"I'll be there in a moment. Help yourself to a table," a loud woman shrieked from the room behind the bar.

They went over to a round table big enough to seat all of them comfortably by the windows with the garden view and fell into the chairs exhausted, waiting for someone to help them.

A stout short woman in her 40s came out of the door. She wore a light brown dress and wiped her hands on her grease stained cooking apron. She shuffled over to the group and Sam noticed that she had small reddish-brown ears hidden in her tangled mess of curly hair that matched in color. Her eyes were human, but her face definitely resembled a minx, with a small nose and long white whiskers along her face. Her puffy tail, with a black tip, stuck out from under her dress.

"What can I do ya for?" she said with a slight accent as she reached the table.

"Do you have two rooms for us to stay in for the night? We are very tired from traveling all day and we have another day's travel ahead of us," Amos said surely.

"I sure do. We are not busy during this time of the year, so there are plenty of rooms to spare. Would you like to eat while you're down here?" The short lady asked. Cedar and Sam nodded eagerly. Sam didn't realize how hungry she was until the mention of food. Her stomach grumbled in annoyance.

The lady nodded back, smiling, understanding the eagerness. Then she turned her head sideways toward the stairs and yelled in a long, high-pitched voice,

"RONIN!" She made her way to the bar to get the drinks and food ready.

There was a moment of silence, but then came a rush of footsteps as someone thundered down the stairs. As he jumped the last three steps happily to the floor, Sam observed it had been the boy from the stream from earlier that day. He had stood up quickly in a goofy way and looked around to see who he was helping. He appeared to recognize the group and promptly fell silent, lowering his head to the wooden floor panels as he hurried towards the woman's side.

The lady handed him four large clay mugs of water and brought over plates of bread, cheese, meats, and soups for everyone.

"This young lad is Ronin," she motioned to the boy, "and I am Margo, pleased to be of service." She put the plates down. The boy looked up shyly up through his ruffled hair.

Sam spoke up. "Ya, we actually saw him earlier today. He was at a nearby stream where we stopped to get water and -" She fell short when the boy frantically shook his head back and forth from behind Margo. As Margo turned to give him a look, he stopped and sheepishly smiled before she swatted him on the back of the head. He winced, pouting in response to the punishment.

"What did I tell you about playing in the stream, hmm?" she said sternly. "Go on now, I'll deal with you later." She motioned toward the stairs and he gave Sam one last spiteful look before leaving. Sam's face grew hot, and flushed with embarrassment.

"I.. I'm sorry. I didn't mean for him to get into trouble," she stammered.

"No sweetheart, he knows the rules and has known them since he was half the size he is now. He just decides he doesn't want to abide by them. It's not the first time, nor will it be the last." Margo sighed with concern for the boy.

"No matter," she perked up. "It's late, y'all eat up and I'll give you the keys to your rooms. Go to bed whenever you like." Margo dug through her apron and handed them two long rusted metal keys with the tags three and four on them.

Amos and Lin ate slower than the girls. Sam, Fern, and Cedar, however, were ready to sleep. In a hurry, they wolfed down their food as if it were their last meal and then made their way to room four.

Sam paid little attention to her surroundings as she wearily climbed the flight of stairs. Their room was on the right side next to room five. Across from them was Amos and Lin's room, room three.

They unlocked the door to see two beds in a medium-sized room with a small window. Her eyes grew heavy as she spotted the bed. Sam only cared about the fluffy mattress and soft sheets that she succumbed to moments later, as her mind slowed and she drifted off to sleep.

13

A LOSS IN THE JUNGLE

Sam stood in the dull light once again. Nothing but darkness surrounded her. She looked forward, seeing a faint light ahead, and followed it. Her feet dragged, the harder she struggled to walk, the slower she got. As she continued forward agonizingly slow, she noticed a dark figure crouched, hiding its face. As she stared down at it, she wasn't afraid. Sadness was the only emotion that captivated her heart.

Once she was close enough, she knelt down and tried to put her hand on its back, but her hand phased through it. Alarmed, she held her hand up and examined it, blinking a couple times, but soon brought her attention back to the shadow.

No matter what she did, Sam couldn't comfort it as she noticed it quietly crying to itself.

Its sadness grew, tears welled in Sam's eyes now. Her throat burned as she choked to level herself.

"I'm sorry," she whispered to the creature. "I wish I could help you."

She sat there, thinking, not sure how to proceed. After a moment, the far off light came towards her. It shone brighter and brighter. Sam shaded her face from the light as she looked down at the miserable silhouette fading into the distance.

The light isn't moving. I am.

Even after the creature vanished, she couldn't tear her gaze away, a desperate longing to communicate welling up inside her.

She opened her eyes to the warm light of the lantern that suspended from the ceiling above the room. The darkness still hung and the stars still sparkled brightly outside in the night. She rolled over to see Fern and Cedar still asleep in the other bed near the door. Sam stretched out her body, feeling a sense of alertness come to her. She sat up quietly to not disturb her sleeping comrades.

Fern snored lightly while Ajax and the pineduck curled up together near the door like little guardians. Sam rolled her eyes and chuckled when she thought back to earlier that day, when the sassy duck wanted nothing to do with him.

The room went unnoticed by her when she first came in. She had fallen asleep immediately as soon as she hit the soft bed. Now, looking around at the unfamiliar sight of the bedroom they rented, she saw it was a quaint room, cozy, and meant to keep the guest comfortable.

The warm light above swayed, lighting the room and casting shadows that danced across their bags and a small table with chairs that sat close to the window next to Sam. In an attempt to coax herself into sleep, she continued scanning her surroundings.

Outside her tiny room, she could hear faint whispers.

Lin, Amos, and... Margo?

She placed her bare feet on the cold wooden floor and crept up to the door, avoiding any creaking planks that might give her away. Sam placed her ear close to the door and strained to listen to the hushed conversation that was happening in the hallway.

"We appreciate everything Margo, I'm glad you remembered us from that long ago," Lin murmured softly. "It is nice to see the place still running."

"Of course, it took a moment, but I will never forget such a kind Priestess and her husband." Margo replied in the same tone.

"I am curious though," Amos started, "the boy- he wasn't here last time, is he your son?"

There was silence for a moment as everyone waited for an answer. Nervousness enveloped Sam as she worried that she had gotten caught and she held her breath, waiting.

"He... no, he is not my son. I am taking care of him for.... a dear friend." The words drew out of her slowly. Margo's careful choice of words indicated her reluctance to continue the conversation.

"We understand," Lin responded. "Thank you Margo, we will see you for breakfast tomorrow and will leave soon after. There is still a bit of our journey left."

There was another moment of silence and then she heard the jingle of a key and the door open. Footsteps traced down the hall as Margo retired to her own room. Sam crept back to her own bed and laid propped up, thinking of the bizarre conversation and the cat boy who loved the water.

She woke to the forest birds and the bright, warm sunlight that stamped the room with its presence. Fern and Cedar stirred as well. Cedar yawned and Fern hopped out of the cramped bed to stretch out her aching muscles.

"Ugh, I feel like a kid again, having to share a bed." Fern put her hands on her back and continued to stretch out. Cedar nodded and groaned in agreement. When they were ready, all three left the sunlit room to find food.

As they made their way downstairs, they could hear Margo humming as she cooked. Lin, Amos, and Ronin sat together at the same large table from last night before and ate breakfast. Sam sat next to Ronin, who ate by pushing his food into the pile on his plate and shoveling it into his mouth.

"Ronin," Margo said in a stern tone. He understood what she meant. He rolled his eyes and started eating less like a wild animal and more like a civilized person.

Sam raised her eyebrow and playfully chuckled at Ronin's reaction.

"I am sorry we scared you yesterday." She leaned in close to him. "And- I didn't mean to get you into trouble."

He nodded in silent acknowledgment.

"Your food looks yummy. What is it?"

Through his full mouth, he responded flatly, "pancakes."

Sam chuckled again, seeing the resemblance to Atlas and his demeanor. Sam looked down at the table and ran her hand over the beautiful designs. She felt an ache of homesickness as she thought of him.

However, the feeling passed soon after as Margo dropped a steaming plate of eggs, toast, and a small variety of fruits and vegetables in front of her. Her stomach growled with excitement. She dug in just as Ronin had a moment ago, starved for the delicious food that sat in front of her. As she was eating, Ronin stopped and looked at her with alert eyes. She looked at him, knowing what he was thinking.

If I can't eat like that, then why does she get to?

Sam slowed down on her eating and sat up straighter, trying to be a role model for the young boy who watched her. Margo joined them and they talked as they ate.

Before long, Amos sat back and patted his stomach, satisfied with his meal. Margo's face beamed with pride at everyone's enjoyment of her food. After they finished, they went to pack up. Margo and Ronin cleaned the tables and plates.

Sam didn't unpack anything, so she was done first. With her belongings in hand, she made her way downstairs to wait for the others. She got back downstairs and helped Ronin clean up after their mess, gathering plates as he wiped down the table.

As they cleaned the dishes, they talked a little.

"Soooo, where are you from Ronin?" Sam tried to be inconspicuous in her questioning.

He shrugged and continued cleaning. When she saw his hands, she couldn't help but notice his dark claws that perfectly matched his fur and skin. There were small webs connecting in between each of his fingers. She leaned back from the counter and peered at his legs and feet. They were also cat-like and long, which made him taller than a normal child would be for his age. She saw the webbing on his feet too.

Now that's interesting, a cat person with fish traits.

She looked at his face, wondering about who he was or what the future might hold for someone different like him.

"You're not from here, are you?" Sam asked, wiping food from the green painted clay plate. He stopped, stray soap travelling down his forearm, and looked outside at water trickling through a bamboo pipe for a moment and shook his head no.

"You aren't either," he said, wrapping his hand around Sam's furless, clawless, pale fingers. He held her hand up to his face to examine them.

"Man, it was that easy for you to tell." Sam laughed awkwardly, shifting under her mask.

"We both don't belong here." He let go of her hand as he responded solemnly, looking at her. Even though he stared at her, she could tell his mind was far off, to a place and a time that he thought fond of.

They finished cleaning in silence, the conversation sent both of them into a lonely wonder. Ronin ran upstairs and distress tugged at her. She hadn't meant to make him upset yet again. Back at the table, she put her hand on her chin. Through the colored light of the stained glass that encapsulated the rounded door, she looked out at to the garden. Sam realized that in the morning light, it was beautiful. The sunlight streamed through the stained glass and painted almost the entire room in wild yellows, greens, blues, and reds.

As promptly as Ronin left, he returned. He jumped into the seat next to her, causing the chair to screech on the paneled floor. Sam said nothing. Surprised and confused, she waited for him to make the first move.

"H... here.." He stammered, putting a dagger on the table hastily. "Its name is *Lotus Blade*."

The dagger was a blade made of polished steel, a delicate lotus flower with a long stem and lotus leaves emerged from it to create an embellished inlay. Double-edged, with a pointed tip that tapered down to a sharp cutting edge on both sides. She took a sharp breath in. The hilt of the dagger was equally impressive, made of a polished material, perhaps ivory or bone. Partnered with a beautiful design of another lotus and its leaves engraved in silver on the end.

She didn't know what to say. It was a beautiful piece of art, but it looked too important to be given away to someone else, let alone a stranger.

"I.. I can't accept this Ronin. It looks too important for you to just to give away," Sam stammered, pushing it back toward him, refusing the gift.

He shook his head, picking it up and pushing the blade out further to her. She took the small dagger tenderly, holding it as if it would snap at any moment. He pulled out another one that was identical to the gifted one. It was a matching pair.

"I want you to have it. We are both different and not from this land, so we are kind of the same in that way." Ronin stumbled on his words, not knowing how to express himself.

Sam sighed. Taking off her mask to look at him through honest eyes. She understood the need for a small connection to anything, and trying to catch a glimpse of something similar to herself in the world around her.

"Ronin," she looked down at the dagger, "I know- it's hard... being alone and feeling isolated from everyone, but we have each other now, right?" Sam looked at him reassuringly. It was hard for her to see such a small child as lonely as she was. "And I will return it to you one day, but for now, I will take care of it and protect it," she said, enclosing it in her hand.

"No Sam, I gave you the dagger so that it can protect you. They are supposed to have a special secret power to protect those who carry them." Ronin whispered while glancing around, holding up his own dagger in his hand like a ninja would. Sam chuckled at the idea of magic spells and fantastical protection, but a part of her, deep down inside, thought it wouldn't be too far off from everything else in the new world.

"That's what my mom said." He added.

"Your mo-" Sam started, but the others came trotting down the stairs with their packs, ending the secret conversation.

The group stepped outside and waved goodbye to the odd pair. Sam smiled, her eyes revealing her hidden sadness as she held the dagger in her hand and waved goodbye to her newfound friend of the forest.

"When should we reach Atlon?" Sam asked curiously. They had been walking for a couple hours and the forest grew thicker with taller trees as the path grew smaller and covered in foliage.

"Definitely before nightfall, if we can keep this pace up." Amos said, looking down at Ajax's who trotted next to him with the pineduck sleeping on his back. "He seems to have made a new friend," he added.

Sam's eyes traveled to Ajax. He had grown since she had first met him in those solitary woods. His horns were more prominent and his scales shone deeper, more vibrant colors than before. She nodded and smiled at the thought of watching him grow into his adult self.

They continued to travel for a couple more hours, listening to the jungle around them, the wild animals rustling the leaves, the birds chirped in a never ending battle of song, and the insects chittering and buzzing along. The smell of the jungle was exotic with flowers, crisp air, and pine. Sam felt calm and energized as she breathed deep into the surrounding air, becoming aware of the sounds and smells. She looked around at the tree trunks that varied in colors of brown, dark brown, and deep red. Some were tall while others were incredibly tall, scraping the sky above and most likely housing the animals that lived there. The nature here differed from the village and the woods that she had lived in for so long. This one was more intense and ancient. It was not just a soft whisper, but lively. Moss grew on the ground where they walked. It sprinkled itself over tree roots, the ground, and the rocks.

"Wow! This place is amazing!" Sam exclaimed happily as they continued down the path. Her body jittering in tune with the life of the jungle.

"Ya, I can't believe the forest could be this big. How do people not get lost?" Cedar responded passionately as well.

"Well... for one, they stay on the path, and don't veer into a forest spirits home," Lin responded.

Sam stopped in her tracks. "I'm sorry... A what?" She raised her eyebrows.

"Forest spirits," Lin chuckled, "or forest guardian, if you prefer. Each Realm has them. They are beasts or protectors of the Realms that they belong to, the Chief and Ajax are considered forest guardians." Lin said, gesturing towards Ajax.

Who then proceeded to proudly puff out his chest and trot along until he tripped over a tree root he didn't see. He and the pineduck stumbled forward and fell. Sam tried to hold in the laugh for her little friend's bruised ego, but couldn't as she helped him up. He sheepishly walked beside her with his tail tucked and head down.

"Ok.. there is just so much about this place. I don't think I will ever fully understand it." Sam shook her head in defeat.

"Don't be too upset, there are many things that even *I* do not know, and I am a Priestess." Lin chuckled. "I'm sure in your world there were secrets, too."

Sam nodded in agreement. Though she remembered nothing about her personal life, she could recall small ordinary things here and there.

Fern glanced at the sun, judging its height in the sky on the temperate day.

"It's about midday. Would you all like to stop for lunch or continue on?" Fern asked the group.

"Let's continue for a little longer. The shade is making this walk easier than yesterday's." Amos answered back. He took out his knife and cut down a rotten tree branch that sagged and blocked the trail. Nodding, Sam agreed. She was happy to be out and eager to continue advancing to the next city.

After a while, their stomachs growled, and hunger grew in the group. But they pushed forward and continued until there was a small clearing in the jungle. Some trees were cut and laid in a circle as sitting spots and there was a stone pit for a fire for cooking or to warm up on the colder days.

A stump called her name as she stretched her weary legs and dropped onto it. It wasn't as comfortable as she hoped, but she enjoyed resting none the less. Slinging her pack around, she rested her staff on the ground, opening it up and revealing a bag of dried meat and an apple.

Sam shared some of her food from the inn with Ajax. Fern did the same with the small pineduck. She threw some bread for her and after a moment of studying the small creature, Fern said,

"I think I'll name her Pine." She glanced mischievously at her mother and father.

Lin held her hand over her mouth to silently laugh, and Amos sighed, shaking his head.

"Fine," he said, pointing at Pine. "But *you* get to take care of it and *no* chickens from Atlon. I am not carrying them home again like last time."

Fern clapped happily, hugging him, "Yes, thank you so much!" She graciously threw more food down for Pine to eat.

As they continued eating, they talked about the upcoming town, sharing what they knew and saw the last time they had visited.

A slight rustle came from behind Sam in the trees. She turned to look in the deep forest, but could only see the crowded greenery. She wasn't too worried about the random life in the forest. After all, it could have been a bird or small animal attracted to the smell of the food. She rejoined the conversation.

Again the leaves rustled, closer this time. With just a glance at Cedar, she was able to see the rest of the group heard it that time too. Her head snapped in the direction of the noise, her eyes scanning the area for any movement. Cautiously, everyone watched. Listening and skimming the surrounding area. Waiting for something to happen. A couple of seconds later, Sam turned back around to look at Amos.

"Maybe it's just a bir-" she started.

Suddenly, Sam was interrupted by a reddish orange tail that stuck out of the tree leaves with a weird hooked object. It hooked onto Sam's staff and yanked it into the foliage. Then, with a burst of laughter, the flash of orange darted out and swung away on the branches into the jungle.

"HEY! That's *mine*!" Blindly, Sam dropped her apple into her bag and darted off the path after the thief.

She chased after the figure who had her staff hanging from his tail and jumping from branch to branch using his hand and a hooked weapon. She could hear behind her Amos calling for her to stop, but she grasped for the sight of her fading staff.

"Get back here!" She yelled fiercely, pushing through vines and branches as she chased him. He mocked her with laughter and kept just barely out of sight.

Sam ran fast and hard, the air beating against her lungs as she pushed herself. Her only focus was finding the thief. Oblivious to the danger, she dashed through the forest, unaware of the tree root that lay in her path. She tripped over it, bracing her fall with her knees and hands that scrapped themselves as she fell, rolling a couple feet through the dead leaves, pine needles and mud. With a limp, she stood and spun in circles, her heart pounding as she searched for her staff or any sign of the thief.

"NOO!" She yelled in pain and anger. Sam covered her eyes with her hands and screamed deeply from her chest, trying to release the anger that was brought on so suddenly. After that, she stood there, listening to her scream that echoed in her head. Her arms fell limp to her side. She stood looking up at the treetops, unsure what to do. She had lost her staff and lost herself in the forest along the way.

The staff was a part of her. Now it was gone. Lost, stolen, right in front of her and she wasn't able to do anything but lose herself as well.

Ajax barreled through the leaves to the rescue, running past Sam, and slipping on the muddy patch of leaves when he tried to stop his momentum. He crashed into the dirt and slide into bushes that sprouted with exotic colors, quickly he picked himself up and trotted over. Amos followed close behind and then Cedar ran up last.

"Sam!" Cedar ran up, hugging her, "You can't run into the jungle like that. We could have never seen you again."

Amos calmed down once he assessed the situation and realized that the staff was gone. He put his hand reassuringly on Sam's shoulder. "We will look for it," he said through heavy breaths, "the only town even *remotely* close to here is Atlon. If the thief wants money, he will sell it there."

Sam nodded in acknowledgement that she heard him, but was glassy eyed as they walked back. She kept looking back through the leaves of the trees, hoping to see that small glimpse of orange. When they made it back to the clearing, Lin and Fern had packed and were watching over their things. Sam went and dug through her own stuff. The mask, dagger, food, other clothes, and armor piece were still there. She sighed in relief that he didn't take anything more, but still felt an emptiness on her back where the staff had lived. Lin copied Amos in reassuring Sam that if they had any chance of finding it, then it would be in Atlon.

The first glimpse they saw were the lights in the trees. Then the gate to the city. The grand entrance was made of intertwining tree roots with moss and foliage growing off of it. Once it had come into view, Sam dug into her bag, putting on her blue fox mask and pulling her hood up. For each step she took, the enraged determination inside her grew.

14

TWIN CITY ATLON

The tired but eager group arrived at the city around sun *fall,* as colors of orange, red, purple, and pink streamed in as an almost solid form through the spaces between the trees and their leaves.

Atlon's citizens lit their candles and lamps, causing the city to sparkle like a swarm of fireflies gathering for their nightly dance. The drained group walked under the looming city gate with only one sentry on watch, welcoming them in. Stepping through what Lin called the *Overlook*, because it stops at the top of the city's canopy above and gives the on-looker an impressive view of the city below, they stopped for a moment and took in the city. Sam noticed that most of the city sat on a giant sloping hill that lightly rolled up as you went.

Market-place workshops, vendors and traders were in the middle along the main road through the city. The hillside had what appeared to be homes dug skillfully into the earth with only the entrances, windows and small stone chimneys visible. At the top of the hill was a much bigger home that monitored the city as its protector.

The most intriguing part of the city to Sam was the towering network of trees, all connected in a mess of ropes, ladders, and bridges. There also appeared to be homes for the residents of the strange city, hidden, scattered in clumps, like small pebbles amongst boulders. The tree houses, constructed from a combination of sturdy stone and weathered wood, seamlessly blended with the massive tree trunks that effortlessly bore their weight. Sam also spotted holes carved into a few of the trees higher into the canopy. With warm light spilling out of them, she realized they were homes for the smaller faunanoid.

Like the tavern before, Atlon incorporated stained glass into their architecture. On all the doors windows were intricate and unique designs in all colors. Sam took a deep breath in. The city smelled of sweet spices, sharp pine, and the crispness of the deep forest.

As they walked through the marketplace, they saw many types of savory meats being cooked in various ways, and other foods presented to them. They walked past breads, vegetables, broths, sweet smelling fruits, and delectable deserts made from pastes.

"We will need to meet with the Chief soon, but for now let's eat!" Amos rubbed his hands together hungrily as he perused the different stalls of food, his eyes scouring for what his stomach cried out for. Sam's main focus, at the moment, was to rest and locate a satisfying meal. Cedar and Lin settled on a salad type dish with many interesting looking fruits and vegetables inlaid in the bowls, and a sweet sauce for the top. Fern and Sam agreed to get a type of sandwich from the vendor next to them. The sandwiches had various types of meats, cheeses, tomatoes, and lettuce in them with eggs and some type of oil Sam couldn't place. Amos came back to the group with a wooden bowl containing chunks of meat, potatoes, carrots, and a fist sized hunk of seasoned bread.

"I was talking to the cook..." Amos dipped his bread into his soup and swallowed a bite as he talked. "He said that we can go up and eat in one of those things." He pointed as he chewed. Sam's eyes ran up the side of a dark tall pine tree. "He called them tree terraces." Sam only regarded them as he pointed them out, but scattered in throughout the marketplace were trees with stairs thoroughly engraved in them that spiraled upwards towards the top.

Sam swallowed. A pit dropped in her stomach as she lifted her gaze to the top of the trees once again. At the top, she glimpsed the edges of colorful pillows behind a fence of over laying branches. Matching Cedar and Fern's wide-eyed shock, they started up the steps.

Concerned, they hugged the tree while making their way to the summit. Sam focused on the patterns in the wooded stairs and the smells of the food they carried. The nagging sensation of looking down grew louder the higher she went.

As they got to the top, it opened into a wide circular space filled with turquoise-colored cushions as the flooring. The cushions outlined the edge of the landing, giving them space to walk around comfortably. There was no other entrance than where they stood by the stairs and thick branches grew upwards in a crossing and weaving pattern as a sort of protective fence. In the gaps of only a select few of the crossing branches were small stained glass pieces secured by moss and deep green leaves.

Sam could see out to other terraces that were both taller and shorter than the one that they had climbed up. She squinted her eyes to see through the darkness of the fallen night. In the lantern light she saw what seemed to be three cat faunanoid with stripes and circles across their yellow fur, relaxing and chatting in an orange cushioned tree terrace to the side of them.

After everyone had found their places, they wasted no time and began to eat with Sam vigorously taking the first bite.

"Omygoshhh!" She said covering her mouth mid-bite. "This is so good!" She swallowed and took an even bigger bite. The oil on the sandwich brought out the flavors of the meats and cheese while the lettuce and tomatoes added in a combination of freshness and a crunch of texture.

I need to get more of this before we leave!

The silence at the shin-high table was palpable as everyone focused on savoring their equally appetizing dishes. Swiftly devouring their food, they glanced around in awe, utterly smitten by the terrace and savoring every moment of the treetop picnic while admiring the beautiful scenery.

The city's nightlife was vibrant due to its well-lit streets, and the increased number of people who ventured out of their homes. Sam leaned over the edge and watched the faunanoid go about their business, buying food for their families, working, and interacting with the others around them. The lanterns that decorated the streets lit up Atlon in a warm, yellow glow. There were also varied stained-glass lanterns scattered on the paths that gave way to a multitude of colors dancing on the jungle paths. From this, Sam remembered the inn and the strange boy. She missed him, looking down at the white lotus dagger that he had hurriedly gifted her, and ran her finger over the flower as she ate. She passed her finger along the edges of the glossy painted lotus engraving, thinking of Ronin, Atlas, and those whom she might never see again.

A moment later, Sam was taken from her thoughts by the sudden alertness around her. She turned away from the spectacle of the treetop canopy, and caught everyone looking towards the stairs entrance. That's when she heard it, footsteps.

She sat up straighter. Swallowing her food, she moved her hand, ready to grab her staff that lay on the floor next to her.

Peering down, she saw nothing beside her. The emptiness shot forth the distressing memory of her staff disappearing into the jungles green.

Her eyes flickered towards Lin and Amos, curious about their plan. Amos raised his hand, signaling to remain calm.

The steps grew closer, anticipation grew heavy in the group. Cedar shuffled uncomfortably. Sam's heart plunged into her throat. The footsteps stopped.

A small head popped up, staring at them.

No one said anything. They stared at the little leopard cub, waiting for it to move first. Sam looked bewildered at Cedar, who also side eyed her with the same skeptical look. The cub vanished for a moment, then pounced onto the terrace as if it was hunting and had finally caught its prey. It playfully bent its head down at Ajax's, who seemed lost, and Pine, who hissed at it, flapping her wings menacingly.

With this distraction, they did not notice the others that came up with the cub.

"Welcome to Atlon," A soft voice purred from the entrance.

Sam whipped her head around to find the speaker and was caught by surprise. A large sleek leopard, so close to her she could feel its hot breath on her face, stared at her with its green-yellow eyes. Terror gripped her heart. She stumbled away, forcing distance between the two of them.

"Calm friend, he is good natured and so am I," the tall woman, Sam hadn't noticed until now, said in a thick accent and bowed forward deeply.

Dreads fell to her lower back with feathers braided into them. A skirt patterned in squares and colors of green, red, and yellow accompanied a black crop top that had short puffy sleeves, complementing her dark skin.

Sam slightly nodded her in acknowledgement and sat back down cautiously. The leopard, uninterested, paid no mind. It simply guarded the entrance to the terrace with its back to the group.

As the leopard faunanoid walked further in, Sam saw she did not need shoes. Her padded paws trailed yellow fur and black spots along her legs and arms. Around her waist sat a brown leather belt that held a small coin satchel. The woman had no need for weapons either. Her clawed fingers shone wickedly in the lantern light. In addition to the leopard spots, Sam observed an unusual dark green paint drawn on her face, chest, and forearms in a lined pattern.

"I am Nakoia. The little one is Meera and our guardian of the night is Ikol." She gestured to the two. At his name, Ikol turned his head in greetings and then back out towards the forest. Meera continued to persuade Ajax and Pine to play with her, but with no such luck.

"May I join you?" She asked, gesturing to the open seat next to Fern and the entrance.

"Yes, that would be lovely," Lin said, setting down the last of her food. Nakoia nodded and sat down smoothly while studying everyone. Her eyes lingered a moment longer on Sam and her blue fox mask.

"So," she said, finally breaking the uncomfortable silence. "How have you been enjoying the city so far?" she asked happily, with a smile. Meera went over and flopped on her back for Nakoia to pet her small white furred stomach.

Sam's eyes bounced from Fern to Cedar to Amos, then lastly to Lin, seeing who would speak first to the stranger.

"We just arrived not too long ago, Amos, Fern, and I have been here before for trading but it was a couple of years ago, when the others were too young to travel, so it is their first time here." Lin gestured to the three girls. "I am Lin, the Priestess of the Whispering Woods, as I said a moment ago this is Amos, and then this is Cedar, Fern, and Samihanee, she goes by Sam." As their names were called, they each did a slight bow of their heads in a greeting. Nakoia, in return, touched her chest with two fingers and then motioned them upwards toward the sky.

"It is very nice to finally meet you all. Chief from your village said to be on the lookout for an odd bunch," Nakoia chuckled. "And here you are, I suppose."

Awareness hit Sam. "Chief... Nakoia." Sam nodded. The rest of the group followed her thoughts and relaxed.

"I enjoy the air of mystery, for a moment.. at least." She smiled to herself mischievously. "Now would you all enjoy a tour of Atlon, the nightlife here-" She stood up, straightening the wrinkles from her skirt, "is wonderful." She said with a smile as she began her descent down the tree terrace. The rest had no choice, so they followed in agreement.

They walked through the market together, taking in the different wares and foods along the way. Sam saw fabrics of all colors and textures, and the continuous smells of pleasant foods as they began the ascent uphill. Whenever the Chief walked past, the people would come to a stop and perform the greeting of touching their chests and extending their fingers towards the sky.

The whole area, protected by a dense forest, was decorated with exotic looking plants of bright yellows, oranges, and reds scattered throughout. Atlon and its denizens were hidden within a lush tapestry of moss, mushrooms, and foliage, providing them with a natural camouflage.

They started on the stone path up the hill that spiraled around the giant slope like the stairs that spiraled around the tree terraces. The doors and windows of the homes were all that were visible. Some had lights on, as people sat outside of their homes enjoying the night air as the group walked past. Others that walked past marked themselves with the same green paint that Nakoia had.

"Um, Chief Nakoia." Sam rushed ahead to walk next to her. "What is the green paint for?" She asked, pointing at the painted lady's forearm.

"This?" She said, looking down and running her hand over the simple design.

"This is the paint of the warrior, all warriors are painted in honor of their service to their people and one of the tests to become a Chief is to be a notable warrior."

Sam nodded, "Do you have to fight much here in the Jungle?"

Nakoia looked off for a moment in thought. She looked deep into the trees and then back at Sam to respond.

"There was a time, yes, before I was Chief where I defended my home from outsiders. Now, though, I protect my people from... bigger things."

Bigger things. I wonder what she means.

Chills ran up her spine at the thought.

Nakoia's dark brown eyes locked onto Sam's, delving into the depths of her soul. Forcing herself to look away, Sam wondered if Nakoia understood her situation.

Is she worried about me being a threat too, like Muninn did?

Worry sprouted in Sam's mind as she festered at the thought. She bit her lip as more tiny sprouts of worry popped up.

"Sooooo, why is Atlon designed this way?" Cedar butted in, sensing that Sam was uncomfortable.

Nakoia looked at Cedar and smiled. "Well, since it is a twin city, Atlon and Atlen are fundamentally the same, except Atlen is a city in the Realm of Sky. They were founded by the twins who were separated at birth, because one twin was of sky and one was of land." Nakoia said.

Lin spoke up then, "Yes, I think I remember hearing this story in my youth. They were brothers and their names were Atlon and Atlen, but they had no clue about one another. Once they found out they existed, they built these cities in honor of each other. In hopes that one day the borders will be opened for travel." Lin looked at Sam, and put her hand on her shoulder, leaning in. "A long time ago, the borders were closed and only those of the Realm could live there. It was a hard time for many." Lin said.

Amos came up, "But one of the kings' ancestors opened the border for trade and travel. The only problem now is the Realms hate one another."

"On a much happier note," She stopped and turned, "welcome to my home." Nakoia gestured to the home that was at the very top of the massive hill. Sam didn't realize they had walked the whole way up already. She turned and looked out over the buzzing city.

"It's gorgeous!" Cedar exclaimed. Sam rotated back around to take in the home of the Chief of Atlon.

Her home was two thick, hollowed out trees that loomed over the forest, disappearing into the dense canopy above. Up to the left, where the branches and leaves grew, hung many lanterns and a bridge connecting from that tree to the tree homes that were scattered on top of Atlon. The taller tree to the right seemed to continue to the top of the jungle, with no end in sight. Under the trees was also a mouth-like gap in the ground that stood a little taller than Amos. It had a long arched opening with no door and stained glass decorated the outline of the gap. On top of the small mound was a fence of jungle greenery that circled around the entire top, creating a barrier from spying eyes. Sam could see a roof peaking over the top of the greenery.

"This tree here," Nakoia pointed to the left one, "is one of the many connections to the homes of the treetops." She then pointed to the right one. "Then this tree is a lookout for us to monitor above the canopy of the jungle for any threats. Now in the middle, here is my home where I live with Meera and Ikol." She gestured for them to follow as they walked to the opening of the home. The opposite side of the hill had the same entrance, so that she could see all sides of her city.

"Ca.... Can I go up top to see above the canopy?" Sam asked reluctantly as they walked toward the entrance. Staring up at the much taller tree on the right, she was curious to see what the tree tops looked like and wished to take a peek.

Nakoia looked at her surprised, "Of course! We should go both at night and during the day. Being so close to the stars at night is just as beautiful as the freedom of the open air!" She chuckled.

"Me too!!" Cedar raised her arm in excitement.

"I would love to as well if it is alright.." Fern added.

"We will *ALL* go and you will see the beauty of the forest the way *I* see it." Nakoia's face lit up. "I almost forgot. We must also tour the treetops. You would love them!"

Amos cut in, "I am sorry, but I am a bit too bulky to be so high in the air. I think I will leave that to you, ladies." He coughed out an uncomfortable laugh.

Nakoia nodded. "I understand. The heights are not for all. Nonetheless, you are welcome to join us if you change your mind."

Lin smiled and placed her hand on Amos's cheek, assuredly. Patting it gently with understanding love.

"I think we will call it a night. Go ahead if you want girls, but remember to be safe. We will head to the Hearths Inn. It is at the bottom of the hill and has a sign out front. Let us know when you get back." Lin nodded, smiling and looking at each of them one by one. They nodded in response, happy to have time to explore the city.

"Wait!" Nakoia raised her hand and stepped forward suddenly, "I was actually hoping to give the Priestess and her strange family a tour of my home... if the Chief is your close friend then you are family and are welcome to stay in my home for the time being." Nakoia flustered, but quickly regained her composure.

Then she added,

"It might be safer for..." She didn't finish her sentence, as she glanced over to Sam, meeting her eyes once again. Sam looked away, flustered to have become a burden yet again. Lin's gaze flickered briefly towards Sam, her impassive face revealing nothing.

"Of course! We would love to. Would you mind showing us where we will sleep?" Lin asked.

Nakoia smiled and began her way into her lustrous home. Sam walked through the entrance and took in a sharp breath of awe.

"It's amazing," she whispered to her herself as she looked all around her at the dazzling forestry that took up Nakoia's main floor.

Directly adjacent to them was the other entrance to her home. Sam looked up and saw most of the light coming from the main oval paper lantern that was substantial and tan colored, then scattered around it were smaller lanterns in various ovals and circles, matching in color. The semi circle dome was made of stone and ran in a circular motion that followed the layout of the home. Inside the mound, there were three disk-like rings.

On the outer rim of the massive round room were plants so vibrant they matched that of the shining gems of the earth. They were of every color and type that a jungle offered.

On both ends of the massive room, there were medium-sized dips that pooled with blue green water. The cool water seemed to flow through tiny cracks in the ground and lead to the plants as a sort of watering source.

Then the middle ring was indented downwards by a foot and filled with dark green pillows similar to those of the tree terraces. The pillows sat on another small ledge, and inside that ledge was a storage compartment that held a collection of books that encircled the whole ring as well.

Now the inner circle was a set of smoothed wooden stairs that spiraled upwards. In the middle of the stairways gap was greenery that dripped with condensation and streamed downward from the skylight as a leafy waterfall, the droplets dripped to the stone floor and watered the plants that lived underneath it.

The group dispersed and looked around in awe of the main room. Nakoia stood back and let them explore. Ikol and Meera got comfortable on the dark green cushions.

"Ajax's.. Pine!" Sam hissed at them, making disapproving clicks of her tongue, then shook her head curtly, making a disapproving face. Ajax froze, hunched over, tongue out, ready to get a drink of the crisp water that lay before him in the pool that Pine had already made herself comfortable in. He trotted away from it when he immediately became distracted by a small insect that flew past him. Pine continued about her business, not noticing Sam in the slightest.

"Sorry haha," Sam blushed in embarrassment, looking at Nakoia with an awkward smile. Nakoia chuckled.

"That is what it is meant for. Do not apologize, the water also cleans itself in its own cycle," she said proudly.

Sam sighed in relief.

The last thing I need is to worry about those two getting themselves into trouble.

"What do you usually do in this room?" Fern asked, scavenging through the books.

"This room is for anyone who wishes to use it. They can read, or spend time with friends and family in the ambience of the jungles garden. I will spend most of my time here as well. This is also where Ikol and Meera stay. They guard it from vandalism, theft, or people trying to go to the upper floors." She walked over to Ikol and Meera and gave them both an appreciative ear scratch. Meera purred, and Ikol settled back in for sleep.

After they took their fill of the beautiful room, Nakoia led them upstairs, leaving Ajax and Pine to sleep with the two leopards. The stairs came out to a circular landing, one with less lantern light but plenty of natural moonlight to see by.

They were now on the inside of the protective jungle greenery that Sam had spotted below. It comprised branches of small trees and thick bushes surrounding it. The stairs lead out onto a still pool of water with large stepping stones to move around on and small fish trickling their way around, darting here and there dramatically. The foliage that hung from the roof and grew from the pond made this section of her home blend in perfectly with its surroundings.

They walked cautiously from stone to stone, each one showing a different earthy color. Once they got to the landing, they noticed that there was a abode with two wooden plank walls covered in greenery. The back wall and the side wall held the roof up with the help of a thick tree truck holding up the opposite end. The trunk was carved out to be different species of faunanoid from the jungle with moss growing in the crevices and corners. Under the roof hung a low hanging hammock, and a floor table with pillow seats close to it. Against the back wall sat a long horizontal bed for those who did not wish to sleep above the ground.

"You can stay here tonight. It is not much. I apologize. I spend little time here. Mostly, I am amongst the people or in the canopy, so there really is no need for accessories." Nakoia said, her hands on her hips.

"Nonsense, Chief Nakoia, your home is a true jewel of the jungle." Lin raised her hands in protest. "This is the most beautiful sight I have seen in a long time."

Nakoia bowed her head in thanks. "Would you two like to spend the night here? The girls can sleep in our tree loft and I will sleep in the canopies," she added.

"No, please we cannot take your home from you tonight, we can go stay at the inn." Lin frowned.

"It is your decision if you want it or not, but please do not see it as an inconvenience to me. Again, I sleep in the canopies amongst the stars most nights anyway." Nakoia gestured towards the sky.

Cedar bumped Sam with her elbow, glanced upwards quickly and locked eyes with her. Sam nodded back, acknowledging their silent code.

She stepped forward. "Chief, would you mind showing us the canopy now? We would love to see it." Cedar and Fern stepped forward eagerly, too.

"Yes! You can leave your packs here and we can head to the top now!" Nakoia responded with matched excitement.

They dismantled the heavy packs and left them on the stone floor next to the bed. Cedar, Fern, and Sam said goodnight to Amos and Lin once they were ready to head up.

"Chief Nakoia, thank you for your graciousness and all the kind help, Atlon is such an amazing city to be a part of, we will go to Hearths Inn, we do not wish to burden you anymore, but again thank you so much." Amos said with a kind nod and Lin bowed in agreement.

"We have never had such a warm welcome from any other place we have visited." Lin bowed her head again.

Nakoia gave them an understanding smile. "You are most welcome. The Inn is truly of the earth, and I am sure you will love it."

Lin and Amos thanked her again and said good night as they headed back down the stairs towards the Inn for the night.

Nakoia turned back to the young woman in excitement and raised her brow with mischief sparkling in her eyes.

"Are you ready to head up?" She pointed, and all three of them scanned the tall tree that led into darkness. It was at that moment that Sam fully grasped the daunting nature of the climb ahead.

Sam huffed, holding onto her side. She stopped on the step to rest a moment.

With her body bent over the side, she tilted her head back to take in the view of the stairs disappearing into the distance above and below her. The inside of the tree had been hollowed out and became a staircase leading to the top. Sam put her hand on the wall and felt with her fingertips the indentions and the patterns in which the people of old used their wood carving and shaving tools to etch through the mighty tree that still lived. There were white capped mushrooms and many other plants growing on the sides as lichen had taken over the inside only in spots where both the sunlight and water could reach. She looked back at Cedar, who made a pained face as her eyes screamed with exhaustion.

"We are almost there, girls. I can see the moonlight shining in." Nakoia kept a steady pace, not winded in the slightest. Sam looked up and to her relief, there was indeed moonlight dancing on the wood in the form of the gaps in the leaves of the canopy. It was a soft, full glow that made the wood of the inside of the tree look pure and magical.

Fern raised her fist in the air in triumph and in celebration of the second wind that came to them as they saw their finish line.

"Come on, guys," Fern said sarcastically as she charged forward behind Nakoia, who continued to lead them with ease.

Sam had to admit, seeing the light of the moon shine in gave her more energy to finish the exasperating climb. They made their way to the top and fought through a protective layer of leaves and thick branches of the canopy. Nakoia was the first out to the top. Soon Fern joined her on the small landing.

Fern offered her hand to Sam, which she gratefully took and made it to the top on wobbling legs. She caught herself and helped Cedar up before joining the others in the wondrous spectacle that lay around them.

Sam caught herself in another moment of awe. As she gazed out to the sea of dark canopy and sky, her mind raced to etch what was before her into her memory.

For what lay before them was a sight to be seen, the sky dark and blue was bright. Bright with the untold numbers of stars dazzling, hanging in the wind, waiting to be told how beautiful they were. Sam could see a line in the sky of light blue and white that shone brighter than the rest. Her eyes could not grow big enough to take in the enormous amount of sky and stars that waited to be seen. Her mouth opened in amazement with wordless speech trying to escape and explain what lay before her, but nothing came out, no words could compare to the light of the sky in the night. The sight ran through her in a wave of goosebumps that formed on her arms.

They stood for minutes or hours. She wasn't sure how long they were there before anyone spoke. Eventually they laid down, propping their heads with their arms, feeling even more as though they lay in a sea of stars. With the vastness surrounding her, she felt small but free.

After a while, she could take her eyes off the stars and the gibbous moon that painted the sight before her. She looked at Cedar and Fern. Their eyes shone with all the stars in the sky and the moonlight danced off of them, turning them into shimmering goddesses of the night. Nakoia sat cross-legged, with her eyes closed, her leopard ears twitched, listening to the sounds of the life around them. Imitating the way she sat, Sam joined Nakoia.

"Thank you," Sam whispered. "I have never seen anything," she looked up at the luminous land that floated above her. "even remotely this beautiful before."

Nakoia nodded and responded faintly.

"You might like it more.... if you saw it with your true eyes and not with the eyes of a mask..." One of her eyes lifted and her finger tapped the blue fox that Sam hid behind, making a gentle rapping sound. "You will not find another place where you can be more free, Samihanee."

She had forgotten she was even wearing the mask. At the mention of it, she touched its glossy cheek. Hesitantly, she grabbed it with her right hand and pulled it off her face. Looking at Nakoia, tears gathered in her eyes, and she cried to herself. Nakoia caressed her cheek, smiling sadly, understanding her pain. She rubbed her hair to comfort her and whispered to her in a motherly tone.

"Find peace in sleep, my child."

Sam laid down and fell asleep amongst the stars.

15

A TINT OF ORANGE

There it is again.

The crouched silhouette weeping to itself. Sam stared at it, unmoving, trying to get a detail or a hint. Anything for her to use to find this person who cried through their silent pain. She sighed in frustration as she walked towards it. Crouching down, she was able to put her hand on its back this time as she struggled to ease its sadness, its pain.

Why are you so sad?

She felt pity for the creature, but knew her words would not reach it.

After a moment, a light glowed above them, illuminating both under its presence. She looked up, confused. In the darkness of her dream, showed all the stars of the night sky, gleaming and dazzling. She recognized the stars. These were the stars of Atlon. They were the stars she slept under at that very moment. She drew a swift breath out and laughed.

"You're here!" she said in excitement, her eyes bright with the renewal of hope.

The silhouette had stopped crying when she spoke to it this time. It slowly looked up at her with its faceless, dark form. She moved downwards uncontrollably, the silhouette watching her fall away into the abyss.

"You're here! You're here in Atlon, I'll find you!" she yelled, wanting her speck of hope to reach across. She watched the stars in her dream grow smaller, filling her eyes with wonder again. She closed her eyes as she thanked them for the help, and fell.

Sam jolted. Before her eyes could wake, her body moved, shaking her out of its slumber and aching at the slightest movement. The backs of her eyelids were bright with morning sun. She struggled to open them, her sluggish mind prying them apart to be greeted with jungle greenery and endless sky. Nakoia was gone, and so was Cedar. She sat up, rubbing her hands over her face, and realized that she had fallen asleep on the canopy's top. Fern was awake and sitting, swinging her legs off the edge. Sam scooted over to her to join her.

"How long was I out?" Sam drowsily asked, slowly looking over the edge. A shiver ran up her spine. Changing her mind, she brought her feet back up and sat cross-legged instead.

"Actually, I woke up a moment ago. Cedar and Nakoia went down to take the things to the tree loft we will stay in. I wanted to wait for you." She said.

Fern leaned back on both of her hands and looked out across the field of green. Vast nothingness rested between them and the sky. Lonesome dotted clouds lazily floated above, making it feel as though they were on an ocean of leaves and trees. In the distance, far to the left, mountains jutted from the tree's horizon and stood in the sky, colored to resemble massive blue hills.

"Where's that?" She said curiously, pointing to the far-off mountain range. Fern turned to look for what she was talking about.

"That's most of the Realm of Sky. They claimed the entire Guardian Mountains and some of the surrounding land." Fern responded, putting her knees close to her chest for warmth as a cool breeze brushed by. "Actually, the back of the mountain range is where the four Realms end. No one has traveled past it since the time of the Elementals." Then she pointed out in the opposite direction, "And waaayyyy that way is the ocean. You can't see it, but we are much closer to that than to the mountains. Then the mountains and the ocean meet on the far end in the middle that way." She pointed out in front of them and joined her two pointer fingers together to make the point of a triangle.

Sam clicked her tongue, thinking of the four realms and what might lie past them. They had mentioned a wasteland before, nothing but barren, hardened land, unable to hold anything.

She squinted into the sun as she looked around. Noticing, far off, in the dense bush of the forest, thick branches jutting out with different colors and styled leaves on them. To the left of the clump, taking up the end, was a cluster of white branches with golden leaves. In the middle, dark brown branches with mahogany leaves, and in the front, light brown with blue leaves. She stared at them in curiosity and saw that after a moment, all the branches meandered their way across the distant, deep forest.

She raised her eyebrow, tapped Fern lightly on the shoulder and pointed at the mysterious puzzle jutting from the wide expanse of leaves.

Fern's mouth gaped a little. She couldn't seem to find the answer to Sam's unspoken, but obvious, question.

"Uh.... mmmm." Fern made the same thinking face as Sam and shrugged.

"Those are the forest spirits." Sam and Fern pivoted around to see Nakoia had joined them on the canopy.

"They heard of there being an ancient one here, so they wanted to come and see. Usually, though, they stay in the isolated parts of the forest or in the Province of the Sacred."

Nakoia shaded her eyes to see better. An explosion of color burst up onto the platform as she emerged in a dress patterned with shades of purple, white, and black.

"Are they going to come here?" Sam asked, curious to see them. Images of what she thought they looked like filled her mind, but she didn't know if they would take her as a threat or a puzzle to be solved. With a sense of anxiety, she decided that, for now, witnessing only the upper parts of them would suffice her.

"No, this is as close as they will get to villages or cities. They take to not interfering with us and expect the same in return. They will judge and watch from afar."

"Great. I *love* being judged," Sam rolled her eyes. Nakoia and Fern chuckled.

"Come, Cedar is waiting with your things at the loft." She motioned towards the wooden spiral stairwell and began her descent down. Both of them stood up and cast a last glance at the tranquil guardians, filling Sam with a sense of serenity, before descending with Nakoia.

It was much faster going down than it had been going up to the top last night. Only a couple of minutes had passed before they reached the bottom. They walked across Nakoia's home towards the other enormous tree rooted next to the hill.

Sam walked up the stairs inside it, only leading up for three spirals, and came out to a wooden rope bridge connecting to a thinner tree that held a home in it. She stopped in the middle of the bridge. Her stomach lurched as she faced the distance between her and the forest floor. A staggered breath escaped her, and she scrunched her eyes shut as she focused. The fear fought its way up, working through her stomach and pushing against the walls of her mind. Forcing herself to move past it, she crouched and compelled herself to focus on her other senses. The birds' chirp echoed above and below her now, singing in tune with the others of their species and the world around them. People's voices traveled from far below in forms of laughter or of jumbled nonsense. Steadied breaths, in and out, calmed her. As Sam opened her eyes, she sought the different colors of the forest, distracting herself, calming her mind. Her chest rose and fell in rhythmic tension as she aimed her focus at that.

I am safe.

Sam opened her eyes, convincing her fear that it was ok. Anxiety still gripped her, but it was more manageable now. She sparred a glance downwards, and her knees became wobbly.

Down to the ground and out into the forest were all the citizens moving around in the morning light that was trying to tear through the forest's dense leaves. The sunlight came through once again in almost solid looking pillars streaming downward and beaming on whatever got in its way. One beam of light she followed to the ground, looking on in admiration, hit the side of the hill where there was a garden on top of the home. She looked at more of the homes on the hill and became aware that above each of them was a garden with different types of plants being tended to.

"Nakoia! That's really neat! Each of these homes has little gardens on top of them, to save room or what?" Sam asked and pointed downward towards the roof gardens.

"Ah, yes, I see you have caught how we grow our food. Each home takes care of a small garden, but here is the best part. It isn't just each individual garden, it is a garden for the city." Nakoia winked and leaned over the railing. With her long arm, she drew a spiral in the air. Fern looked over to, and once they saw it, they both gasped with delight.

The entire hill was a giant garden in the shape of a spiral leading to the top, and the cobblestone walkway and the earth homes supported it like a stone wall.

"Sam! It is like our herb garden back home," Fern replied happily.

Sam glimpsed something past the big hill. It was a second hill, exactly like that one, but smaller. She patted Fern on the shoulder excitedly and pointed it out to her.

"We must have not seen it in the dark! Look and even the roads curve and spiral around. Wow this place is like a giant garden hidden in the woods!" Fern and Sam looked over to Nakoia passionately, beaming like the sun that showed through the leaves. Nakoia winked at them happily and then they continued on their way across as they admired Atlon in a new light.

Sam caught up with Nakoia once they started walking again. "Soooo, I have been meaning to ask someone this question." She looked at Nakoia.

She nodded, "Go on."

"What's with the stained glass?" Sam gestured her hand to the tree loft. This one, she saw, was decorated with a random pattern of nature.

Nakoia lifted her hand and wagged her finger, contemplating on how to explain it to Sam. They had just reached the home and Nakoia put her hand on the smooth, colorful glass that graced the edge of the door that stood before them.

"This is something that goes back to the twins. We believe they used stained glass as a way to connect with one another and to the world around them, as well as how they told their story. So, in honor and respect, we continue this tradition." She ran her hand down the glass. "Each family tells their story through the stained glass outside their home, and the Chief's hill is decorated with the story of Atlon. But since no one lives here, it is decorated with the nature that lives around us.... No one is here, so there is not a story to be told.. yet." Nakoia looked proudly at her city's culture, satisfied with how she answered Sam's question.

Her body buzzed in excitement, and her mind brimmed with wonder and curiosity about the city. She stared at the glass, wondering when someone might come along and change the design to give the home a story.

Nakoia opened the door, and they went inside one by one. Inside was a medium-sized room with two doorways leading to two smaller rooms and a bathroom connecting in the middle.

The whole loft, inside and out, was made of a brown sanded wood that was soft to stand on. The small home was decorated only with a couple of pieces of furniture and plants that they had seen from the forest.

Sam peeked into the room on the left and saw Cedar lying in the bed with her arm shading her eyes and her leg hanging off it.

"Hmm, that looks comfortable." Sam laughed, and Cedar looked up, smiling. She rolled her eyes dramatically as she got up and Sam looked into the room on the right, to see it was symmetrical to the one she had just been in.

"What took you guys so long?" Cedar asked, "Nakoia had to go back up there to make sure you didn't fall through the canopy or get eaten by something." Cedar laughed sarcastically at her joke while she stretched out her back.

"Psh, we didn't take *that* long," Sam made a face at her, and Fern intervened.

"Besides, it's not like we are in a hurry. We still have to find your land dweller, for the King's Journey, before you can move on." She shrugged nonchalantly.

Cedar waved her hands up and down. "Woah, woah, how do we even know that they are here in Atlon?"

"That is a good point," Nakoia chimed in.

Sam got quiet. She didn't want to tell them about the dreams.

It is something a crazy person would deal with. What am I supposed to say? I see people in my dreams!

"Sam?" Cedar raised her eyebrow curiously, she spotted Sam's expression.

Sam sighed, and rubbed her brow in defeat.

"Ok, if I tell you, will you please not think I'm crazy?" She said, meeting each of their eyes.

"You're freaking me out. Just tell us already." Fern said.

"I- I can see the people in my.. dreams," she said, reluctantly. Her face got hot, and she covered it with them, not wanting to meet their reactions.

"Ahh, so you have met with Muninn then, I assume?" Nakoia looked from girl to girl. Cedar and Fern seemed unfazed, nodding as well, but Sam was speechless.

Cedar responded, "It is Muninn sending you these dreams Sam, this is not an uncommon thing for her to do. She sends messages to the Chief in his dreams all the time."

Sam, still speechless, crouched over, balancing on her toes, and held her face in her hands. Speaking through her hands, she responded.

"So- what you're telling me is... is that this is a *normal* thing that occurs in your *normal* life?" She asked, breathing deeply into her hands, that now smelled of dirt and pine.

Someone put their hand on her back and rubbed it up and down, chuckling.

"Well, Muninn and Huginn aren't big deals for nothing." Fern said through her laughter.

Sam lifted her head to look at Fern, who was bending over next to her. She smiled softly.

"I have been working so hard to make sense of it all... Am I ever going to get used to this world?" She groaned.

"*No.* You will not, ancient one, but the world is too vast for it to be familiar. I think the mystery is the fun part. No?" Nakoia looked at her mischievously. Sam stood, taking in what she said and relaxing a little. Even if she didn't feel comfortable with it all right now, that did not mean that she would never be. Reflecting on this helped calm Sam's thoughts.

"Alright, well then, we have *two* goals while we are here in Atlon," Sam said, now determined.

She put up her pointer finger. "To start, we need to find our next ally." Then she made the number two sign with her hand. "Two, we get my staff back."

Cedar and Fern both nodded firmly.

"What staff?" Nakoia asked.

She caught Nakoia up to speed on the events that happened during their travel to Atlon. After that, Nakoia said she would tell the vendors and Ikol to keep a lookout for the staff. Each of them agreed to split up and search for someone who was either a skilled runner or climber to assist them in the race.

"O and one more thing, in my dream this person was crying, so maybe look for anyone who is incredibly sad..." Sam gave an uncertain shrug.

The three of them shot her a confused look but didn't argue as they left to do their tasks.

Sam started the search throughout the tree lofts. Cedar went to look through the city on the forest floor. Fern went to find Amos and Lin to fill them in on the plan. Lastly, Nakoia went to warn the vendors of the stolen staff. Once everyone was gone, Sam looked around at the other tree lofts, mostly clustered in a few dispersed spots with random homes scattered throughout, with no real pattern to the layout. She looked at the tedious job ahead of her and shriveled a little. Reflecting on the enormous pressure and limited time they faced in collecting a team and reaching the kingdom. She closed her eyes and sighed.

One step at a time.

She looked up through the morning light and scent of fresh jungle air and began her search.

Sam groaned. Her body was tired and her mind had fizzed out. She had seen too many tree lofts, and she never wanted to see another green leaf in her life. The entirety of the upper city had been scoured, and she sat on a higher level with her legs dangling from the bridge while her head leaned forward, resting on the twined rope. She observed some people who lived up top had long monkey tails that they used to hold things like a third arm and no shoes, so that their feet could feel the trees or earth beneath them. Others were cat people like Nakoia, with different colors and patterns on their fur.

However, she also saw a few faunanoid who were other jungle creatures.

Two interesting thoughts flashed through her mind, igniting her curiosity.

A snake man, with the body of a human and the lower half as a snake, he traveled by coiling around the tree branch to tree branch.

Then there was also a woman who lazily hung in a hammock off of her tree loft's edge. Sam nervously leaned over, looking at how far down she would fall if the hammock were to break. A long fluffy black and red striped tail slowly rose from the hammock and slumped out, relaxed. The woman also seemed to enjoy a leafy treat as she laid there.

Sam brought her thoughts back to the present moment as she looked down at the forest floor in the midday glow of the warm sun. She watched the tiny ants of people mosey around from stall to stall or talk with their friends and family. A light breeze picked up, and she caught the scent of food rising from below. She took it in, thinking of the corresponding taste and what the delicious scents mystery food might look like. Sam sat there for a moment longer, planning her next steps. She could still keep looking but also make her way to the source of the foods that called out to her and her growling stomach. As she lifted her head, she looked to her right and rubbed her forehead, feeling the irritated indent. At the end of the tree lofts, she spotted a path leading downwards. If she could navigate through this area, she would finally be able to go down and enjoy her lunch.

She thought back to the morning and regretted that she didn't have breakfast.

In response, her stomach growled at her again.

So it would be brunch then.

She nodded to herself, confirming her full proof plan. As she got up, a bright flash of the golden sun caught her eye. She turned to see what it came from, and as she looked, she saw a reddish-orange tail disappear to the front side of one of the bigger lofts. She furrowed her brow.

There's no way.

Anger bubbled to the surface as she recalled the other day, her chase, and her staff, stolen.

That was the same color she chased furiously through the dense forest, the color she despised but begged to see again. Her heart fluttered. She couldn't take the chance. If it was the thief, then this would be her only chance.

As she approached the home, she tiptoed up to the back window, curious to catch a glimpse inside. It was dark and empty except for the natural light that streamed in on a junky room. She crept up to the window that was next to it. This time, when she looked in, she saw someone. They had the same color fur and a long monkey tail. Desperate for answers, she leaned up further, peering in. Once she could see more, she saw that it was a small pale child playing with his toys. Disappointed, she continued to the side of the home.

The home had larger windows that dominated its side, adorned with excessively flashy decorations. She could hear loud voices before she looked. The first one, deep and strong, spoke with authority. The other was younger and louder and spoke with retaliation. Then the last one was softer, but sneer and cruel as they spoke.

"Finnigan!" The deep voice boomed, controlling the air. "Where have you been?! You haven't been home in days."

"Fin- dad- it's Fin, and nowhere... Just out and about in the jungle," Fin, the louder voice, proclaimed in annoyance.

"I named you boy. Your name is Finnigan, that of your grandfather. Do not disrespect him with your nonsense," the father bellowed even louder.

The soft voice snickered. "You're in for it now *Fin*," emphasizing his name in mockery.

"Shut up, and get out of here, no one is talking to you," Fin retorted. "Dad! Look- I found this in the jungle! Pretty cool, right?"

At that point, Sam's eagerness to see the situation grew too great. She peaked into the large room. It was a combined gathering room and kitchen. The kitchen windows were the windows that Sam looked through at that moment.

The younger child had his back turned to her. The stocky father and the taller, older one were standing close to the entrance of the tree loft on the right side. They all had orange-red fur with long tails. The boys wrapped them around their waists a couple times, but the father had his out as it flicked in annoyance.

Sam caught her breath, and the hair on the back of her neck stood on end. In the older boy's grasp was the staff, her staff, being presented to the father as if it were a gift to be given away.

Sam's anger grew, barely being able to contain herself. She began to get up, to confront them and claim what was hers. As she moved to do so, the father forcefully knocked the staff out of his hands. It clambered on the floor, clanging, then creating a defining silence. She sat back, frozen, waiting to see what would happen next.

"This is what you have been doing with your time!" The father yelled. Fin was speechless in defiance. His excitement turned to anger in one swift motion.

"Scaling the jungle like a wild man! You are the heir to this family, and you squander your privilege!" He scowled. "This is the last straw. Your mother, if she were still here, would be heartbroken at the disappointment her child has become."

Finnigan seemed to snap at this, his face contorting with anger. He snatched up the staff and got close to his father's face. "Don't you *ever* speak about my mother like that. She deserved more than to spend the last of her days with a sorry man like you." He spit in anger as it seethed through his teeth.

"Get out of my face!" He howled in rage, waving his hands, he continued, "Go to your room and find something useful to do for once and get rid of all that worthless junk you've been stealing!" The father turned and pointed towards the darkened room that Sam had previously looked in. Fin huffed and looked over towards the younger one sitting at the table.

Sam ducked and closed her eyes, praying that he didn't see her. The sound of loud, stomping footsteps echoed through the air, coming from inside the loft. Then a slammed door confirmed he was in his room. She crept back towards the corner just in time to see him hop out the window and angrily stomp the other way towards the bridge to the forest floor, her staff clutched in his hand.

She looked back inside the kitchen window. The sitting child stared off into the distance with his hand supporting his face, as their father huffed and stomped to the third doorway adjacent to where Sam was, slamming the door, leaving the room in silence.

Pity filled her heart as she watched the interaction between the thief and his broken family. She shook off the thought, her mind reflecting on the lie he had told his father about the staff's origin, and that he had taken it from her to begin with.

Steeling her determination, she let him get a little distance away before she stood up and followed the heated thief through the shadows of the day.

She stayed a good distance behind and watched as he strapped her staff to his back and jumped from branch to branch downward. He used his whole body to maneuver through the tree, including two unusual hooked swords that had previously been on his side.

They hooked at the end, creating a semicircle, and both were double edged. He used the hooks on the end as an extension of his arms and grabbed branches to easily swing down. With each passing moment, Sam became more aware of the distance growing between them. She hurried to the tree terrace that was connected to the rope bridge and frantically raced down the stairs, trying to keep her eyes on him as she spiraled down the tree.

Sam jumped down the last couple steps and felt the steadiness of the earth under her as the thief landed only a couple of yards away. Still not on the main road, their area was deserted enough for Sam to confront him confidently without having the eyes of many on her mask-less face. The world had given her an opportunity, and she took it. His back was turned to her, and she blocked the exit between the back of a few shops and the main road.

"What's up?" She asked.

Sam raised her eyebrow smugly as she drew her sword.

16

THE START OF A JOURNEY

The orange thief swirled in surprise, becoming aware that he was caught. He stared up at Sam with his piercing brown eyes, waiting for his audience to make the first move. Sam glanced down at her staff, that glared back at her, waiting to be rescued.

"Ya, so…. That's *mine*." She said sternly, pointing at the staff with the tip of her sword.

Finnigan looked over his shoulder at the glinting staff strapped to his back and then looked back at her with sarcasm plastered on his face.

"Pssh," he waved his hand dismissively and stood, "*No* it's not and if you haven't noticed I'm a little busy so kindly…" He motioned for her to leave. "Go away." He stood with his hands on his hips and his eyebrow went up with a retaliatory smirk on his face.

With her other hand, Sam ruffled through her bag and grabbed her fox mask.

"How 'bout-" she placed it on her face in cold familiarity. "Now?" She flashed a smug smile, feeling as though she had caught him off guard. He narrowed his eyes, understanding the situation more clearly. The thief took a step forward and Sam steadied herself for the expected brawl to come. She widened her stance, squared her shoulders, and stared down at her opponent. Finnigan's hands brushed the hooked swords that dangled from his waist. Sam gripped the leather hilt of her sword tighter as she bounced back and forth on her heels. He took another step forward and then staggered, disheartened. Up until now, his gaze had been fixed on hers.

His eyes trailed to Sam's side, and they grew wide with fear. Confused, Sam looked down. There was nothing there. Behind her, though, a soft, deep bellied growl arose.

Shocked, she turned to see a black spotted cat and its piercing eyes locked onto the thief with a menacing glare. Its small but sharp teeth showed on its snarled face.

Ikol.

Sam slowly moved towards the side, sheathing the sword and making herself invisible to the fury of the hunter. She glanced at Finnigan to see him backing away as he laughed uncomfortably.

"Heyyyyy, big kitty, I- I meant no harm..." He stuttered.

Ikol hissed, bearing his fangs even more and hunched over, ready to attack.

"Woahhh woah, ok- ok," he continued to back up, pressing against the store's back. He shakingly took the staff from his back and threw it down. The metal clanked as it hit the ground and rolled towards them, stopping a few inches in front of Ikol.

"Take it, I didn't want the dingy thing anyway, it isn't worth the trouble..." he said, once again shooing her away.

"And take the mean cat with you. He is such a fun killer." Finnigan forced a laugh, trying to ease the situation.

Ikol looked back at her, and she eased past him to pick up her staff, not taking her eyes off of Finnigan. Once it was in her hands again, she felt the familiar engravings and could sense a rush of relief surge through her. She breathed, and it felt as if the weight that sat on her chest had melted away. The staff in its rightful place on her back, she was complete.

Not saying anything, she looked back at the thief. Sam motioned for Ikol to follow and as they walked away, she made a face, whispering under her breath.

"You're dingy."

Ikol and Sam left the small alleyway from behind a glass smith's shop.

To show appreciation for her rescuer, she knelt down and patted him on the head, scratching his ear to thank him. He leaned in and purred softly, in a grateful reply.

"Thanks, Ikol."

"Can you find Nakoia and everyone else and let them know that I found my staff? Now we are just on the lookout for our land dweller." She finished speaking, and he looked at her for a moment longer before disappearing into the cobbled streets of Atlon.

She stood back up, feeling as though she finally accomplished something. It had been a moment since she felt adequate enough for the tasks ahead of her. With this small victory, she grabbed hold of it and worked hard to not let go of the feeling.

She looked back, gazing at the entrance they had just left and thought about Finnigan, the arrogant thief.

Is he still back there? Or did he disappear into the jungle?

Her curiosity got the best of her and she walked back to the corner, doing her best to soften her footsteps.

Discretely, she peaked around. He was facing the other way, looking at something. Unmoving, he had his hands on his waist and head tilted towards the sky. He swiftly kicked some wooden boxes near the shops, causing her to flinch at the sudden movement. Sam hid. She heard him cursing to himself, his bitter words echoing through the air, she couldn't resist taking a quick peek back out.

He was crouching down, weeping softly into his hands. The image stapled to her mind as she thought of her dreams.

A flush of emotions ran through her. Surprise, dread, anger, then pity.

She understood this was her new cohort, recognizing the way Finnigan sat there crouched and cried quietly to himself as the silhouette did in her dreams. She leaned against the wall, her stomach churning as her thoughts raced.

"What are we supposed to do *with a thief?*" She hissed to herself, closing her eyes and putting her hand over them in annoyance.

Sam focused on her breathing, listening to the world around her, leaving behind her worries. Muninn sent her those dreams to show that, for some reason, he was what they were looking for, whether she understood it or not.

This faunanoid needed help, and if he was to be her land dweller for the King's Journey, then she was going to help him.

She opened her eyes and rounded the corner, making herself known by her loud footsteps as she approached. He looked up from his hands, seeing her through red, watery eyes. He grimaced and looked away.

"What do you want? Did you come back to gloat?" Finnigan said in a congested tone.

She didn't respond. Once she was next to him, she did what she did in her dream. Sam crouched and gently put her hand on his shoulder.

"I- I'm sorry," Sam said, scratching her scarred upper arm awkwardly. "I saw what happened with your father and younger brother," she admitted.

He looked at her in disbelief. "So you have been *spying* on me?!"

Her face flushed with heat, "Well... not *necessarily*. I was already looking for my staff and once I found you, I followed you here-" She paused as she searched for her next words.

"Hey! I don't need to explain myself to you sir... you're the thief here." She pointed at her staff in reminder of the recent events.

He rolled his eyes but didn't respond.

"Why did you take it, anyway?" She asked, searching his face to see any resemblance of a familiar emotion.

He said nothing.

She nudged him.

He looked at the ground, picking at the dirt. "I *collect* things I like."

Annoyance washed over Sam. Rolling her eyes, she attempted to mask her frustration by rubbing her forehead.

"I'm sorry," he said bluntly.

She looked at him once more, and again realized whether she liked it or not, that this pickpocket was going to be the one to help her achieve her goal.

She sat down on the ground, relaxing a little more.

"You don't have to explain to me. I can see that your family life seems a bit rough around the edges." She looked up to the sky, smelling a stew permeate the air.

He laughed at her comment.

"That doesn't even begin to explain it." He smiled to himself through his sad expression.

They were silent for a time, listening to the city and the life that was happening only a wall away from them. She searched for the right words to say that would convince him to join their group.

"Come with me..." Sam blurted out.

"And my sister, leave Atlon and travel with us," she said.

He looked at her in surprise with his mouth agape. Finnigan snorted back a laugh.

"I can't leave! My little brothers are here. I *definitely* can't leave them alone with my dad." He shook his head more profusely, running his hand through his coarse orange hair.

"AND I don't even know you! You could be a *murderer*!"

With a steely gaze, she stared at him, her mouth pressed into a tight, straight line. He rolled his eyes. Both of them shared the understanding that his statement was utter nonsense.

After a moment, she shook past it and continued.

"It wouldn't be forever," she sat cross-legged, "and it might be good for you to get a change of scenery, get out there, into the world, breathe in some freedom and have room to think about what you want." She pointed at him. "Then, once you feel more.... confident in yourself, come back to take care of your brothers," she said.

"I don't know- I don't know if I could leave my littlest brother with my dad or even my younger brother. They're too like-minded and can be hard on him," he sighed.

"It sounds to me like you're trying to find excuses not to leave," she looked over at him, "listen- you can either stay here, hate your father and your life and continue stealing," she motioned with her left hand. "OR you can come with us and travel the four Realms and find yourself along the way." She lifted her right hand and weighed both of them. "You can't save your brothers if you're also drowning."

He put his head back in his hands and didn't respond.

There was nothing more she could do. Unless she physically dragged him out of Atlon with her, he had to decide for himself what he wanted to do. Sam sighed and stood, dusting herself off.

"I'm sorry about your home life, but it's up to you to change it. My sister and I leave Atlon tomorrow at noon. I can't force you to do anything," she paused, "I'll leave it up to you to decide what you want to do."

She left him there, his thoughts hanging in the air as he sat on the ground.

At the junction where the alley and road converged, she came to a stop, allowing a moment for him to soak into the idea before she turned one last time.

"See you tomorrow... Fin."

They all met at Nakoia's home to talk. Ikol had let Nakoia and the rest know of the staff, but Sam finding Fin and him turning out to be their land dweller was news. They all sat in the circle of pillows and spoke, catching up. Sam had told them what she said to him and how they will leave Atlon tomorrow around noon.

"That way, we can spend the rest of the time together before we are separated for who knows how long," she said with a sad smile.

The pain of missing those around her sunk in as she thought about moving on. Her comment brought the mood down when they realized that she and Cedar would be leaving.

Cedar looked at her. "Do you think he will come?"

Sam shrugged. "I don't know, but I have a feeling he might."

"Fin is a good boy. His family life has been hard since his mother died, and his father was hit hard and hasn't truly recovered from the loss." Nakoia added. "This journey would be good for him, to cleanse his soul and maybe find himself, like you said."

"Yes, but we can't force him to do anything. Unfortunately, he has to decide on his own whether he wants to leave or not," Lin added.

"Well, he would make a valuable addition to the team you need, the way he evaded us in the jungle before we arrived, if he races like that then you will have no problem in the land passage of the King's Journey." Amos nodded.

They all agreed in silent nods. Sam looked over at Ajax and Pine, who rested peacefully unaware alongside Meera.

Subsequently, they all made the choice to satisfy their hunger by lunching on the tree terraces, relishing the delicious food as they prepared for the upcoming journey.

The sky settled into a quiet orange and blue over the forest. Fin sat squatting on the thick branches that overlooked his home. The home he grew up in, with his mother, and two younger brothers and his father. He sat silently, thinking about the decision that had to be made, nervously picking at the tree bark, making it rain bits of wood onto the bridge below.

Memories of his childhood came rushing back, where he would spend hours playing with his baby brothers, running wild and causing all sorts of mayhem. Stormy nights also crossed his mind as he fondly remembered how his mother would comfort him as he lay in bed, creating a sense of warmth and security.

Most importantly, he mourned over the loss of her and his jolly father after the birth of Justin, his youngest brother. Their absence casting a shadow over his days. After their mother got sick and passed, their father was never the same. Like solid stone, he became unyielding and merciless.

A bird singing its melancholy tune to the dusk brought Fin back from deep within his memories. He continued to pick at the branch ruthlessly as he watched Justin try to snatch a bug and Brant, the middle child, read a book.

The weight of regret settled in his chest as he thought about the idea of leaving. He couldn't leave the two of them with the *'wall of harsh emotions'*. With a sigh, Fin's eyes trailed to his father, Rolt, searching for his familiar face. It was clear to him that his father's sadness had morphed into anger, creating a challenging situation for him and his younger brothers. If he left, no one would be there to watch out for them.

He looked up, through the small slits in the canopy, out to the endless sky. He could travel the realms though and find the parts of him that felt as though they were missing, like the unfinished puzzle with its pieces lost to the void.

A shifting in the leaves made Fin aware of another's presence. Someone was watching him.

His ears twitched. Alert, he listened for more movements as he scanned the jungle around him, looking for the source of his discomfort.

Suddenly, another noise caught his attention, and he swiftly turned his body towards the source. He narrowed his eyes and carefully examined the rustling leaves. Something caught his attention as he looked at the sun's rays falling to his left. They were obstructed by an unfamiliar object.

His heart quickened, tensing as the object's shape became clearer.

The moment he spotted the dark woman staring at him, he locked eyes with her, sensing the imminent danger. She pounced on him with the swift and powerful grace of a leopard.

His heart leapt out of his chest. He lost his balance on the branch and fell backwards. As he tried to catch himself, the intruder grabbed him.

She laughed heartily as she pulled him back up onto the branch.

"Nakoia, you gotta stop doing that." Fin rolled his eyes and let out a couple of hard breaths.

"Hmm, well that's what you deserve for stealing that poor girl's staff, Ikol told me and he said he also gave you a scare today as well." Nakoia turned her head and raised her eyebrow playfully.

Fin groaned in annoyance.

"I can't believe you *let* him do that. He is terrifying enough as it is. I thought he was going to *ACTUALLY* kill me!" He raised his hands dramatically, and it was Nakoia's turn to dramatically roll her eyes at him.

"You're lucky you're not in any trouble over this." She narrowed her eyes at him.

He turned his attention back down to his brothers, his stomach twisting.

"So," she said curtly, changing the subject, "I came up here because our mutual friend told me that she offered for you to join them on their journey...." She looked at him. Fin did not meet her eyes. He continued to pick at the bark, focusing on the task at hand.

"Hmmmm?" Nakoia prompted him for a response.

"I- I don't know... I can't leave them," he gestured to the children playing below him. "Especially with him." He pointed to the house.

"Do not worry about that. This isn't about them, this is about you. Besides, I can handle my brother, however hot tempered he may be." She paused to sit more comfortably. "When I found out that you were the one who stole her staff and the one that she had seen in her dreams, I knew it was for a reason. Do not waste this opportunity to find yourself."

He laughed. "Ohhhh, she is having *dreams* about me? I must be something special then."

Nakoia chuckled. "This is serious, Fin. You can do great things if you put forth effort."

Fin grew restless, losing interest in the conversation. "Ya sure, but maybe I want..." He paused, looking into Nakoia's dark eyes, searching for the words. When he couldn't find it, he looked back down and grew to a whisper. "I don't want greatness."

Nakoia stood elegantly on the branch. She put her hand on his head. "And that is why it calls to you, my nephew. This is your decision, so I will not force your hand, but I tell you now, this is your path. Do *not* abandon it."

She jumped up into the branches, and he watched her disappear into the trees.

"BOYS! DINNER!" Rolt barked loud and clear from inside.

THE START OF A JOURNEY

Fin sighed and jumped down from branch to branch as easy as the fish swims or the bird flies and moments later he was on the tree loft's paneled bridge. He went inside wordlessly and sat down, still thinking of the offer and hoping the right decision would come to him.

Dinner passed with the small boys bickering over the nonsense of their lives. Rolt and Fin spent their time in solemn silence, not paying attention to the boys' arguments, just eating and being buried deep within their emotions. Each passing moment gave Fin the confidence in the choice he should make.

Frogs chirped in the distance outside Fin's window as he wrote a letter to his brothers and father. He decided against telling them. But to just go, he would let nothing change his mind. Not his dad yelling harshly at him about how he was a disappointment or Justin's attached crying, no matter how much that upset him. He would sneak out and leave the letter in his room. They wouldn't notice until it was too late.

He finished the letter and sealed it with the wax of the family crest, placing it neatly on his nightstand. Then he rummaged through all the things in his messy room he had collected over the years, some his, some not his, all of it shiny or shiny to him at least. Once he had a pack of clothes, his hooked swords and some other things he deemed worthy to take, he laid down on his bed to sleep. With his arms propping his head up, he lay there, his eyes wide open and refusing to blink. Unable to sleep, his body buzzed with anticipation for the upcoming adventure. He didn't know how long he stayed awake, but after his brain exhausted itself by playing out various scenarios in his mind, his eyes grew heavy and he drifted to sleep.

Sam woke nervously energetic about the day with the distant chatter of people and the sun pouring through her green and yellow stained glass window. Her room was round and supported by light wooden panels that curved with the wall. To be closer to Lin, Amos, and Fern on their last day together, she made the decision to stay at the Inn for the night.

The question lingered in her mind: Would Fin opt to join them on their journey? And as she contemplated this, she couldn't help but imagine the potential outcomes if he chose to stay behind.

How would we be able to compete in the King's Journey without a land dweller? The dreams she received from Muninn pointed to him. So what would happen if it was someone else?

She shook her head to expel the negative thoughts that haunted her.

No.

Sam knew deep down that he would come.

Ajax was sprawled out on the edge of her tiny bed, making it seem even smaller. He took up half of the end of the grass stuffed bed. She got up, pulling the sheets off and ruffled his head, which turned into a scratch behind his ears. His antlers were undergoing noticeable changes. They were increasing in size, protruding more prominently from his head and sprouting a new, smaller section on each.

A small, sleepy quack reached her ears as she leaned over Ajax, and she spotted Pine nestled snugly between him and the wall.

She chuckled.

"I bet that's uncomfortable."

Sam emerged from her underground room and made her way down the winding hallway, towards the charming lobby that also served as a cozy dining spot. The morning sun gave off a calm air of peace that streamed through the same patterned stained glass windows that decorated Sam's room. Light and dark wood panels adorned the floor in an intricate pattern, while the walls and roof featured a mixture of dried mud and large river rocks for added support.

She found Fern at one of the smaller tables and sat to join her. Her tea steamed in the cup, releasing a delightful floral fragrance as she took a sip.

"Hmmm, that smells so good! What is it?"

"It is jasmine tea with honey." Fern smiled.

With care, she placed her delicate cup on the table and exchanged it for an empty cup, identical in design, which she placed in front of Sam. Fern lifted the white clay teapot, its repaired cracks adorned with a deep green metal, resembling a flowing stream on the earth's surface. As San examined the small cups, she noticed that they were made of the same type of sparkling rock, mirroring the cracks of the teapot.

She watched the polished cup glisten, entranced by its color, as Fern poured the floral tea into the cup. She picked up and coveted the warmness by bringing it close to her chest and breathing in the soft steam that rose from the amber liquid.

Fern pushed a jar of honey over to her, and with the honey dipper she watched the sticky golden glob seep from it into the tea. She took a sip and her whole body warmed from the taste of jasmine as it lingered in her mouth. She took a breath and sunk into her chair, thinking about what she might want to eat for breakfast. After a while, the others joined them to eat and talk about the day ahead.

They left the beautiful inn about two hours later. Packed and ready to travel on. The group, with no sign of Fin, now included Nakoia. Since it wasn't too far, they had promised to accompany Sam and Cedar to the edge of the forest, which would only take an hour or two to reach. Before they officially left town, they stopped by the stalls and bought some food that would keep for a week's journey.

Sam walked through Atlon's Overlook Gate and looked back at the jungle city with its yellow lanterns swaying in the wind, adorned with its historic stained glass and exotic greenery. She hesitated, her heart yearning for one more glimpse of the sea of stars that laid above her or to be in a tree terrace eating and enjoying time with her family.

If she stayed in Atlon, though, the rest of her journey would be forfeited, losing the possibility of seeing the rest of her family's world and losing the opportunity to discover her memories.

As she turned away from the captivating and incomparable city, a mix of sadness and excitement filled her heart, wondering what adventures awaited her in the rest of the realms.

It's time for me to move on.

It's time for my journey to begin.

They started their trek to the edge of the forest and out of the deep jungle.

The insects around them chirped in tune with the frogs that sounded their deep bellied croaks for the afternoon sun. An hour had passed when the jungle lessened and turned into a small patchy forest, with blotches of trees and less greenery surrounding them. During that time, Nakoia took Amos and Sam aside to speak with them privately.

"I do not wish to frighten you, but we have been followed by a rather large wolf, since we left Atlon."

Amos and Sam met each other's eyes in silent understanding.

"Yes... we call him The Hunter. He must have been following us since the village. We believe that he is tracking Ajax." They all looked at the Qilin that happily trotted ahead of them.

"I understand. These creatures are valued and hunted for many reasons." Nakoia said, looking thoughtful. "If he is hunting him, then we should attack before we separate, no?" She asked, looking from Sam to Amos curiously.

"He is a mighty beast, I'll give him that. There is not much we can do in the way of killing him," Amos said as a matter of fact.

"We *could* trap him." Cedar poked her head into the conversation.

"That would work. We could surprise him in the hills out in the open and trap him there." Sam replied. "I'm assuming that the Hills of Yoid are pretty barren?"

"Yes, yes, that could work. I will join you!" Nakoia said passionately. "It has been too long since a good hunt." A dark gleam shone in her eyes that made Sam uneasy. She had just met Nakoia and never seen her fight, but knew that it would be the fight of a true predator.

"Let's come up with a plan on the way there, then. That way, we can set it in motion when we get out of the forest. Until then, we need to stay aware of our surroundings in case he attacks, but we keep this on the low. We don't want the lack of surprise gone." Sam had chimed in looking at Cedar, who would be the one that would let the whole forest know in no time.

The four of them nodded in agreement, but it didn't take long for Cedar to realize it was a snide remark on her part.

"Rude!" She said playfully. "I can be hush-hush if I need to be!"

With a sarcastic nod, a smirk played on her lips before she erupted into laughter.

17

Hills of Yoid

It had begun to rain *in the woods,* not a terrible pour but a small dribble that tapped the leaves and made them move faintly. They stood at the edge of the forest looking at a vast land of nothing but rolling hills, as if the desert had turned green. A couple of tall, thin trees and random formations of rocks jutted out of the light green tufts of grass that spread over the land. No one wanted to break the silence as they stood, their gaze fixed on what awaited them, the tension thickening with each passing moment.

"HEYYY!"

In surprise, they turned to see a young man trotting up to them with his pack swishing back and forth and two hooked swords dangling to the side. Sam smiled and waved at him in greeting. He came up, joining the group, bent over with his hands resting on his knees to catch his breath.

"You decided to join us after all," Sam said with a mischievous smile growing on her face.

"I thought you guys left me!" Fin said through sporadic breaths.

"Bahhh, they wouldn't want to leave their precious land dweller behind," Amos said heartily, slapping his hand on Fin's back roughly. Fin made a pained face but laughed along with Amos. The group chuckled in response to their interaction. Sam noticed the tension in Fin's demeanor with Amos, a clear sign of his complicated father-son dynamic. Nevertheless, observing their exchange was an amusing sight for Sam.

"For those of you who haven't met him, this is Finnigan!" Nakoia announced to the group.

Fin blushed shyly and waved. "It's Fin."

Nakoia flashed Lin a look, and Lin held back a smile. Sam glanced between the two. She could see there were unsaid words there as well.

Cedar and everyone made introductions. They sat down on a formation of rocks close to them and settled a camp. The three that were traveling rationed their food out while Amos gave them tips on camping and survival in the wild. As they talked, there were many things that Sam didn't know, but luckily, Cedar and Fin made up the gaps of knowledge.

As everyone finished eating, Lin spoke to the group. "Fern and I have decided it is time for us to head back home."

Heads snapped to her direction in unison, their expressions filled with surprise as they looked at her. Sam had believed that they were going to continue on with them until after the Hunter situation was dealt with.

"When did y'all talk about this?!" Amos stammered, obviously caught off guard.

"Well... we *both* agree we miss home.. and Atlas. And we don't really see a use for us anymore," Fern said, disappointed. "Cedar has been practicing her fire summoning. You have Nakoia and... well, whatever he can do." She pointed to Fin.

"Which is a lot if it might add-" Fin responded, puffing out his chest.

Cedar side eyed him and snorted, and he shot her a look in return.

"Bear, you will be fine. It is time for us to depart and go home. I miss our youngest," Lin said, putting her hand lovingly on Amos's cheek.

"I am not worried about us. I am worried about you both being by yourself in the woods." Amos looked down at her as he put his hand on top of hers.

Lin raised an eyebrow. "You know I can take care of us. The forest will blaze with the heat of the sun before he could even get close."

Sam shifted at the intensity that she saw in that moment. Lin radiated with a flameless and heatless fire. It would be a revelation for Sam to see Lin unleash her summoning abilities at full strength, making her question just how powerful she truly was.

Sam looked at Cedars' blistering red hair and sharp hazel eyes, wondering if she carried any of her mother's power in her. The memory of the night Cedar discovered her power came to her. She felt the ghost of the heat that permeated the woods that night, knowing it to be the spirit of the flame. This led Sam to believe there was more to Cedars' ability than what was shown now.

As she glanced down, her eyes fixated on her pale hands and the scars that marked her body. With no powers or claws to defend herself, she relied solely on a staff and a crudely fashioned sword. The only thing protecting her was the armor that was gifted to her by Amos and a mask that hid her true identity.

Useless.

She grimaced.

If I had left on my own... Would I have survived?

She shut her eyes, clasping her hands together in her lap and gripping her knuckles.

I can't do... anything.

Nakoia's voice broke through her thoughts, bringing her back to the present. Sam grit her teeth, feeling the tension building in her jaw. Her face a picture of intense concentration as she masked her emotions with the façade of attentive listening.

"If it makes you feel better, I can have Ikol take them to the Inn that is outside of the Deep Forest Province." Nakoia whistled a calling tune. In response, Ikol stealthily slinked out of the woods and seamlessly joined the group, lying down beside Nakoia. Sam cracked a smile at the leopard's ability to remain unseen.

"*Oooof course* he was with us the whole time, cause when is he not?" Fin gave a sarcastic nod.

Ikol glared back at Fin and bared his teeth, giving off a low warning growl. Nakoia chuckled, then looked at Amos and Lin for an answer.

"I- well, I guess, as long as you three give this area a wide berth and avoid any areas where he might be, then you should be safe," Amos said.

Lin gave him a decisive hug. Despite Amos's agreement, there was no way to halt Lin's decision once she had made up her mind.

Cedar was crying as she hugged her mother and sister goodbye.

"I'm going to miss you guys so much," she said as more tears fell.

"It's ok darling, we will miss you too, but this will be *good* for you. You will grow stronger and be able to call the flame with ease. Make sure you practice every day." Lin kissed her forehead, and Fern hugged both of them at the same time.

After, Lin took Sam's hands into her own. "Sam, I know you are going on a journey that feels long and treacherous, but do not be discouraged. You will find what you are looking for. I know it. And even if it's not what you thought it was, you *always* have a home in the village. We will wait for your return daughter." Sam's eyes welled, the dam of emotions both hidden and unhidden cracked. She hugged Lin tight as tears rolled down her cheek. Smearing them across her face, she hugged Fern as well.

Sam cried, hugging them, understanding that they were doing this for her. Her family, who had not only found her, but helped her recover, taught her their ways, and selflessly put themselves in danger to protect her. She hugged them tighter. If something happened to them, it was her fault.

"I- I'm so sorry." She choked out, her eyes stinging as more tears welled.

"What?" Lin and Fern pulled away, confused.

"This is *all* my fault. You wouldn't be in this situation if it wasn't for *me*. The Hunter wouldn't have been following us. And everything that has happened since I met Cedar wouldn't have happened. It's all my fault." She tried to control herself, but her voice broke and lost itself as she talked. She couldn't bring herself to meet their eyes, her shame felt tooraw and to painful.

"Sam, I'm sorry that you feel this way, but that's the stupidest thing I have ever heard you say." Fern said.

Shocked, Sam looked up at the two of them in disbelief. Her mouth opened, but no words formed as she shook her head in disagreement.

"For obvious reasons." Lin took Sam's hands into her own. "That's a lie. You have helped us grow just as much as we have helped you grow. *Never* think that you are a burden on us, Sam, because that's far from the truth."

Sam nodded, trusting the sincerity in their words and the sorrowful expression in their eyes.

"We'll miss you," Fern added. "Promise to write from time to time."

"We will." Cedar bumped Sam's shoulder affectionately and instinctively reached out, enveloping her in a comforting embrace. Sam could only manage a nod, her eyes watering as she fought to compose herself.

With that, Fern picked up Pine from the back of Ajax. She quacked in soft defiance, but settled into Fern's arms after a moment.

Lin embraced Amos, their foreheads touching in a moment of silent connection.

"Stay safe. I will see you soon." Amos said.

"You too, my otso."

Ikol led the way on a small, lightly treaded path across the grass. Fern and Lin followed behind, turning back and waving every once in a while. The group stayed and watched as they grew smaller and smaller, following the line where the forest met the hills and eventually disappearing from sight. With the two of them gone, the group set off towards the Hills of Yoid, their anticipation growing.

They traveled over the hills for another hour in the drizzling rain and dark clouds. Sam's hood pattered with droplets when they heard a rumbling noise from the distance.

"Is that thunder?" Cedar looked up curiously at the gloomy clouds.

"I don't think so..." Fin removed his hood and pointed in front of them.

From behind the hill before them the point of a long pole and the top of a colorful banner. It swung back and forth as it grew longer. The ground vibrated underneath. Everyone stopped to watch as heads poked out as well. Galloping over the hill at lightning speed, a massive group emerged, too many to be counted.

Sam took a deep breath in.

Centaurs?

The herd sprinted towards the group, their thundering footsteps shaking the ground as they ran past them before abruptly turning around. Sam found herself surrounded by a diverse group of centaurs, each with their own unique characteristics. As she looked around, she saw a mixture of horses, cows, sheep, and even some that surprised her.

Three bunny centaurs clustered around her. Staring in wide-eyed curiosity, she shakily found her mask and discreetly put it on under her leather hood. Their attention momentarily diverted, they impulsively jumped off and seamlessly integrated themselves into the bustling crowd, never missing a beat in their circling.

She got closer to Cedar and hissed, "I didn't know other types of centaurs existed." Sam shot her a glare, as if she was blaming Cedar for not letting her know.

"What is that supposed to mean? What centaurs were you thinking of?" Cedar hissed back.

Sam's mind flashed to the centaurs of old, the tall horse warrior that she had seen in stories.

Sam opened her mouth to respond, but was cut short.

"Good morrow! Why do you travel through the tribes of Yoid's path?" A deep voice boomed through the crowd. A gap opened and a centaur that stood a foot or two above Amos emerged. His human torso had a light caramel complexion, while his horse's body was a deep, sleek black. He wore no shirt except a spear and bow strapped to his back. Sam noticed he had a pointed beard added character to his face, and his long black hair was styled uniquely, half down and half up in a top bun adorned with two obsidian pins featuring intricate gold designs.

Amos stepped forward, "These young ones," he motioned to Fin, Sam, and Cedar. "are traveling through to the Realm of the Sea. The Chief of the Deep Forest and I are accompanying them because we have a beast following us."

The tall centaur observed everyone in turn. He turned to Nakoia, giving her a deep bow, his eyes filled with respect, and she reciprocated the gesture with equal grace.

"Apologies. I have not traveled outside of the jungle in a long while, so I haven't been able to meet the new chief of the tribes yet. It is nice to finally meet your acquaintance. I am Chief Nakoia."

"Likewise, I am Uldous, Chief of the Hills." He stamped his spear. In response, the clambering crowd stamped their spears and banners, creating a thunderous echo.

"If you are being chased by a monster from the forest, we would love a hunt!" The horse centaurs of the crowd muttered, jittering with excitement. "If you agree to it, of course." He added.

Nakoia and Amos locked eyes, a silent understanding passing between them as they came to a mutual agreement.

"We planned on trapping him. If you would like to have a couple of your warriors and hunters join us, then they would be appreciated," Nakoia bowed her head slightly in thanks.

"It is decided then!" He turned to his tribe and in a projected voice, he declared, "we camp here!"

With a forceful motion, he slammed his spear twice, the echoes reverberating through the air. In response, they mirrored his actions, creating a synchronized rhythm. Then, the tribesmen and women scattered in every direction, each with their own tasks, as they began to build their camp.

Sam walked next to Nakoia. "Why are there so many of them traveling together?"

"The centaur tribes are nomads. They travel the lands and set up their homes every other month throughout the hills," she responded.

"I don't think I could live that way. I like our cottage too much," Cedar said, her voice tinged with nostalgia as she glanced to the side. Sam also caught herself reminiscing about their home and feeling a pang of homesickness.

It took a couple of hours to settle in. The small group eagerly pitched in to help set up, doing whatever they could.

As they pitched a nearby tent, Sam marveled at how the tribe blended seamlessly with the rolling hills. The cotton cloth tents, in dull tans, browns, reds, purples, greens, and blues, were adorned with squared designs that lent a sense of uniqueness to each structure.

Uldous's tent was situated close to where they had stopped. The design of the building was grander and more extravagant than the others, with a banner on top adorned with a centaur shooting its arrow, symbolizing the tribes of Yoid.

There were fires placed where the faunanoid gathered. Sam and Fin walked around looking to help anyone and basked in the merriment that the tribe created. People gathered around the fires, enjoying their meals and drinks, while others busily moved around, attending to their tasks. There were blacksmiths with a travel forge, and many horse centaur sharpening their weapons or having their armor repaired. Bunny centaurs scanned the perimeter with their watchful eyes. Sam and Fin observed them in intrigue.

Fin leaned close to Sam and glanced at her. "Do you think that they are useful... as guards...?"

"Pfft, don't be rude. I'm sure they are *fast*," Sam said pointedly. Fin snickered and Sam shook her head as they walked on.

They continued to adventure around the encampment for a while longer before returning to their group who sat around a fire as well. Fin and Sam settled in with their plates of food next to Uldous and two other companions.

"You then are not from her province, but are traveling through. Has it been a fair road then?" Uldous asked, waving the cooked leg of a bird as if it were a pointer.

"Yes, we have been traveling for a week. I am weary and ready to be home. These three, however, have yet to begin their journey." Amos put his hand on Cedar's shoulder and the three of them murmured in agreement.

"May I ask what adventure you follow?" He asked curiously. "And can we be of help? I enjoy a good quest."

Sam's eyes fixated on the ground as the group watched her, and she nervously buried the tip of her shoe in the dirt. Her eyebrows furrowed with uncertainty as she shrugged at Amos. She couldn't decide if she could trust this centaur or if it was wise for others to know her true identity.

Nakoia quickly understood and responded. "They are looking to create a team for the King's Journey. It is something they have always wanted to do."

Uldous looked around, hesitant, but dismissed it quickly. "Ahh yes, that is coming up at the end of this warm season.

Well, we will have to come and watch if you end up taking part."

"Thank you, that would mean a lot to us." Cedar said gratefully.

"Have you found your land dweller yet?" Uldous asked. "We have plenty of fast runners in our tribe."

"That would be me." Fin said proudly. "Wait ya, that's why you asked me to join, right?" He deflated for a moment as he looked to Cedar and Sam for confirmation.

"Hmph, the skinny long tail? I am sure we have faster runners than him." He laughed heartily and gulped down the rest of his drink. The other centaurs snickered and did the same.

Fin raised his eyebrow and smirked.

"Wanna bet? I'm likin' those pins in your top bun."

Sam stopped eating. Glaring at Fin as he pointedly avoided her gaze.

At that, Uldous took him more seriously and nodded. "Ok, if you win, you get the pins, and if my racer wins, then they replace you."

What is happening right now?

Fin made a sarcastic thinking face.

"Mmmm, deal."

Sam choked on her water.

Both, with a burst of energy, sprang up and slapped their hands together, grinning madly as the air buzzed with energy. At the unspoken signal, the centaurs surrounding him hurriedly dispersed to set up the competition.

"Grand! A race sounds glorious!" Uldous boasted.

Before Sam had a chance to stop the interaction or even take another bite of her food, everyone was gone and the plans were underway, the news of a competition spreading the camp like wildfire.

Fin put his finger up, stopping him. "As long as there are hills *AND* forest. It has to be like the King's Journey race."

"YES! Even better, we can have a mini tournament here!" Uldous said proudly.

Sam thought of the Hunter lurking nearby and tried to protest. Amos insisted it was a bad idea as well. But the two stubborn headed ones were already walking away to prepare for their game. Cedar, Amos, and Sam exchanged hesitant glances before reluctantly agreeing.

Sam sighed, concern tugged at her heart.

"I guess as long as everyone stays together, and Ajax stays near us, it will be fine," Cedar said.

"Also, a race sounds interesting and we can finally see what the boy can do." A smile curved on Amos's lips, while a glint of interest lit in his eyes.

She nodded. It would be a good opportunity to see Fin in action. Reflecting on the day he stole her staff, Fin's impressive speed became apparent, and now they could witness his running prowess first hand.

The race had taken a while to set up, but they created a perimeter of onlookers around the painted trail that Fin and the other racer would be traveling. The eager crowd, full of energy and anticipation, shuffled restlessly while their flushed, cheerful faces reflected the effects of numerous drinks.

At the starting line, Fin and the centaur made themselves ready.

"This is Eelias," Uldous made introductions. "He will race your dweller today!" He looked at Sam, then smirked at Fin.

Eelias nodded rigidly at them and went back to stretching. He was a bunny centaur with white spots covering his black fur. Freckles dotted his cream toned body and face.

"He doesn't seem too friendly," Cedar whispered to Sam. She nodded, silently agreeing, then stepped up to Fin.

"Hey, I know I didn't really explain to you what we were traveling for," she said. "It's something I don't enjoy telling everyone that we meet. But... if you win this race, it'll be real, you'll be a part of our team and our friend. And I will tell you the full story then."

Initially, he chuckled without comprehending the gravity of the secret she carried. When she didn't join in, he frowned.

"Don't look so upset Sam, you know I got this. I'll make us proud." He pointed his thumb at himself and flashed his familiar, arrogant smile.

She made a face, uncertain if he was cocky or just dumb. Either way, he was about to race, and they were about to find out if he really had what it took to be their first racer.

"Besides, I'm in it for the nice-looking pins he has. I think they will look *great* in my hair. What do you think?" Fin added, ruffling his own hair, making it shaggier and more matted than before.

Sam snorted, adding, "Try your best, Fin. That's all you can really do." She turned, joining the others away from the starting line as he went and dug his heel into the dewy grass and waited for the race to begin.

He was going to do it, he was going to win. Fin was tired of not putting any effort into what he did. He wanted to prove to others and to himself that he could achieve what he put his mind to. He knew he could beat this small bunny in a silly race, especially once they got into the forest. His eyes briefly flickered to his shorter adversary, and he honed in on the task, heightening his senses.

"The starting marker will be the arrow that will land between the two competitors!" A cow centaur with an arrow docked in her bow announced.

He hoped his legs would carry him as swiftly as his heart pounded.

The arrow left the archer with a *thwup* of the reverberating bowstring.

All watched as it whistled, singing through the air.

Fin closed his eyes, focusing himself. Letting all other things go.

The whistling cut short with the sound of impact.

The world slowed as he opened his eyes and ran.

The familiarity of the strain on his muscles as he pushed forward and continued to move relaxed him. He felt his feet hit the sturdy ground and pushing his toes into the earth to propel himself forward. Fin understood this. This made him happy. He pushed himself harder. Trying to keep his attention on his speed and the waves of the hills, but he could see his opponent next to him, keeping pace and working to push as well. They flashed past the unnoticed people around them, who cheered and screamed louder as they went by. Eelias pulled ahead of him. Fin knew that because he was a quadruped, he would be faster than him, but he also knew that when they reached the forest and the trees that Eelias wouldn't stand a chance.

The forest grew close now. Eelias full body ahead as Fin looked for his route through the trees. His eyes locked onto one. He found it. Fins eyes filled with a sinister darkness, and a sly smirk played on his lips.

Taking out his hooked swords, he crouched so low to the ground his knees brushed against the damp grass. He pushed off the side of the low hill and leaped, rising into the air, holding out his swords, outstretching his body as far as it would let him. He sensed his muscles stretch all the way, as far as they would go. His hooks locked onto the thick branch of the closest tree. His gaze fell upon the bunny centaur, who had not yet made it to the woods, and a mischievous smile appeared on his face. He pushed off the branch and raced through the trees, losing sight of the other racer.

Those pins are mine.

The race through the woods was formed to be a giant arch that looped back towards the camp. Fin barely needed to use his swords because of his momentum as he flew through the treetops. The wind thrusted him forward, and the droplets of rain slapped against him. He could feel the arches in his feet as they landed on each of the branches for less than a second as he danced through the small wooded canopy.

While the hillside was teeming with spectators, the forest had only a handful of onlookers. Nevertheless, those who ventured into the forest were awestruck by the agile movements of the long-tailed opponent.

The rain picked up, Fin slowed down to check where Eelias was. A couple of yards behind him, the bunny struggled to keep up. He wrapped his tail around a branch and stopped. Leaning over, he laughed, mocking Eelias. The centaur ignored him as he pressed on. Fin wore a smug grin as he pressed forward as well, surpassing him effortlessly, only to come to a sudden halt and taunt him again.

Abruptly, he stopped as movement caught his peripheral vision. He noticed something massive further in the woods. He squatted on the branch and watched. His eyes grew in terror. Looking back to Eelias and to the figure, he saw that the bunny was being hunted. Eelias continued to run, unaware of the beast looming in the trees. The wolf grew closer.

Panicked, Fin yelled. "Eelias! Look out!"

Eelias faltered, not sure what was happening. This caused the hunter to seize the opportunity of the distraction.

He sprang forward.

Eelias dodged, scrambling to the side, barely escaping the swiping claws. A growl rose from the Hunter and Eelias cried in fear as he ran, scrambling back to the hills.

Where did this thing come from? It's HUGE.

Urgency rose in Fin's body, his legs forcing him to move before his mind could come up with a plan.

Fin caught up in no time, using the branches to his advantage.

"Hey you big fur ball," Fin spat, "look up here." He swung one of his hooked swords at the Hunter, missing but completing his true goal. The beast snarled. Its eyes locked onto him and grabbed at Fin's soul, almost tearing it out. The Hunter jumped up, using his enormous back legs, snapping his jaws and gnarled teeth at Fin. Leaping to a different branch in time, he watched the wolf's paw striking the branch with a force that shattered it into numerous fragments that scattered in all directions.

He went faster, trying to escape. He could see the clearing now. Eelias had made it out, crashing through the leaves, alerting all the others that the race had been interrupted.

Come on! Just a little further.

He was going to make it. He could hear the massive wolf so close behind. The trees grew shorter and smaller as they neared the edge. Fin's fear dared him to look back. His eyes stayed plastered to the clearing ahead.

The last branch arrived. Fin used the strength in his legs to jump as far as he could into the hills. He could see the centaurs running around in a panic, trying to understand what had happened. He closed his eyes and leaped into the harsh rain.

The rain had fallen harder, darkening the clouds along with the merriment. They watched from under the tent in small talk as the screams began.

Sam stood, alert. Moments later, centaurs that were watching the race ran out of the forest in all directions, creating a panic. The group sprinted forward, out of the tent's protection from the rain and towards the commotion. As they looked on, Eelias burst out, his speed creating a blur, and Fin soon joined him from the treetops. They all watched as he jumped out as far as he could into the air and summer-salted into a run. Sam stopped in her tracks as they finally had a clear view of what everyone was afraid of. The sight sent shivers down her spine. Out of the woods prowled the greened eyed beast.

18

Night of the Wolf

Fin sprinted toward them, his feet pounding against the ground. The archers took their shots and volleyed a swarm of arrows at the giant wolf, who stayed out of reach in the tree line and paced back and forth, his eyes never leaving the sight of his prey. Sam grimaced, annoyed with this never ending nuisance. Now that they had the chance to fight, he was being a coward. She stared, disgusted at its behavior.

"COME ON!" She bellowed from her chest, baiting the Hunter from his haven.

The crowd settled a safe distance to watch the interaction. Cedar tried to stop her, but Sam brushed her off.

Enough of this. If he wants to fight, then let's fight!

"COWARD!" The word echoed on the stormy day. Silence deafened the air. She pointed her staff at him and he snarled.

"LET'S END THIS HERE!"

He stopped pacing and stared at her now. His eyes burned with a fiery hatred, their intensity matching the sharpness of his fangs protruding from his mouth.

Fear washed over Sam as the Hunter turned his full fury onto her.

She took a step back, faltering in her decision.

I had the courage moments ago. Where is it now? Did I even mean what I said?

Her heart raced, and her arm that held the staff trembled in fear. With a deliberate motion, she slammed her staff on the damp grassy knoll, in hopes to lure him from his safe haven.

However, it didn't matter, he stared only a moment longer before he turned and vanished into the dense undergrowth. The nomads and her group kept their eyes fixed on the spot where he had stood until the memory of where he prowled blended seamlessly with the surrounding landscape.

"Bold words, young warrior," Uldous broke the silence. He dispersed his clan from the field.

Sam jolted, caught off guard. She glanced back and forth between him and the forest a moment longer before her heart settled back into her chest.

"Hopefully not shallow words," she chuckled, her body trembling.

He stared at her for a moment before speaking.

"They only become shallow without the act."

As he walked away, she nodded, her eyes fixated on him, contemplating his transformation into the newest chief of the tribes. He was not only a warrior, but a guardian of his people's safety, earning their trust through his actions.

She looked at Amos and Nakoia. "We need a plan. He needs to be gone *tonight*."

"Let's start planning, then." Fin walked up to them, out of breath. "Who won, by the way?" He put his hands on his hips.

"Technically, Eelias did." Cedar pointed at the clearly shaken centaur, who was speaking with Uldous.

Fin looked at Sam upset, "I'm sorry." And with a pained face, he looked away, unsure what to do next.

"Fin- bro, do you think we were really going to replace you?... With a bunny?" Sam snorted a laugh and Cedar added, "Lots of *good* fighting he did." And rolled her eyes. He flashed a smile and laughed with them.

"I guess our race is undecided, then. Eelias tells me you defended him and let him escape while you distracted the Hunter. I thank you for your service." Uldous bowed and held out his hands, presenting the gold lace hair pins to Fin.

Fin stammered, "But I didn't win-"

"Nonetheless, you proved yourself to be valuable to the people around you, and besides, once you got to the trees... I knew you would win," Uldous winked at him. "You deserve them."

Fin grinned as he thanked him and picked up the pins.

"But you must have your hair done as mine is. This is the custom if you wear the pins." Uldous added after. "Meet with the seamsters tonight when you are free. They know how to do the custom styles for hair."

"I'm at a loss for words. Thank you so much!" Fin's eyes gleamed at the pins.

"Now, onto more pressing matters, it is time to come up with a plan for *that*." He gestured to where the wolf had lingered in the tree line only minutes before.

"We were just talking about that. It is time that he was dealt with," Nakoia spoke up. Uldous motioned and led the way to his tent where they formed a plan to trap the beast, and the sun sunk past the hillside as they rested for the time to come.

The time arrived quickly while Sam had wished it to never show. She was aware that it was foolish to desire something so unattainable. Yet, as she mentally went through the plan again, her stomach twisted and she felt queasy. Of course, this was bound to happen. It needed to happen. This monster was a burden and a danger to her family, her friends, and now the people around her, so it was time that he was dealt with.

But. Is this the best way?

Sam continued down the rabbit hole of anxious thoughts and began twirling the bead in her hair. Her chest felt tight, as if someone rang out a wet cloth inside her. Her breathing was erratic. She tried to center her mind on the dark hilly horizon in front of her, focusing her breath and her thoughts, as she racked her brain for the positives of the situation.

Amos, Nakoia, and Uldous are incredibly skilled fighters. If anything goes wrong, Cedar can summon fire. Fin had his agility and hooked swords, and I have...

She looked down at her staff that lay next to her. It shimmered under the gentle moonlight, as though whispering, *I am here for you.* She touched the engraving and ran her fingers down the floral designs. With her knees pulled up to her chest, she placed her chin on them and let out a sigh. The gibbous moon had only just risen into the sky, giving way to a moonlight world. The stars shimmered brilliantly, not quite as radiant as in the overhead canopy in Atlon, but still performed a captivating celestial dance for those who watched.

Her mind thought back to what they had agreed on, and her stomach flipped again. To avoid the tense silence, she constantly sought things to occupy her mind. Looking around to see the surrounding emptiness, she slipped her mask off, cleaning the sweat and grime from her sore face and used a piece of cloth to wipe down the mask. It had gotten dusty in the day's commotion. When it was clean, she laid it next to her.

With another sigh, she sprawled out in the ankle-high weeds, making random noises with her mouth. Sam heard a familiar laughter close to her and strained her neck to see Cedar standing above her with a bowl in her hands. She sat down next to Sam and placed the bowl on the laying girl's stomach.

"Here," she laughed again, "I thought you might be bored."

Sam leaned up on her elbows to see the bowl was brimmed with fruits, she grabbed a slimy white piece with her fingers and ate a couple bites. The taste was subtly reminiscent of a cantaloupe. Laying back down, she continued to eat the fruit as she stared upwards.

"Thanks. This isn't half bad," she said as Cedar grabbed a few as well.

"Do you think you're ready for this?" Cedar asked nervously. She was never the type to hide how she felt about something which always felt refreshing to Sam.

"No."

Cedar fidgeted with her hands. "Well- I'm here, I have my med kit and if things get bad, I can summon fire to help, and Fin's here too. So are Nakoia and Dad. You don't have to worry, ok?"

"It's not that," Sam said. She intentionally avoided looking into Cedar's eyes. Sam was fully aware of her own weakness and uselessness, yet she also understood that the others would never openly acknowledge it.

The emotion clawed its way up her thought as her mind screamed to tell Cedar how she felt. Unable to resist the urge to speak the truth. Sam gazed up at her, meeting the child's hazel eyes that overflowed with concern.

"I don't have these amazing powers or super awesome fighting skills. My weapon isn't even sharp." She laughed dryly at herself as she motioned to her sword. "How am I supposed to do anything?"

"What?! No Sam, you are *amazing*." She waved her hands for emphasis. "You are so smart and brave. I don't know why you are so hard on yourself."

"What would I have done if you guys weren't around?"

Cedar didn't respond, so Sam continued.

"I came out of that hole and you helped me. Amos saved me from the Hunter, then you saved me again, then Lin saved me," Sam said, exasperated. "I... want to help people. I am *TIRED* of being a burden on *EVERYONE* that I care about. And to be honest, I don't see that changing soon. Unless I train my butt off to become a better fighter, because that's all I *can* do," she huffed, exhausted from her rant.

She turned over frustrated, keeping her eyes on the ground and tearing the grass and weeds out of the ground in clumps to keep herself from breaking down in front of Cedar.

"Then, do that. Become the best staff fighter, or bow archer, or sword master," Cedar said, sternly. "I know you're upset. But I'm tired of seeing you wallow in your self pity. *None* of this is going to change. Like you said, you're not going to magically get powers or become a faunanoid like us. You're stuck with what you have and you're going to have to accept that and move on because this pity party you have thrown for yourself since you came out of the cave has gone on long enough." Cedar crossed her arms, solidifying her argument.

Sam opened her mouth. Then closed it, not sure what to say. "I have not-" She sat up and made a face, "I have not- been throwing myself a pity party... I'm sorry that I'm a *little* upset that I woke up like a thousand years after everyone I know *DIED* and now LITERALLY EVERYTHING is different. So- my bad," she scoffed.

"And it isn't going to change back, either." Cedar covered her eyes with her hands. "Sam, you have been sad since you woke up, and rightfully so, but you are missing out on so much more because you can't stop thinking about what isn't here anymore! Please, your grief has gone on long enough. It is time to move on and enjoy what you have!"

Sam remained silent, but her hurt expression spoke volumes. She thought that Cedar understood her pain, but now it felt as though her truest friend had betrayed her.

"I think I need to be alone right now," Sam turned away from her.

With tears welling in her eyes, Cedar quietly slipped away, the sound of rustling grass the only disturbance. Sam covered her face with her hand, trying to fight the sour feeling in her throat and the sting of her eyes. She replayed what Cedar had said in her mind.

Does my grief block my vision of the present?

Sam didn't know what to think. She couldn't think. Her mind hit a wall as she tried to push past their conversation, her anguish creating a mental block.

She laid back down, setting the empty bowl next to her. With nothing to distract her, she continued to sulk and speculate about Cedars' echoing words. She dozed off, blinking in and out, and tired from crying. Sam closed her eyes on the night sky.

"Pst," someone nudged her shoulder. Adrenaline charged through her, and she threw her eyes open, flinging herself forward.

"What- what happened?" She stammered as her mind tried to make sense of the situation.

"You're supposed to be the bait, not it's dinner, dummy. They sent me up here to check on you and good thing, too." Fin mocked. Sam brushed in and out of existence as her mind forced itself awake. She looked groggily at Fin, her eyes begging to be closed again.

It's been a while since you sent Cedar back in tears," Fin said in amusement. "What did you say to her to get her in a tizzy?"

Sam rolled her eyes dramatically at him, waking up more. "Whole lotta non'ya is what I told her."

Fin made a snarky face at her, but settled in. "I like how I'm *part of the crew*, but still get told nothing."

"I- ya, you're right- I'm sorry, but that one is a bit personal for real, not just because it's you," she said apologetically and starred out at the tree line.

"O! I brought you this! A gift from Uldous." He handed over a bow and a single arrow, drenched with something that smelt harsh.

"Thanks," she grumbled, taking it, putting it on her other side.

"Sooooo," he rubbed his hands together for warmth. "are you going to tell me the big secret or what? I ran super fast just for this, plus bonus points. I even fought off a giant wolf and saved a cute bunny centaur. Is that honorable enough for the great secret or what?" He put his hand on his chest and spoke with a fancy accent that made Sam laugh.

"I suppose I should tell you. It is kind of a long story, though," she responded.

Fin made a point of getting comfortable and leaned back onto his hands for effect, "Well, good thing we have time." He turned to face her while she determined where to start. They sat in silence for a moment. She rubbed her face, gathering her thoughts, and decided to start from the beginning.

After a while of confusing storytelling, they sat in silence as Fin registered the information that he had received.

"Woah, that makes sense why you look different, and the mask thing, I guess." He looked down at the blue fox mask and it stared back up at them, sleeping and solemn.

"That's why you want to enter the tournament? So you can win a boon from the High King and speak with Huginn." He looked out into the distance, a thoughtful expression painted over his features.

"No turning back now I guess, *O ancient one*." Fin snickered.

"Ha Ha Ha, you're soooo funny," Sam said sarcastically and smiled at him.

The wind blew rough, rolling over the hills and through her hair, giving her a sense of freedom for a moment. She inhaled the fresh night breeze.

"Thanks for waking me. I feel better now, but if you don't also want to be the center of attention, then I would skedaddle." She clicked her tongue twice and shooed him away.

"Fine, fine, I'll get out of your hair. Just know though.... You're technically really *REALLY* old." A smile curved on his lips as he ran down the hillside and into the darkness. She laughed mockingly at him as she watched him go.

Sam watched the moon rise, and it sat above her when she felt a chill in the air. Not the chill of the night, but the chill of fear. A shiver ran down her spine. She was being watched. Suddenly, she became alert, sitting upright and focusing intently on the trees camouflaged in the night that concealed any potential threats. She scanned the distance, quieting her breathing. Her heart skipped a beat. She stopped.

There, staring at her from the trees, were the eyes of an enraged beast.

Sam stood with the bow. She didn't need to be a good shot, she just needed to be decent enough. The wind blew harder, and they stared at each other, unmoving, waiting and watching for the other to make the first move.

The words of Uldous rang in her head.

They only become shallow without the act.

She drew back the bow, he growled and launched into a bound towards her. Sam could feel herself shaking again. Her heartbeat was in her ears. Closing her eyes, she steadied herself, and shot the whistling arrow that dripped over the land. It sang in the air as the one did earlier that day, hitting the ground with a slick thud.

Nothing.

He continued running. She grabbed her staff and braced. She needed to trust the others to do what was necessary. He was about to reach the edge of the hill and jump to her when a flash of heat and light lit the dark crevice underneath the two of them, lighting Sam's face in the color of flames. The Hunter stopped, sensing the threat, but it was too late. He was snared in a trap made from his own hubris.

A ball of flame came up and torched the arrow, creating a barrier of flames between the two. He snarled in frustration and snapped his jaws at her.

Her chest tightened, holding onto the moment.

It began to sprinkle. Drizzling the fire, creating a smoke screen above the flames.

Sam watched with a firm expression, keeping her attention on him. He hadn't noticed the flammable sludge encircling the hill or the horrid smell it produced.

She stood taller and more courageous in his mistake, staring him down and narrowing her eyes, meeting him at his level. He looked around at his prison of fire, growing angrier and howling toward the moon for revenge.

Sam and her comrades at the bottom of the hill watched in horror as he hunched over, his body beginning to morph. Her eyes grew wide with ladened fear.

He sent out a painful roar and continued to change.

With shallow breathing, her face contorted in shock and disbelief.

As his arms grew shorter, his back and legs seemed to stretch out, creating an unusual and disproportionate appearance. Now standing on two legs, the Hunter took on a more humanoid appearance. He bellowed deeply, sending dread into the hearts of his enemies.

The silence after his transformation was deafening. No one moved. No one wanted to draw the attention of the true monster the beast had become.

Sam's breathing became weak and hollow. She watched as he turned, putting his sights on the people closest to him. As he extended his newly formed fingers, sharp claws emerged from them.

Nakoia and Uldous jumped through the flames, entering the battle. Amos stayed back. Sam could see him growing bigger and beginning to shift as well.

"NO! RUN! GET AWAY!" Sam yelled through the roar of the fire, waving her hands and running towards them.

They hadn't expected this. He was too strong for them now. She couldn't risk losing anyone. Despite their inability to hear her, she clumsily kept running downhill towards them. She watched Nakoia run towards her opponent and Uldous fire a volley of arrows. While she was sprinting down the slope, they vanished over the top. She lost her balance, falling and rolling down the hill, scrapping her face and her arms. In the midst of her pain, she found the strength to steady herself. Without hesitation, she snatched her staff from the ground and started into a sprint up the hill.

"SAM NO!" Cedar yelled from the side.

"Let them handle it!" Fin called out.

They ran after her.

Paying no attention to the commotion behind her, she pressed on up the hill. Halfway up the hill, she suddenly heard Uldous let out a cry of pain. With her staff securely strapped to her back now, she scrambled up the steep hillside on all fours, frantic to reach the top of the nearly vertical hillside.

As she reached the top, arrows flew out past her, lighting on fire as they went through the wall of flames and striking the side of the hill she was just on.

She watched Nakoia and Berserker Amos fight the morphed terror up close, while Uldous fought from afar with his bow and arrows. The beast had a bloody scar running across his snout with a couple of arrows sinking deep into his torso.

Blood dripped from his claws and spouted from his wounds, splattering all when they collided in battle. Amos had grown bigger and more ravenous than Sam had previously seen. He rammed the Hunter with his shoulder, knocking them both to the ground as Nakoia went for the monster's head, wrapping her legs around his neck.

Uldous waved at his men to approach with roped arrows to trap him. When he turned to the side, Sam noticed a savage gash that traveled alongside his flank. She began furiously running around the tall bright flames, trying to find an entrance to the fight. The Hunter broke free from Amos and swung his claws at Nakoia. She swiftly dodge backwards, barely escaping his grasp.

The Hunter rolled over onto his stomach and boosted himself up, charging Nakoia, whose back was up against the flames now. Just as he lunged into the air for the attack, Amos grabbed his leg and pulled him backwards. Nakoia escaped to the left side, joining Uldous and wiping the blood and sweat from her face. Sam continued to madly search for a way in as she watched Amos throw the Hunter by his leg, further from his allies.

Rain fell heavier now, wetting the ground and causing the fire to dampen out. Cedar pushed her arms out and her face contorted in pain and concentration as she forced the flames higher.

The archer centaurs jumped high over the flames and joined Uldous. He pointed and spoke, but Sam could not hear them over the roar of the fire. As the Hunter lay on the ground, gradually moving to get up, the centaurs circled with the ring of fire and aimed their bows, waiting for the call.

"Cedar! Let me in!" Sam looked at her, defeated. Fin and Cedar made eye contact, exchanging a nervous glance.

"Come on! We can't let them do this by themselves. We need to help," Sam pleaded.

Cedar looked at her once more before giving in. Closing her eyes, she focused on lowering the flames closest to them. With the height of the barrier now manageable, the three of them promptly made their way to the inside. Cedar released her grip, and the flames grew back, regaining its previous heat and strength.

Sam drew her staff, her friends shuffled next to her, readying themselves.

The Hunter got up, slower in his actions. He ran awkwardly towards Amos, who now stood in the center. They met head on in a battle of strength. Amos steadily began to take over the match, putting the Hunter on one knee, then the other.

Uldous raised his hand. The archers took position, raising their bows higher and pointing the arrows toward the sky. Amos gave one loud, final roar and pushed the weakened beast to the bloodstained grass. Uldous gave the signal and yelled.

"FIRE!"

Sam watched, her mouth gaped.

The archers released their arrows with the ropes connected to them. They flew through the air, creating a cross-hatched pattern and trapping the tired beast under them.

It felt like time had gone on forever, but also stopped simultaneously. They waited, watching for signs of movement or life as the net kept him down.

Amos was far gone into his beast form. He stumbled around aimlessly, bloodied, as Cedar ran to calm him. A couple of minutes went by as they watched him slowly grow back to his regular form. He laid on the ground, resting and breathing heavily as Cedar began cleaning the blood from him. Sam rushed to their sides. Cedar teared up as her hands trembled over her injured father. Examining Amos sent a surge of dread through her. He looked weak and his breathing was ragged and labored.

"He will be alright," she said calmly, taking a trembling breath, comforting Cedar as she worked.

"Can you put out the flames, Cedar? Let's get some medics in here now," Nakoia called from Uldous.

Aided by the rain and with a swift motion of her hands, Cedar wiped out the flames, leaving only the evidence of charred ground.

With Cedar resuming her work, Sam approached their prisoner. Fin joined her a couple of paces behind and Nakoia caught up to Sam, putting her hand on her shoulder, shaking her head.

Hesitantly, she stopped, waiting to see if it was safe. Nakoia continued forward and stood next to the unconscious beast.

"So, what should we do?" Sam said as she approached cautiously. Her eyes traveled to its face with gray and brown fur matted in thick, dark blood. His face was calm for the first time, no anger or malice showed.

"I guess it's time. We need to end this before he gets back up..." Nakoia trailed off.

Sam looked at the defeated beast and felt pity for it, which quickly turned back to indifference when she remembered how much harm it had brought the people around her.

"I- I can't." Sam turned, her eyes closed.

Nakoia nodded, her eyes narrowing as she focused. She raised her arm, transforming her hand into a deadly clawed blade.

For a moment, there was nothing.

Then, out of nowhere, a noise on the smoldering hillside drew Sam's attention.

"Ajax?" Cedar was looking past the hill where Sam couldn't see. But a second later, Ajax's horned head popped up as he trotted past Cedar and the injured Amos.

"Ajax." Cedar repeated, trying to stop him, but missed grabbing his leg. He continued trotting up to Sam, Nakoia, and the defeated Hunter.

Ajax nonchalantly bleated at Sam as he went past her.

"Woah, woah, woahhh." She leaned over, blocking his path with her hands and body. Ajax speedily moved around her with no trouble and continued on his trek. Nakoia stopped, and Sam turned to watch as he went up to the Hunter. He bleated gently and licked the monster's nose.

"Ooooookayy, we are done with that now. Let's go." She got in between them and ushered Ajax from the scene.

As soon as she took a step to lead him away, a sharp, intense pain surged through her leg, making her gasp.

She loudly yelled, stiffening in pain. The torment grew worse. She felt her breath being taken away from her, frenzied she glared at the source.

One menacing green eye beamed hatred at her and he sneered as his teeth dug further into her leg. She screamed even louder this time. The echo of the cry rolled through the rainy hills and into the forest. She collapsed as he let go of her. Her body curled into itself for protection as she grabbed at the wound.

Nakoia dragged her away from his thick jaws. Sam grew weak and tired, her body grew cold. Fin and Cedar ran up. He grabbed Ajax and held him off the ground away from the beast.

They gathered around her with their backs to the morphed wolf as they tended to her leg. Dazed, she could hear words but couldn't understand what was being said to her. Sam watched, her eyes blurring as he licked his teeth clean from her blood, his mouth curling upwards in a sinister smile as he met Sam's eyes once more. He began pulsating and shaking. Weakly, she pointed at him. They turned to watch in horror as he began becoming smaller and smaller. He lost his fur in chunks, shedding it off like an animal would shed a winter coat.

His legs and arms became bare.

His skin turned a dark tan color and his shaggy hair was gray and brown, like the color of the fur he no longer had.

And his face became that of a boy.

19

THE STRANGER IN A STRANGE WORLD

He woke, in the dark.

Pain coursed through his body as he moved. He groaned as he tried to find where it was coming from, slowly moving around he found that the aching was coming from his shoulder and a couple of other wounds on his back. He gingerly touched the tightly bandaged area and looked for blood. Inspecting his clean hand he saw something that he didn't quite understand.

His skin was smooth, and he had fingers with no claws or fur. Confused, he held both of his hands up toward the soft light and scrutinized them, flipping them around and examining his palm, the back of his hands, and his small useless fingernails.

It got worse as he looked down and saw, just like his arms, his legs were bare except for a small rough hair that ran down it. Frantically he grabbed at his legs, grabbing his feet and toes. Then putting his hands on his chest and face, trying to figure out what bare creature he had shifted to. In a panic, he scrambled up and tried to leave the darkened room he woke in, but the pain and the ropes he hadn't noticed earlier stopped him from getting any farther. He fell back down with an excruciating grunt.

That's when he started noticing his surroundings. He looked around and saw that he was in a small tent with a wooden pole holding up the colored cloth. He could see warm torch light coming from outside and the shadows of the people who stood near it. He continued to glance around and back at his hands, growing more desperate and panicked with the thought of being trapped in an unknown species body.

The fight flashed through his mind in chunks. He hadn't planned on changing into the stronger form but when the red haired one created a fire ring around him, he grew frightened. He had felt a pull to these people, he wasn't sure why but he tracked them and watched them. Interacting with them was not in the plans but then the obnoxious one with the staff challenged him and he couldn't see anything but a fog of red after that. So many things had happened the way he didn't want them too. He was being stupid and he was angry for making such a careless mistake. He should have just stayed in his territory, alone and without any problems.

He started pulling at the rope trying to see if it would loosen, it was no use. He groaned in frustrated defeat and realized it was too loud when the shadows outside turned and started to move. One disappeared and the other turned to looking in the gap in the cloth. He shrunk back into the corner, making himself small and hopefully invisible. Still trying to think of what he could do, his mind felt overcrowded as it raced. He grew scared thinking of what was going to happen as he hugged his knees to his chest, holding back angry tears as he watched the entrance for his captors to appear.

"In my many years, I have learned to trust the Qilin, whether I agree with them or not."

"Ahh, Cedar, that burns." Sam yelped out in pain, she had woken up only moments ago to Cedar treating her new leg wound.

"Don't be a baby, you know I have to disinfect it. Do you want to die from giant wolf germs?!" Cedar said dramatically looking at her, her expression telling Sam that she had enough of the over exaggerating.

Sam grumbled but kept the rest to herself, only breathing in sharply or making a face when it truly hurt.

Fin had brought her some water, once she saw the cup she became aware of how dry her mouth felt. She grabbed the mug and lifted it in the air in a toast of thanks and gulped it down in moments. Slamming the clay cup down, she laid back on the hay pillow wrapped in cloth as Cedar finished up wrapping her leg in tight bandages.

"Soooooo....." Fin said awkwardly trying to start the conversation they were all thinking about.

"Ummmm," He scratched his head, Sam noticed that he had gotten his hair fixed to look like Uldous's.

"How long was I out?!" She sat up quickly.

"And when did you have time to get the man bun?" She pointed to his pins and freshly combed hair.

"Psh," Cedar interrupted before Fin could say anything.

"He was freaking out so much that he passed out. They sent him to the hair people. Why does this group consist of babies?" Cedar asked rhetorically.

"They were very nice to me and understood why I was so upset," he added, crossing his arms.

"Aw, you were scared for me, that's so sweeeet," Sam said in a baby accent as she made a face at him.

He rolled his eyes and walked out saying, "This is what I get for TRYING to be nice. A bunch of sassy women."

Cedar and Sam laughed. As she laughed she felt the soreness course through her leg and tried to calm down. She looked at Cedar who was rummaging through her medic sash, mumbling to herself about the things she needed to stock up on. Sam rubbed Ajax's head who had been there sleeping the whole time. She remembered how he walked up to the Hunter and sniffed him as he had done to her when they first met. Her mind forced the memory of her argument with Cedar back up, and through a sorrowful face she scanned her fiery medic for any signs resentment from last night.

"Hey. Cedar, I-I'm sorry, you know I love you right." Sam said apologetically. "I didn't mean for us to get in that big fight earlier."

Cedar's eyes began to well up with tears and she pursed her lips. She came over and laid across Sam and the bed vertically.

"I'm sorry too, I know you are having a hard time, I shouldn't have pushed it. I love you too."

Ajax bleated sleepily and looked up.

"I know this is weird, but... Ajax acted as if the Hunter was important to him. He went right up and sniffed him like he was a bunny in a meadow. Did you see that?" Sam said running her hands through her now unbraided and freshly combed hair.

"Nakoia washed and brushed your hair when you slept... There was a lot of blood and mud in it, from when you collapsed. And ya, I saw that. I don't know what he was thinking," Cedar added, eyeing him.

"Me either but while I was sleeping I heard Muninn's voice saying over and over again to trust the Qilin," she said thoughtfully. "There is more to this, I can feel it. Did you guys kill him?" She asked worried about how she might answer.

"No. Once he turned into a boy, no one had the nerves," Cedar said, frowning. "Who knew he was so young this whole time.. Where is his family?" She looked troubled at Sam.

"We need to speak with him," she said without a doubt. Sam started to get out of the bed. "Do you think he speaks?" She added thoughtfully. Cedar began to get upset with her as Sam continued. "What a little turd, to be giving everyone this much grief." She stood weakly and at that point Cedar took over.

"OH no you don't! YOU need to stay in bed! Your leg almost got bit off and you're over here trying to walk around on it! What's the matter with you?!"

Sam was taken by surprise again, she sat back down on the bed and looked back down at her throbbing calf, the blood was seeping through the bandages again and she was starting to feel dizzy. It didn't take much convincing after that to get her to lay back down.

"I guess.. You're right.. I should take it easy. We still need to talk to him though," Sam said. "We can't let anything happen before we get this mess figured out." She looked at Cedar.

"That's fine, I will go with Fin, and we will speak with him." Cedar said calmly reassuring Sam. "Now, here is some water by your table, you need to get some more rest." She wiped the sweat from her brow and sat in the chair next to the bed and watched over Sam as she drifted into sleep once more. After she knew she was asleep, she nodded in affirmation and headed out of the tent to find Fin.

"Watch her, she will try to leave, don't let her." She told the cow centaur who was sitting on the ground outside, she nodded in response to Cedar and moved closer to the entrance, blocking it and Cedar went off to find Fin.

She found him quickly, he hadn't gotten very far after he had left the tent.

"Hey," Cedar reached out to tug on his sleeve. "Let's go check the Hunter out and see if we can get some answers while Sam sleeps."

Fin gave an indecisive look, and Cedar interrupted before he could respond. "O don't be a baby, he is literally tied up and injured.

"Ugh," he rolled his eyes. "Then why did you ask me?" He snarked back.

Cedar looked at him like he was dumb. "I didn't," she said flatly and led the way.

Fin thought back and once he realized she was right, he grumbled a few words of protest under his breath but followed her anyways. They walked through the forest of tents and past Uldous and Amos's tent. Cedar's eyes hovered over her fathers tent as she reminded herself to check on him after they had spoken with the mystery boy.

Seeing the stressful glances, Fin spoke up. "I'm sure he will be fine, he seems like a tough enough guy."

"Ya," she sighed, "sorry I'm being so rude, I guess everything is just getting to me." She looked back at him quickly and kept walking ahead.

He shook his head, "Don't worry about it. I think everyone is on edge right now."

They got to the small tent with the two massive centaurs guarding it. They stepped in the way of Fin and Cedar, stopping them from entering.

"We are with Uldous, we need to see it and see if it can speak," Cedar said.

"We know who you are," the brown haired one on the left said in a gruff course voice.

"It isn't safe, it's awake now and dangerous for just the two of you small things," the one on the right said in a snarky tone as he laughed.

Cedar and Fin turned to face each other in an annoyed way and then looked back at the two centaurs. Cedar lit her hands in flames.

"Move, before I start catching things on fire." She retorted.

The one on the right smacked his teeth and both grimaced as they moving away to let them pass.

"Be careful," he said, "or don't," he added in a much quieter snarky voice, the centaurs laughed in unison as they passed into the blue, red, and green tent.

With no light source inside of the shelter, it was much darker than they had expected. Fin and Cedar stayed near the entrance until their eyes adjusted.

Near the back, scrunched up and small as it could be, glaring with the same green eyes of the monster, was a boy, about the age of Cedar. They stared back, in awe and in confusion, scared to move forward but not wanting to leave. Their curiosity kept them trapped.

"What now?" Fin said awkwardly, leaning towards her. "Does it speak?"

"I don-" Cedar started.

"IT," the boy said in a ferocious tone, "can." His words spit venom at them.

They both stammered, uncertain of how to proceed. Cedar sat where she was, hoping that it was far enough out of reach from the boy.

"Sorry. He," she said, trying to cool the tension. She patted the floor looking at Fin. This time he looked at her as if she was out of her mind, but with another firm look, he reluctantly sat.

"Yes, MY bad. He. The Hunter.... The killer," Fin said sarcastically, turning to Cedar, trying to remind her that this boy wasn't just a child.

"Let. Me. Go." He said calmly but they could see the raging storm on his face.

"Really..." Cedar started. "Let's see, you have been hunting us for weeks, maybe even a couple months. You have attacked us multiple times, and NOW you turned into this." She gestured towards him and his plain form. "So, no," she said slowly. "I don't think so," she flashed a fake smile at him.

He glared at her but didn't respond.

"Would you like to explain to us what type of creature you are? Since you finally uncovered you can, in fact, speak?" Fin said, trying to move away from the uncomfortable topics.

The boy snorted and laughed. "Nothing your petty Realm's can handle."

"So, you're from beyond the Realm's then?" Fin asked.

The boy said nothing but turned his head, clearly upset he had given them an answer.

Fin began to count on his fingers. "You can speak, you say your from the outer realms. You turned into not one," Fin raised his eyebrow, "but two different wolf forms. And you enjoy hunting, killing, and maiming." He looked at the boy through his eyebrows. "Am I correct so far?"

"Are you usually this obnoxious?" He snapped back.

"Yes, he is," Cedar replied.

"So I guess all we are needing from this completely normal introduction is your name." Fin said.

He said nothing but turned all the way around to face the back of the tent.

"Nothing?" Cedar huffed, standing and putting her hands on her hips. "What. Is. Your. Name?"

"Back off! You think you're safe over there past that silly little line." He pointed at the line drawn in the dirt. "But I can reach you just fine!" He began to growl, "I can tear you apart with these hands just as well as my others! I DARE YOU TO TEST ME!" He yelled and stood in his anger, prowling above them.

Fin backed away, he could see that the boy and Cedar were in no mood to speak to one another.

Cedar's body felt flush and hot as she stood and looked at him. She radiated a heat, not a heat that lashed out with flames radically but a heat that could burn away forests in an instant. She stepped over the line, and approached the boy, when she was only a nose distance away she spoke softly, small flames beginning to wave downward in her hair.

"You have attacked my father multiple times, you have tried to hurt my friends as well." Her hazel eyes began to glow bright red, the boy's forehead started to bead from the heat.

The ground at Cedars feet began to sizzle and smoke.

Fin glanced quickly between the grass and the two of them. "Cedar," he hissed, "the grasssss!" She ignored him, then the grass caught fire.

"The fact that you are alive is a question in itself."

Fin began to watch the flames spread wider, "The grassssssss!" He whined, laughing uncomfortably.

"You are lucky I don't burn down this tent with you inside of it as I watch."

The boy didn't stray. "You think a little spark scares me?" He asked. "I know of magic that your mind couldn't even begin to comprehend!"

"I can do much more than that, I assure you."

Fin stared in wide-eyed shock at the blazed grass that had crawled its way slowly to the bottom of the colored tent.

"The tent!" He groaned putting his fingers on his temples while he let out an indignant fake cry.

They stared at each other, neither backing down, both seeing who would cave first, ready to hold what they said to the truth. The air was hard to breathe with the spreading rage, at this Fin snapped.

"Ok, this is too much, we will come back. Cedar, you need to relax," Fin said reluctantly moving forward. He went to grab her but her skin was hot to the touch.

She looked at the boy a moment longer, then turned, leaving the tent quickly and smoldered the growing baby flames as she left. Not looking back to see if Fin was there or to see the smug looks of the centaurs as she ran off. She rushed to a quiet place between some of the tents, trying to calm down as she began to cry. Anger had never been so adamant in her life but seeing how much he had hurt the people around her, it controlled everything she did when she was near him.

How could someone do something so terrible and be ok with it!?

Fin squatted in the grass next to her and stayed quiet while she tried to calm down.

"That was.... intense," he said carefully trying to find the right word.

"Ya, well the anger is justified!" She cried out, "He has attacked Sam, and Ajax, and my dad more than once. You have seen what he can do!" She stood in a rush and walked angrily back and forth, not sure what to do next.

"DAMMIT!" She slung a ball of fire down, it hit the ground with a *woosh*, flattening out and then quickly rising up in a mini mushroom cloud as it set the patch of grass ablaze.

"We don't need to worry about him right now, we got some information, right? Let's meet up with Nakoia and talk with her," Fin said, trying to calm Cedar.

She moved her hand up slowly and down fluidly as she silently watched the fire. Fin's eyes were mesmerized in fearful curiosity as the small flames increased and decreased in ferocity with her hand.

"I want to check on my dad and Uldous first though," she decided and wiped her face, finally putting the fire out. If the grass had not been singed, Fin never would have thought the fire was there at all.

As they walked, Cedar turned to him, "Sorry about earlier, I'm just-" she sighed heavily. "Ever since I have been able to call the flames, I have been so- angry and bursting with energy all the time!" She looked forward and quickened her pace.

"We don't have Elementals in the City of Atlon but you don't need to apologize to me," he laughed. "You were scary as hell in there! I can't believe you did that!"

She laughed with him, relieving some of the stress she had.

Thinking back to what had happened, she replied, "It scared me though."

"Ya he seems pretty feral..."

"No. Not him. Me." Cedar stopped and looked at him.

"I'm scared of me."

20

WHERE THE WATER MEETS THE LAND

Fin swallowed, "I don't-" He scratched the back of his head in anxious confusion.

"No. Stop." She put her hand up. "I am not going to put that *whole* emotional load on you. I'm sorry for even mentioning it.... It is just something I have been thinking about since I could summon. But now is not the time for this, nor for me to pity myself," Cedar stated, more determined. "Let's go check on the others and then we can get some food with Sam."

Fin nodded, and his stomach rumbled in agreement. He didn't feel equipped to help her with her summoning problems, so he was relieved when she changed the subject to something he felt equipped for: food. He changed his thoughts to the many things he could eat and his mouth watered.

"Alrighty then! I am *soooo* ready for some grub," he responded, slapping his hands together in excitement.

They entered the tent Uldous and Amos were staying in. Amos was speaking with Nakoia and Uldous, who had a plethora of bandages wrapped tightly around his body, concealing the nasty gash he received in the fight earlier that night. They stopped talking and watched Cedar and Fin join them. Cedar walked over to her father, wrapping her arms around him in a warm embrace, while Fin settled on the ground near Nakoia.

"Sam's asleep. She is recovering from the bite," she told the group as she sat on the grass bed next to her father.

"I heard what happened. They just filled me in. I hope she will be ok," he said.

"We went to see the boy just now," Fin added.

Upset, Amos turned to Cedar. "He is dangerous. You should not have gone by yourself."

"Fin was there."

"Ya, I was there," Fin blurted out.

Amos glanced at him and raised his eyebrow. Fin's face turned red, and he cowered, trying to make himself smaller.

"Tell us what happened. Did he speak?" Nakoia asked, changing the subject.

Cedar and Fin filled them in on what they had learned and their half of the conversation with him while expertly leaving out the part where Cedar threatened to burn down the tent.

"This gives us much to think about," Uldous replied thoughtfully after they finished recounting their story.

"Yes, I agree. I was ok with hunting and killing the beast. But now that he has transformed into a child-" Nakoia trailed off.

"We have too many questions and shouldn't do anything rash until we answer them," Amos added.

Nakoia stood. "You two should rest today, and *if* you are feeling better tomorrow, we can go see him." She turned towards the two younger ones. "For now, let's leave these two to their beds."

After Cedar and Fin said their goodbyes, all three left the tent to let Amos and Uldous rest.

"We were going to find some food for us and Sam. Would you like to join us?" Cedar asked. She was getting hungrier from the smell of the food nearby. With a pained expression, Nakoia shook her head.

"I need to think. I have much to go over. Thank you though. I will eat later."

"Please don't make yourself upset about what is happening," Fin comforted his aunt.

"And Make sure to actually eat if you're hungry. Sometimes food can help with this sort of stuff, ya know?"

"Of course, thank you Fin, I will keep that in mind." Nakoia smiled softly. "Now go to your friend. I'm sure she is hungry as well."

The next day, they gathered, wounded but resolute and determined.

"We need to figure out what is going on," Amos stated.

Nakoia and Uldous nodded in agreement.

Sam, Cedar, and Fin stayed silent but exchanged nervous glances. Sam's leg felt sore, but after having it cleaned and daubed with a healing paste, it felt much improved. After resting since the battle, she couldn't contain her eagerness as she anticipated meeting this strange boy.

With Cedar's warning in mind, she proceeded with caution, being mindful of not overexerting her leg.

"There is still confusion on what exactly he has turned into, that being said, keep your guard up." Nakoia added, narrowing her eyes to the three, making sure they understood she was speaking mostly to them.

Fin had revealed to Sam last night as they ate about what had happened between Cedar and the Hunter. Her eyes traveled to Cedar. She wished she had been there to help. Her blood boiled at the thought of him continuing to threaten them, especially with the position he was in. Fin had also spoken to her more privately about Cedar's voiced concern after the fact. She could see that this newfound power was raw and untamed, making it incredibly challenging to control without unleashing its impact on her emotions.

As she touched Cedar's shoulder, she could sense the unspoken worry in her gaze. Sam squeezed her hand, silently conveying a comforting empathy between them. She didn't necessarily understand her power, how it worked, or what it felt like to summon fire, but she understood her friend who has been there since the beginning, her sister, was in pain and anxious about this unknown spirit she now controlled.

"We shall speak with him in my tent. It is the largest and most secured. Let us gather while the men bring him to us. And let the boy sweat on his walk to the blade," Uldous said, his demeanor firm.

As they walked to the tent, no one spoke. Sam's mind traveled to the discussion they would soon have and to what the outcome would be. Barely seeing the beast transform before she passed out, she hadn't been able to see what he appeared as yet. Fin described him as a boy that was Cedars age with dark skin and shaggy matted hair.

I want to see him for myself.

The lingering thought that the other night was an odd occurrence stayed with her, causing a sense of unease. She couldn't ignore the nagging sensation that something was amiss.

This feels different, but I can't put my finger on it.

They arrived at his large tan tent, its canvas flapping gently in the breeze. It had a blue and red stripe that encircled the bottom with square patterns on the stripes. As Sam examined the size of Uldous's tent in awe, she realized that it had to be at least a couple of yards taller. They were all easily able to sit inside of it.

Amos settled himself on the left side of the entrance, while Nakoia claimed the right side. Uldous, on the other hand, positioned himself on his elevated bed made of grass and hay directly across from them. Sam and Cedar sat on the side with Amos, and Fin sat on the other side with Nakoia. Everyone guarded a section, encircling and ensnaring the Hunter if he tried to escape again.

Once they were settled, Uldous motioned for two of the leather bound warriors to retrieve the Hunter. They nodded and trotted off towards the direction of the guarded tent. The room was filled with an uncomfortable silence, as everyone sat still, not knowing what to say. Sam could feel her heartbeat in her feet as her legs pressed into the hard ground. She tapped her finger on her knee along with the rhythm, trying to calm her senses. As her eyes meandered the room, she caught Fin picking at the grass nervously. A frown appeared on her face as she thought about the different paths this interaction could go.

While they waited, Sam glanced around and noticed Uldous's sparse collection of belongings. There was a bed, a small weapons rack with a bow and long curved sword, a couple of furs and cotton clothing to keep warm, and a bowl of fruits that caught her eye. She wondered if this was how minimalistic all the nomads in the tribe lived.

They heard the guards coming back, and stood, waiting for him to be brought in. Sam fidgeted with her clammy hands. She nervously chewed on the inside of her mouth, her fingers finding solace in twisting her untouched braid, careful not to dislodge the bead.

"STOP.... BEING.... SO.... DIFFICULT!" The guards launched the Hunter through the cloth flaps and into the tent.

His hands were tightly bound behind his back, with ropes constricting his chest and arms. The two guards came back in, their disheveled appearance revealing the challenging time with him. One had her hair pulled ajar to the side, and the other had a couple of scratches on his arms and face. They stormed in after him, irritated, holding the ropes and guarding the entrance with their backs.

He hit the floor with a grunt and remained there for a moment, catching his breath. In silence, they waited, their eyes fixed on him, anticipating his next move. Sam was astonished. Her mouth gaped open. The stark contrast between the boy's previous brutality and his current form left her bewildered. She laughed, slapping her forehead with her hand in disbelief and astonishment at the irony of the situation.

"You really are a child!" she said alert, her eyes scanning the room to meet the gaze of others. Overwhelmed by what she was seeing, she struggled to make sense of it all.

"He's a child," she said again, repeating herself and pointing at him.

"You are a ch-" she stopped. He was looking at her with the same green eyes that she had known for a long time. She crouched in front of him, taking care to keep her leg extended out, meeting him at eye level, unafraid. Amos took a cautious step forward, his concern for Sam's well-being clear in his expression. She continued to look at him. She could see a familiarity in his face.

But what was it?

Her brow furrowed, examining him up and down. He had bare arms and bare legs. No claws, no fur, no fangs. The more she tried to make sense of it, the more her brain tangled and knotted.

"You're.. like me," she said, looking at him and coming to the realization that he was more than just some monster from the woods.

"You're human. How is that possible? How are you a human?" She said fiercely, pleading for an answer at this point.

He spit on the ground and then averted his gaze from her. Rage propelled itself forward, and she scowled. Suppressing her emotions, she rolled her eyes in annoyance at him and stood up, making her way back to her designated seat.

"How do you know this?" Nakoia asked, leaning forward and examining the boy.

"He looks like me and has nothing that any of you have anymore." Sam struggled to sit down with her leg in pain from the previous movement. He doesn't have fur, claws, or a tail, and he looks like me. This boy is a human child now. He did *something* to himself to turn into this." She gestured up and down towards the kneeling child.

"I'm sorry, a what?" Uldous intervened. He stared expectantly at Sam for an answer, and her eyes darted to the floor.

"We might as well tell him the truth, Sam, now that he has seen the child like this," Cedar replied softly.

She nodded, agreeing, and slipped the fox mask off her face with trembling fingers.

"I'm a human, not a faunanoid, and probably the last one too." Her voice was so low that she could barely hear herself over her heart in her ears.

Amos relayed the rest of the story to Uldous, while Sam shifted uncomfortably, the weight of their stares weighing on her.

"I see," Uldous thought for a moment, stroking his pointed beard. "I guess humans must have been brave warriors then," he said and turned his attention back to the child.

"Well, they say you can speak- so speak."

The boy said nothing but sneered at him. As Sam fiddled with the loose end of the bandage wrapped around her leg, a thought suddenly struck her.

"Did he shift before or after he bit me?" She looked at Nakoia. The boy's eyes widened in surprise, but he swiftly composed himself, returning to a neutral expression. Nakoia noticed as well and took a moment to respond.

"After," she said.

Sam thought aloud to the group.

"You bit me, and I am the only human here. Then the next thing we noticed was you convulsing and turning into a human." She stopped and studied the boy.

"So, correct me if I am wrong..." she leaned forward. "But you can shapeshift into the things you bite."

He glowered at her.

"Wait, I don't understand," Cedar broke into the conversation. "I don't see how just biting someone could help him shape shift."

"I agree with Cedar. There is more to it than that," Amos responded.

"It was your blood!" Fin blurted out. Everyone stopped and turned to him. The wind ceased, leaving a stillness in the air. A heavy silence filled the room, with everyone holding their breath. No one spoke. Fin spoke softer this time, "He- he drank your blood..."

He shifted uncomfortably as well, "It- makes sense, he bit into your leg, all of that blood got into his mouth and he- he drank it... and he is what you are now."

All eyes went to the boy, and his fell to the dirt.

"That's it then," Uldous broke the silence. "You are a shape shifter by blood."

Sam leaned back. Her head spun, overwhelmed by a whirlwind of thoughts and emotions.

How was this possible?

He started as a giant wolf, then transformed into a monstrous beast, and now he was a human boy who can shapeshift by blood. She could hear the others asking him useless questions, but she couldn't understand what they were saying. Their words muted. She put her face in her hands, steading herself, breathing heavily she ran her hands through her hair. It had grown quiet with frustration, so Sam took this opportunity to intervene with another thought.

"Well, I was probably the worst one you could have bitten. I don't know if you know what a human *is*, but I have no special powers or neat little traits." Sam snickered, "So, you might have just screwed yourself out of that cool, shifting thing."

At that, the boy looked at her for the first time without anger but with shock and distress.

"What.." He croaked, his voice cracking.

"I am a human, from way before all of this, '*an ancient one*'." Emphasizing, as she waved her hand backwards as if it would transfer them back to her own time. "I woke up about a year ago. And I don't know how your powers work- but if you turned into what I am, well- I am *without* powers. Soooo, you probably just screwed yourself, buddy." She didn't feel pity for the child, she felt a sense of victory over him finally. After being tormented and fearful, she finally felt as if she had won the battle with him, even if it was a fluke.

"No- no, that doesn't make sense. I have turned into many creatures and turned back into my other forms. That's what I am, a shifter," he stammered. "I can't just lose my power."

"You bit or killed creatures from THIS time, not from MY time… and WE didn't have powers in my time." She began to feel twinges of sadness for him as he struggled to desperately comprehend what was happening. As she searched the group, she could see the uncertainty mirrored in the faces of the others. The anger welled inside her, as she couldn't bring herself to feel any compassion for a killer. However, he still seemed to have trouble processing what she had told him.

"No, no," he shook his head, "That's not true, it…. It can't be, I-" He stammered into silence.

She closed her eyes, turning to the side. Unable to watch the desperation in his actions and words.

"So, what should we do now? He doesn't seem to be dangerous anymore, and he is just a kid." Fin leaned backwards on his hands and stretched out across the thin mat he sat on.

"I don't think anyone feels comfortable with…. what we had originally planned." Cedar looked down at the floor.

"No, we will not. There are lines we must draw for ourselves," Nakoia paused. "This can be the punishment for his crime, losing his power." She looked around, waiting for someone to intervene. No one spoke up, so she looked at the boy. "Where is your family child? Are there more of you?"

Without uttering a word, he shook his head in defeat.

"Then we should drop him off at the desert border. He said so himself, he is not from here. Exile him from the Realms for his violence," Cedar exclaimed.

Sam nodded, agreeing with her. She didn't know where that was, but at least he would be away from them and not be their problem anymore.

"When I am healed, I can take him to the border." Amos replied. The boy scowled at him.

"Ikol can assist-" Nakoia added but was interrupted by a rustling at the tent entrance. They turned to look and heard a soft bleating. Ajax poked his head through. He came into the tent fully, shaking out and stretching.

Sam groaned. "Ajax not again." She struggled up to get him, but as she stood, he trotted under the guards and went up to the child smelling him.

All in a moment, Ajax looked at the boy, meeting his face and touched noses with him. The boy jerked his face back in alarm, but said nothing. Then Ajax laid in front of him, looking at Sam and the eyes of the room were on her now.

She rubbed her face in distress. "Ajax... *what* are you doing?" She annuncuated all the words as she stared down at him. The little Qilin picked his head up and stared at her. They spoke in silence, not needing to say anything. The words of Muninn echoed in her mind.

In my many years of being here, I have learned to trust the Qilin, whether or not I agree with them

She regretted saying it aloud, but she needed to trust Ajax, as Muninn had. If not, she probably wouldn't be here. She rubbed her face again stressfully as she gathered the strength to speak her thoughts.

"We must trust him, whether or not we agree, the boy will come with us." Sam said assuredly.

Voices of objections rose from the room.

"What!?" Fin and Cedar said in unison. The group was standing now, yelling and arguing. "He can't come with us! He will kill us in our sleep!" Cedar exclaimed. The boy snorted.

"You're really going to trust that little creature?" Fin made a face. "It doesn't know."

"HE knows, that's *LITERALLY* the point of his entire species." Sam responded, at which Fin looked sideways in irritation, making a face.

"Look, I *know* this sounds ridiculous but, I mean... just look- if he can trust this mess." She waved her hands up and down towards the boy again. "Then there must be a really exceptional reason why, and I will not be the one to fight it." She sat stubbornly, unmoving in her decision.

"We should discuss this more," Amos said tenderly. "We shouldn't rush through something this important, Sam. You don't want to put your lives in senseless danger."

They sat in silence for a while. Sam listened as the wind hit the sides of the flapping tent, whapping on the sides in thick waves.

A voice broke through the broad curtain of silence.

"Bram, my name is Bram Alder. And you didn't kill me when you could have.... so- I am in your debt." He looked up in honest certainty as he met each person's eyes, meeting Sam's last.

"I'll go with you."

Their departure day was a windy one. The sun shone on the fast-moving clouds and the grass that rolled across the Hills of Yoid. It had been a couple of days past the meeting that was held in the giant tent, and Amos was now well enough for travel. Sam packed her things, her mind filled with thoughts of the conversation they had two days ago.

Since they were closer to the sea than the mountains, they finally decided to head to the ocean. Amos spoke with them and told them there was a port town that doubled as a border town between the two realms. She wasn't sure who they were looking for next, but she had a trust in Muninn to show her, just as she did with Cedar and Fin.

Uldous gifted them bison and oxen to ride. Fin and Nakoia were getting them packed and saddled while they said their goodbyes. Amos and Cedar were speaking with Bram. Everyone was still uncomfortable with the decision for him to join them. He had not transformed back yet, whether or not he could was still undecided. In an attempt to quell her anxiety, she reminded herself that Ajax had gone to him for a reason.

"SAM! YOU READY?" Cedar yelled as she ran into the tent just as Sam had finished gathering her things.

"You seem excited?" Sam laughed as she slung her pack over her shoulder.

"Are you kidding? I've always wanted to see the sea!" Cedar squealed and ran back outside as Sam followed.

"Really? Well, you're in for a treat," Sam chuckled as they walked towards the stables. Her mind flashed to an image of long green grass swaying back and forth in the sea salted wind, the golden sand sparkling as bright as the sun, and the white-capped waves of the ocean as they rolled over all the different shades of blues. She felt warm and fresh thinking about being where the water meets the land, and felt the excitement from Cedar seeping into her.

They reached the group of oxen and bison that were scattered and lazily mowing over the grass. Everyone was together, chatting near the trough. Ajax bounded joyfully from Sam's side and ran up to them. He looked back, waiting for them to catch up. Bram was standing alone by the bison, feeding it some hay.

"Hey guys!" Fin waved, causing everyone to divert their attention to Sam and Cedar walking up.

"Are you ready? Do we have everything?" Sam asked as she joined.

"I believe so. The cattle are packed." Uldous stood taller than the oxen he was next to and patted downward onto its neck. "These are a parting gift from us. They are supplied and are yours to keep. They will return to us when you no longer need them once you reach the lake port and we will take care of them until you need them again." Uldous fixed the strap tighter on the ox.

"Thank you again," Sam said gratefully.

"For everything," Nakoia added as she glanced at Bram.

"Of course, Nakoia, I am proud to have helped our neighboring Province, as I am sure you would do the same." He said with a slight bow.

Amos looked at Sam and Cedar wistfully. They could tell he had not wanted this moment to come, but as the sun rises, so must it set. They were ready to finally begin their travels and continue on their quest.

"Do you remember everything we talked about?" He asked restlessly. "Where to go from here? Which direction to travel? How to ride the oxen and bison?" He shot out questions in rapid fire without taking a breath.

"Yes, we do." Sam put her hand on his shoulder. "We go south for a little while until we hit the stream. Then follow the stream's flow and it will get bigger and turn into the small river." Sam took a pause. "We send the mounts back once we reach the ocean." She gestured with her hand. "Then we take a boat, follow the river toward the port town." She nodded enthusiastically at being able to recite the entire plan.

"And you remember which way is south?" He asked anxiously. At this, Bram interjected.

"I do, in case she forgets," he motioned with his head towards Sam. In return, she scoffed.

Amos nodded quietly, grimacing, then whispered, "Do you have a back-up plan for him?" He eyed Bram wearily. Sam smiled and nodded back at him. She understood his weariness, but Sam noticed that Bram was beginning to feel more comfortable with the group. Although he was known for his extreme anger, he had calmed down over the past few days.

"Ok. Well-" He didn't know what else to say.

"We are going to miss you," Sam said as she hugged him, "And thank you for everything that you have done for me." She let a couple of tears fall as they hugged.

Cedar came up to hug her father goodbye and talk with him as Sam went to Nakoia and Uldous.

"Thank you both as well, really. I don't know what we would have done without either of you." Sam looked at the both of them, acknowledging their tremendous support.

"Sam, even though we have just met, you have shown me great strength and perseverance. I am grateful for our meeting and we will make sure to attend the festival to show our support." Uldous bowed deeply, and Sam returned the gesture with a bow as well.

"Your adventure will be great, in both good ways and bad," Nakoia took her aside to speak privately. "You will need to be cunning and aware of everything around you. This world is beautiful, but sometimes it is not what it seems." She looked at her. "But with these people by your side, I believe that you will be fine." Looking at Bram she added, "I know what I said about him, but his eyes now are different. I see something in them." She trailed off.

"We will keep an eye on him, at least until he proves himself," Sam said, in hopes of making Nakoia feel better.

"Yes, of course, and Fin has always had strong instincts. I know he can be a goofball, but lean on him for guidance if you need it." She raised her eyebrow. "His wisdom may surprise you."

Sam murmured her thanks, using her palm to wipe the tears away, and they hugged once more before Nakoia left to say goodbye to Fin.

Making her way to the oxen that were gifted to her, she gently ran her hand along his side in a warm greeting. His breath was powerful and full, filling the air with a sense of vigor. As he turned, she could feel the muscles under her hand flex and ripple with each movement. Grateful for the presence of a reliable mount, she comfortingly patted his side.

With the help of a shorter centaur, she mounted the ox that was gifted to her and waited for the goodbyes to end. Bram was mounted on a bison and he pulled up next to her as Ajax continued to joyfully run circles around the riders. They looked at each other, and Sam, not really knowing what to say, stayed quiet, waiting for Cedar and Fin to join them. Her heart ached with longing, a mix of sadness and reluctance as she thought of leaving behind the familiar faces and the newly forged bonds.

Sam's ox was red, brown and cream with white horns longer than her arm, and they bent upwards at the end of them. If he turned his head, his horns would swing around, hitting anything in proximity. The other ox was similar, but had more brown than red patches on his fur. The two bison looked the same with dark brown fur and a curly, tough mane that started from the middle of their bodies and covered their heads.

"Hey." Bram's small voice broke the silence. He shifted uneasily. "About when I attacked you guys..."

"Which time?" Sam said calmly, but with spite.

He cleared his throat and looked away. "The first time." She stayed silent, waiting to see what he would say. "You had a smell on you that I- remembered. I had seen you and her and another person that day in the forest. It was a scent with an... unpleasant memory. But it has worn off you and it's gone now. I don't smell it anymore, so I was confused and angry-" He didn't want to explain further. She could clearly see he felt uncomfortable sharing this part of him.

"Apology accepted, flea bag," Cedar and Fin had mounted and joined them towards the end of the conversation. "Now let's get going. We have a journey to start," Fin said. Sam could see on Cedar's smiling face the sad tears of what she was leaving behind.

"What'd you say?" Bram turned to Fin as he raced off, laughing on his bison. Bram chased him and they bickered back and forth as they raced over the hill and out of sight.

"Do you think this is a good idea? Taking Bram with us? We barely know anything about him?" Cedar asked.

"I don't know... But we are going to have to see what happens I guess," Sam said, lacking confidence but hopeful.

As they turned to leave, Uldous called out, "When you return from your quest, we will have a feast to celebrate in your honor! It will be grander than any festival there has ever been!" He reared up and waved his sword. Amos and Nakoia stood watching them leave. Sam and Cedar waved as they disappeared over the grassy knoll.

"How much longer! Ughhhh I'm so tired!" Fin whined and flopped on his bison facing down into its thick fur.

"Why is there someone always complaining about traveling?" Sam asked in annoyance.

"Calm down monkey brain, it hasn't even been that long," Bram retorted.

"Look! Even Ajax is tired!" He pointed at the little creature sprawled across Sam and the ox. In a defensive manner, Ajax let out a bleat at Fin, as if he were being wrongly accused, prompting laughter from Sam and Cedar.

"Well, the sun is going down, and we have been traveling for a while." Cedar looked towards the setting sun. "We could make camp and continue tomorrow."

Sam agreed, her body aching from sitting on the rocking ox for so long. They dismounted and began setting up camp for the night.

The smoke from the fire traveled towards the stars as they ate around the campfire. The cattle lay behind them, sleeping soundly, and Fin watched their surroundings. After eating, they fell asleep in between the two tall hills that watched over them. The day and night had been noisy with the talkative wind, but as morning came, it was quiet as the sun rose.

"Do you hear that?" Sam asked. The fire had died down to only red coals sizzling in the black ash piles. Everyone stirred, waking up.

"It's the fire," Cedar groaned sleepily.

"No, it's different. It sounds like wind or something," Fin added straining to listen. They listened and became aware that they could hear water.

"It's probably the river we have been following," Cedar shrugged. Bram climbed the hill towards the sunlight and the others followed. As they reached the top of the hill, they saw the source of the commotion.

Upon reaching the top of the hill, Sam stood frozen in awe, her mouth agape in speechless astonishment. The shocking revelation hovered over them as they discovered what they had been looking for. She didn't say a word, but her face light up with a brilliant smile as she marveled at the breathtaking view in front of her. Two dragonflies greeted them, stopping only for a moment to share in the beauty but then quickly continued on their way.

The sun was rising on the vast horizon, rays of light beamed out a sunlit yellow, turning orange and then a red pink as it grew closer to the sun. Hitting the scattered clouds and making them send out their own dark shadows across the fresh morning sky.

The smell of salt and the wild, untamed wind hit them as they stood at the crest of the hill. The group's shadows, long and dark, lay across the many hills they had previously traversed. Foamy soft waves licked the golden white sands tenderly as the grass green hills merged into the salty blue waters of the ocean.

End of Book I

INDEX

Unsure how to pronounce a name? Well here you go.

Samihanee (sam-ee-ha-nee)

Qilin (kee-lin)

Amos (aw-moh-s)

Bram (br-aw-m)

Muninn (mue-nin)

Huginn (hue-ghin)

Captain Ryner (rye-ner)

Ronin (roh-nin)

Nakoia (na-koi-ah)

Ikol (eye-cohl)

Meera (mirh-ra)

Finnigan (fin-ih-ghin)

Uldous (ol-jus)

Eelias (eel-li-as)

ACKNOWLEDGEMENTS

First, I would like to take a moment to thank and appreciate God for everything he has done for me in my process. He picked me up from my lowest and gave me writing to help spread joy and wonder to others.

I would like to express my gratitude to my family, friends, colleagues, and my beta readers for their invaluable support throughout my work.

I also feel compelled to recognize the significant role played by Mythology and ancient religions in my book. Without them, my inspiration and idea for my stories would not exist. Mythology has taught me the wide expanse of knowledge and culture of the timeless people from around the world.

Thank you to my sister Tiffany, who helped me storyboard and who also created the cover of my book. And to my friend

Jenny for dedicating her time to helping this book be the best it can be.

Thank you to Xander, the person who I couldn't make it to the starting line without. You pushed me to start and I will be forever grateful to you for helping me get past my fears and doubts. You struggled with me at my lowest points and you celebrated with me at my highest. Without you, I probably would have still been "planning out" my story.

Lastly, I would like to thank the one person who helped me through my entire book. He read every single chapter when it was sent unedited to him. He told me I was amazing and helped me through every step of the way and tricked me into not giving up on myself or on my story. He helped me edit the entire book and working tirelessly to make sure it was up to par. His words of encouragement and help made this book possible. Thanks dad, I love you.

About the Author

SHELBY GRAGG IS A fiction writer specializing in fantasy and science fiction, where she weaves stories that explore themes of sacrifice, adventure, family, perseverance, and identity.

With a bachelor's degree in Early Childhood Education, Shelby's work is often influenced by her passion for mythology and storytelling. When not writing or working as an elementary school teacher, she enjoys reading, video games, and exploring the outdoors with her family. Shelby is currently working on completing her *In-Between Chronicles,* continuing to bring her unique blend of of wonder and depth to life.

Also By

S.J. Gragg

The Four Realms Saga
Of Sea – Book Two

Made in the USA
Columbia, SC
27 March 2025